SHE IS A
HAUNTING

D1638890

SHE IS A HAUNTING

TRANG THANH TRAN

BLOOMSBURY

LONDON OXFORD NEW YORK NEW DELHI SYDNEY

BLOOMSBURY YA
Bloomsbury Publishing Plc
50 Bedford Square, London WC1B 3DP, UK
29 Earlsfort Terrace, Dublin 2, Ireland

BLOOMSBURY, BLOOMSBURY YA and the Diana logo
are trademarks of Bloomsbury Publishing Plc

First published in the United States of America in 2023 by Bloomsbury YA
First published in Great Britain in 2023 by Bloomsbury Publishing Plc

Text copyright © Trang Thanh Tran, 2023

Trang Thanh Tran has asserted their right under the Copyright, Designs and
Patents Act, 1988, to be identified as Author of this work

A catalogue record for this book is available from the British Library

ISBN: PB: 978-1-5266-5708-4; ePub: 978-1-5266-5709-1; ePDF: 978-1-5266-5710-7

2 4 6 8 10 9 7 5 3 1

Book design by John Candell
Typeset by Westchester Publishing Services

Printed and bound in Great Britain by CPI Group (UK) Ltd, Croydon CR0 4YY

To find out more about our authors and books visit www.bloomsbury.com
and sign up for our newsletters.

For my mother and hers, and hers

To the angry girls, to the ones figuring it out:
you are always enough

mouth

THIS HOUSE EATS AND is eaten.

Memories mar the wood, pencil in the heights of children, and wear the scuff marks of well-loved feet. There are echoes that do not stop echoing, trapped in nooks and old curtains, until they're found again—still screaming or laughing, voices dead or gone. What parts are undigested lie waiting. There is no real organ here to rot, only soft wood that termites consider and wasps hollow. But shut the door tight and something can still die.

The body becomes full of things it did not ask for.

So, when a door opens, it is this: the first page of a menu.

1

I AM A TOURIST in the country where my parents were born. Even my clothes have been here before me. All made in Vietnam by Vietnamese hands, then sent overseas where a Vietnamese American girl (that's me) picks it off the rack and one day brings it to a place she can't call home but the clothes can, if inanimate objects could claim shit. I'm not bitter or confused, at all.

My fingers tighten on the cart I'm pushing out of Đà Lạt's airport. People stream around me, laboring under giant backpacks, which really is the only thing that would make it more obvious I don't belong. Like hell I'd do one of those "finding yourself" trips though.

I only have this summer to make up the money for UPenn.

Lying to Mom about getting a full scholarship was the only way to stop her from taking out loans, when she works seventy-two-hour weeks at the nail salon already. My Walmart on weekends and scooping out "Ice Custard Happiness!" part-time every summer at Rita's was just enough to cover SAT registration and college application fees after my little sister's club expenses. That leaves Ba. His money is the thing that's gonna make it happen, and I have to see him.

That's his condition.

"There he is!" Lily yells, bounding off the cart to sprint toward the idle cars. Ba steps out of a beat-up truck, opening his arms for my sister. He's still slight, tanned a reddish brown, with black hair trimmed thin. Lily's already telling him everything he's missed in the past, oh, four years of sparse calls.

"Jade," he says when I finally catch up.

"Dad." There're too many sounds in my mouth. This untrained tongue. I don't know how to say *hello* or *I miss you* in Vietnamese. We'd never said either much, and I don't miss him. I hate him.

Ba squeezes Lily's shoulder, but his eyes stay on me. I'm almost as tall as him now. "Where's your brother?"

"He stayed in Saigon with Mom," I say. Bren barely remembers Ba, or so he claims, so he'd rather hang out with our cousins on Mom's side for the rest of the trip.

We stare at each other before I toss both suitcases into the back, shuffling aside wood planks. I take the middle spot up front since the seat belt's shit, which makes Lily's face do a fake-angry thing until Ba gets in the truck. It shifts into gear, and we're on our way.

It's quiet, then quieter as the other cars and motorbikes fade away. Lily's voice is as familiar as a heartbeat, filling the space

3

between us. The air cools against my face, smelling sharply of pine and flowers rather than Saigon's smoke-tinged lungs. Green and gray, soft hints of yellow, and a pink sunrise unfurl to my right.

Mountains rise from the mist like candles in an uneven buttercream. I want to smash them down with my thumbs. It's ridiculous that Đà Lạt is so beautiful when I am this angry.

"We're fifteen minutes from the city," says Ba. "Closer to our house."

I want to correct him: it's not my house. I don't belong here. *Stay the summer, five weeks, and you get what you want*, he told me during the April call. Will I? Ba spent years building the perfect houses that aren't ours, all time lost in a black hole where a thirteen-year-old girl had to become a father for her siblings.

"How's your mom?"

"You could call her." My attempt at casual comes out bitchy, which Lily confirms by lodging an elbow in my rib. I step on her toes. "But she's fine." It's the first time Mom's come back in decades, since she stepped onto a boat drifting for an American dream. From the moment we landed in Saigon from Philly, Mom started crying, then sobbing and laughing as she hugged her sisters and brothers. Her family is overwhelming in the best way, which means the entire week was food and karaoke, and so much of her laughing. It gnaws at me, how I could've taken this visit away from her just for tuition money.

Ba slows around another bend on the road. The forest closes in, branches near enough to brush the truck hood, like braided fingers urging us back to the earth. We're so tucked away no one

4

would be able to hear a scream. Glass blinks between treetops, the dark eyes of abandoned houses.

"The French left them, after the Americans ran," Ba says. I roll my eyes. Communism: bad for real estate.

The truck veers onto a dirt driveway where pines cluster all around. The heady fragrance of flowers thickens, luring us closer. We stop.

The house juts upward, yellow and tangled in vines. Roots crisscross the body, grow into wood, and drag it whole into the hill. Hydrangeas climb the crumbling walls beside tall and thin windows, their white blooms kissed with lazy bees. They're the most loved thing here.

I stand in its shade, dizzy when I look up, either from jet lag or all these damn flowers, I don't know. An antique balcony, with iron bent at odd angles, leans from the second floor.

Below it, a girl sits on the stair's railing, balancing, precarious, her hair as shiny as oil over cast iron.

Beside me, Ba introduces his business partner Ông Sáu, who joined us from the other parked car. The bald man waves. "This is my niece, B—"

"Florence," the girl cuts in with a sawtooth smile.

"Nice to meet you, Florence," I say, emotionless and pleasant in the same way I greet white people. No handshake though. I drag the suitcase by her, hoping I don't look as greasy as I feel.

Her midriff is exposed beneath a loose bomber. She quirks a brow before twirling a hand as if ending a magic trick. "And you, as well." She speaks in English, accented with Vietnamese tones.

5

The two business partners are oblivious to our awkwardness as they talk about upcoming repairs before the house's grand opening. While Lily fidgets at our dad's side, Florence is close to me at the top of the steps, her brown eyes clever and wrinkling as though we share a secret. She slides down the railing. Part of me is pulled along, wanting to learn how her perfect mouth moves between our languages.

It's the sound of Ba's laughter that drives me indoors. I'd thought only Mom could coax that joy out, but I am wrong, as always, about him. Mistakes take one moment to unravel, and I've nearly made several just now. Too much is riding on these next five weeks to entangle myself in the false hopes of reconciling with Ba or knowing this girl.

The door shuts behind me, and it's like I'm back in the thick heat of Saigon. Something here is newly sanded, freshly painted. I smell an unfamiliar life pressing itself around me before a sweet scent roots me back in Đà Lạt. Pastel blushes of hydrangeas are potted along the windows, their large shadows unfurled over empty rooms. Needing escape, I take the curved steps two at a time and land in a hallway of closed doors. All the doors, except one. A blade of light slices into the darkness, and I follow.

The room swallows me in brightness. Crown molding weighs the walls with such fancy, sharp edges that I expect Michelangelo's angels to be among them. The bed frame, carved with roses, has a headboard in upholstered velvet, also fancy, and I flop down without fuss. My suitcase falls over as the voices outside fade and a car starts.

I stay that way for a while, alone, because the truth is this: Ba left us, all three of us with Mom and no child support. He doesn't get to come back.

———

I nap past noon. Everything aches when I remember where I am. Between jet lag and my devotion to seeing as little of my dad as possible, it takes several minutes for me to admit that my stomach's close to eating itself. "Shit."

I blink away the pale ceiling and get up. The sheets cling to me, their print barely concealing a sweaty outline of my body. Gross. The windows look out to a swath of pine over the hills, and hydrangeas turn their heads up, sneaking a glimpse inside. I unlock the one closest to the desk and fumble for the lift, but something fuzzy squishes against my fingers. Bugs—many-eyed, too-many-legged, and sometimes no-winged—litter the entire sill. "For fuck's sake," I mutter.

They're not smashed or wrapped up in webbing. It's as if they dropped dead. Even the webs along the glass panes are quiet with spiders turned on their gray backs. It doesn't surprise me how Ba would spray poison everywhere and call it home.

Ignoring the carcasses, I try the window again. When it doesn't give, I move on to the others. Pull up, push, breath held and unheld; none budge. I guess I'll just shrivel right here.

My stomach growls.

"Fine," *you traitorous organ.*

Quietly, I move into the hallway. A different door has been left open this time. Beyond it, branches extend across emerald

7

wallpaper. At first I mistake them for the roots digging deep into the house, but moving closer, I see they're drawn. Birds sit on the trimmings, watching over the gorgeous claw-foot tub and gold-plated fixtures. Ba's restored this room already, as much as he can anyway, since some of the wallpaper's been eaten away by age.

My hands are sticky with sweat and probably bug guts, so I hurry to lather up at the sink. I pick under my short nails and think of what to say to Ba, if anything. We'd barely talked before the April call.

Before scholarships, $60,000 a year. After: $38,755. That is this summer's worth, plus the interest that would've added up for loans. Figuring out the other years will be future Jade's problems.

My anxiety decides then to create worries from nothing. *Don't look into the mirror.* It's a bad distraction. The Healthmind page pops up in my brain.

First, acknowledge the thought. This is an intrusive thought.

Next, accept and let it pass. There is no meaning behind it.

I look up. My reflection stares back. I'm alone, except for the birds' glossy eyes watching over my shoulder. I turn the faucet off and leave. The faucet drips behind me, but since I'm not responsible for *this* bill, I don't spare a glance.

The house is ridiculously large, at least twice the size of our town house back in Philly, even with all the thriving hydrangeas inside. My steps slow in the sitting room, where mostly blank space looms above the fireplace, dark and tunnel-like. It's made starker by walls as pale as soup bones. Mom, Bren,

Lil, and I beam from cheap picture frames, shrinking even more in this vast room. This house was designed to make people feel small. I don't have to go close to know the pictures are old.

My stomach forces me away. Finding the kitchen is easy: the sizzling pan calls me. Ba hovers over a stove in the well-lit room, glancing when he hears the creak underfoot. "I'm making bánh xèo."

That was Bren's favorite; it was the one food he took every bite of at three. And it's been at least three years since he's even asked for this. Suddenly, veggies did not taste so good to him, but I think it's because he didn't want to be reminded who made them best. "Okay, but Lily's a vegan now," I say.

Her ponytail tilts to one side as she tells me, by motion only, to shut up. Quick to cover up my blunder, she says out loud, "I'll eat it without the meat and shrimp." I give her a thumbs-down; I didn't start eating tofu at least twice a week to let Ba get away with it.

I light incense at the small altar in the kitchen's corner, burning three for Quan Âm's statue and one for my grandma on Ba's side. Prayer isn't required in Mom's house, and we don't go to the temple outside of Tết, but it always feels weird to step by the altar and not pay respects. Ba works rice flour batter into the pan, his presence too real, so I close my eyes.

Dear Bà Nội, please make your son not annoy me so much. Watch over us, and my mom, and Bren too. Then, remembering she didn't know any English, I ramble through a poor Viet version. Ash flicks from the incense down to the rice-filled container. A wooden plaque bearing her name sits on the level below Quan Âm.

Bùi Tuyết Mai

The only photo of her is tucked in Ba's wallet. "*See, Jade*," he would say, showing me. "*You have her eyes. Đôi mắt bồ câu.*" Big as a dove's. But didn't he see that they are like his too? That mattered to me more, since I didn't know his family like I did Mom's. He is the youngest of six, the only one to make it to the US, and he never shared anything about them. He and Bà Nội spoke on the phone weekly but never us; the language barrier was too steep.

Settling at a table pushed against the wall, I stir the nước mắm so the garlic and sliced chili peppers swirl throughout. After shooting another look that very clearly said, "No fighting or I'll kill you," Lily heads to the bathroom. My little sister's sweet, until she's not. Ba moves at the corner of a glance, the paint smeared on his jeans crinkling.

He places a plate in front of me. "Did your mom tell Brendan not to come?"

"He's eight. He decided for himself." The acid in my stomach bubbles up, and my head tilts back so our eyes meet. "You can ask them in person if you fly back with us, but the deal is that I stay here, right?"

"I know what the deal is. I'm his dad. I'm your dad." The displeasure is clear: Don't talk to me like that.

I'd rather not talk at all, Dad.

You asked me to come. *You* dangled the money in front of me. I'm an ambitious gremlin, so of course I want it. I will take it, but that doesn't mean I have to respect you.

The smell of crisp crêpe, yellow with turmeric and heaped with glistening pork belly, shrimp, and bean sprouts, makes the acid simmer down in my stomach. I wish, for a second, Brendan had come too. He would've known the names of all the dead bugs. He would've been Lily's backup, so cute or annoying that Ba and I wouldn't ever have to talk to each other.

I ladle nước mắm into a small bowl and stick to facts. "My windows wouldn't open, by the way."

"I repainted them," says Ba, wrapping lettuce around his bánh xèo. "I'll fix it later." I imagine the space being perfectly sealed, coated with dry paint, holding in heat. Of course he would paint them as is. He always loved a good shortcut.

"So," I say, swallowing a mouthful. "You and Ông Sáu are making this into a bed-and-breakfast?" A wild concept, honestly. I'd rather dine and sleep at home for zero dollars than listen to some old people do their anniversary boning through the walls.

"That's right. We'll start taking reservations for the busy season as soon as you and Florence finish the website."

I stop. "What?" Shrimp falls from my bánh xèo. The website was always part of the deal, thanks to programming classes, but he'd said nothing about a group project.

"She translates everything into Vietnamese for you. Google gets it wrong all the time," he says. I couldn't care less about Google screwing up. This summer needs to be as uncomplicated

11

as possible, which means no distractions, no teamwork, and no friendships. "She's also good with computers. Born here but did boarding school in the US."

"I don't even know her," I argue, even if it sounds immature.

"She's going to be a student at Temple next year. You'll know her."

"I don't want to be her friend." A laugh escapes my throat. How can he understand? Not only is UPenn my first choice for college, it is where my life will change too. Where I can be close to home, Mom, Lily, and Brendan, but not actually be home. I feel inadequate in ways I can't put in words, confused in others, but that can change in college. I can figure out who I am, and who I like, without consequence. Halle, my best friend, is the one other person I want to keep close. Was—I mean. I forget she's not mine anymore. "Fine."

We eat in silence. The house surrounds us like a cocoon, and I wonder if Ba believed it would birth us as something new and precious. No, that gives me too much weight.

I have my assignment.

A bead of sweat slips onto the greasy dish. "What are you calling this place?"

Against the straight lines of too-perfect cabinets, his back is slightly arched, probably aching from work. He sets unused batter onto a refrigerator shelf, breathing out the slight rot of things left too long.

"Nhà Hoa." *Flower House*. Simple, lush, and all-consuming.

2

EACH MORNING BEGINS WITH Ba disappointing me. Condensation gathers on each window, covering its glass in a sheen. Water pools under my fingertips at every touch, then slides like teardrops. The windows stay stubbornly shut and keep in a sweltering heat. It's been three days, but it seems longer—slow, like the time I imagine it'd take to melt a house of this size into a wax glob.

It's hard to concentrate here. Turning back to Nhà Hoa's website on my phone, I add, "Come to Đà Lạt to sweat your ass off in a precious French colonial home." Ba was wrong about Florence being good with computers; she's *incredible* at website coding. It's more complicated than what I've learned, and my plan had been to use a template. She left a placeholder for each of the six rooms, which have their own themes.

The marketing foresight would've impressed me, if not for it crumbling my other plan to send entire portions for Florence to translate at the very end. Now, I need her to tell me what the themes are before I even start. I, one-hundred-percent, regret answering yesterday's invite to do the work together with "no thx." Usually, I don't even use shorthand, so my confidence in avoiding the hot girl must've been overflowing.

At ten, I compose a straightforward text requesting this information. What I get, five minutes later, is a game show. *What's behind door #1, bedroom to the back?*, followed by several nonsensical emoji. "Star, triangle, light bulb," I mutter, scowling. To my dismay, there are emoji for each room.

When I send her my five-week schedule for website creation instead of playing along, her next message has a thumbs-down emoji and in all caps, *BOOOOOO NO FUN*. She lists the themes after—Marie Antoinette, Paris at Night, Napoleon, French Countryside Getaway, and the token Lovers at War thrillingly described with two dancer emoji, the French flag versus the Vietnamese flag, a knife, and a heart. She leaves the last theme for me, in what I assume is a gesture of goodwill.

It's easy to imagine those dark eyes crinkled with mischief. My reply is simple. *Wow.*

Her name flashes on my phone a second later: *People eat that*—poop emoji—*up.*

Tempted to send an emoji back, I toss the phone aside. She talks to me as if we're friends already. Familiar. Warm. She's probably that way with everyone, so this isn't special. I snatch the phone back up, but there are no new messages.

It's too damn hot to think.

I wipe sweat off my forehead, side-eying the windows Ba had promised to fix and didn't. A few more bugs lie dead on the sill over the desk, despite my cleaning it yesterday. Nice to have a visual of my ideal temperament: dead inside and unbothered.

Before I decide to stay in bed forever, I roll off. Underneath the reigning teenage mess of a room, the Marie Antoinette theme becomes clear. The headboard is plushy and dusty pink, a color that's threaded all around. A painting of a three-tier cake hangs near the door. It nails that whimsical style that teeters between "could be in a museum" and "shit, that's a waste of paint." The iced flowers are smooth under my fingertips. Since cleaning this temporary room ranks low on my priority list, I leave to check out the other rooms.

The décor hints at opulence but suffers a muted glamour, so I use words like *old-world charm* and *hidden treasure* in my notes app. Each piece of furniture has been polished to a gleam, yet tiny scratches relay their imperfections. The restored chairs still bear the curve to someone's pert vintage ass on the cushions. The French Countryside room is a frothy cream, with twin beds and linen sheets. My palms press into the deep cuts on the door frame, where someone long ago recorded their children's height. They must've planned to stay here forever.

In Lily's room, Paris at Night, everything is romantic and moody. A star chandelier sways above the bed, a combination of glass and metal spikes that she seriously shouldn't be sleeping under. I cross to her window, which overlooks the back of the house. While Ba directs the renovation crew laying out stakes and soil for a patio, Lily tends to the vegetable garden. It's not as big as the hydrangeas, but the growth is hefty and green. How does he even have the time to care for all this?

I don't stay long before going to Ba's room. This is probably what I'd planned all along in my secretive heart, the one that hides thoughts from me and simply wants instead.

You didn't say I couldn't readies on my tongue as I glance across my shoulder to the empty stairway. A standing fan blows hot air at my neck when I slip inside. The blades spin, and I flap my shirt as if it might cool me, as if the motions could stop my mind from racing.

My sight shifts from the clothes folded over an ottoman to the digital clock that sits out of place. Everything here he chose to take with him to this new life. He spent most of last year traveling between Vietnam and the States, not sharing news of his "venture" until we called to get info for financial aid applications. He'd wanted the house to be ready first—a surprise no one asked for.

I close in on the nightstand, where several notebooks are stacked together. The paper is wrinkled as though it's been wept on or doused in water. I flip through the pages, over messy writing that switches between English and Vietnamese.

It isn't a journal, I'm sure of that, since Ba taught me—when I was seven—that it was naive to keep my secrets where people could read them. The lock on my dollar store diary had broken easily in his big hands.

Stella is so pretti. I wis she wuz my Fren. I like her so mu—

"Stop it." My voice is firm against the memory, but it's too

16

much. There's something about this house, and its cloying perfume, that draws every unwanted thing from me.

"*Who's Stella*," he asked, voice edged in something dark.

It doesn't matter how I answer.

Girls like boys, you understand? That's it. You're too little to know.

Except I wasn't. There've been Jenns, Margie and her twin Max, and a Sierra since. The lesson had been learned anyway: Don't keep a diary, and don't do anything that lets people know who you are. Each name had been kept close to my heart, until Halle and I became friends freshman year. Then I whispered those names to her in the night, as precious as birthday wishes. I've never told her or anyone about the diary though. That hurt, and secret, I've pressed into a stone in the pit of my stomach.

Your dad betraying you is one of the worst feelings in the world. I wonder, *How about a daughter?*

Stomping my finger pads across the paper sends a powerful trill through me. A list of repairs starts at the beginning and continues for a few pages, numbers interspersed between crossed-off items. The scribbles are messy, and farther into the notebook, Nhà Hoa's hand-drawn floor plans gaze back up at me. Rigid lines, narrow hall—but the furniture moves in each iteration. Notes on color and style are scribbled beside each shape. Ba's been home decorating.

"Amazing." The same man who hated picking out home décor so much that he once came home with the first curtains he fished out of the sale bin: mustard-yellow and velvet monstrosities that outlasted his relationship with Mom. I'm too cheap to replace them, and Mom considers his efforts charming rather than mediocre.

These drapes hiss on their rods when I slide them through. The view is similar to mine: endless green and brown. "Enjoy panoramic views in our Napoleon room," I say. "Where assholes will find themselves at home in avoiding their loved ones for years at a time." Silence lingers, except for a distant thumping elsewhere in this house.

I leave his room as I found it, with the notebooks' spines mismatched and the door ajar. Only the master bedroom left now. I study my list carefully. In a slow spin, I count the rooms again.

One.

Two.

Three.

Four.

Five.

There is no sixth bedroom.

Florence must've counted wrong when she was here. You couldn't be a prodigy in every subject, even if it's basic math. Shaking my head, I scroll down the website's mock-up, delete the extra placeholder, and face the master.

Its glass doorknob is cold to the touch. When I twist it, brightness hits my eyes in one searing flash. No curtains hang against the white-paned windows. The balcony doors are open, swinging in Đà Lạt's breeze.

A real king-sized, four-poster bed imposes on a large portion of the room, its corners sharply carved spears.

"Update Lovers at War to: sex dungeon," I dictate into my phone. The wood sighs under my feet. I see why Florence named it so. There's a mix of European design and Vietnamese artwork.

This is a room to marvel at and be marveled in, where sunlight is as bright as waves called to shore. Standing in this house is as claustrophobic as being in a forest clearing, surrounded by woods that have seen more than you—this spot, most of all. It is bare and clean, and even emptied, I feel like I've trespassed.

I arc around the bed for the balcony, frowning at dark splotches of moldy wood right at the door frame. These doors must have been left open during yesterday's storm. The clouds come and go so quickly, sky turning deep gray and the moodiest of blues, and pour rain. It'll get wetter in August, but I'll be gone before the worst of the season.

My heel catches on a squishy floorboard when I try hopping over. Ugh. It oozes delicately, making it easy to imagine the floor breaking apart. Being discharged from the hospital would be a pleasant way to end this visit early. Ba, however, would argue that I did not follow our arrangement, which we still need to iron out. Lily being around complicates things somewhat, though she should know I'm too petty for real reconciliation.

I test the balcony's steadiness under my toes first. When it doesn't give way, I step outside. Vines curl into the iron, fastening in thick ropes that reach toward the balcony doors. Leaves shuffle, and for a second I think a daddy longlegs is creeping among the foliage. Only it doesn't scurry away. I squat for a closer inspection because if there are spiders, I shouldn't have to clean bug carcasses up every morning. A strand of hair is tied in a neat bow, fluttering.

It unravels when I pull one end.

The hair dangles from my fingers, longer than Lily's. Darker, and longer, than mine. A fierce wind blows, stealing it to a sky that threatens more rain. I scowl. Our hair tangles in everything. At home, our cat Sir Meow-a-Lot has a fifty-fifty chance of barfing up one of our hairballs rather than his own. Bren tried convincing us to get pixie cuts, but if I'm not allowed to shave Meow-a-Lot down to his pre–birthday suit, we're even.

It had to be ours since no one else has been here.

Wooziness overtakes me when I stand, and the world spins and blurs with bright dots. My skin tingles, as if pulled by a magnet to the ground below. I reach for something to steady myself; ice-cold iron bites my hands. The vines' fuzz brushes over my knuckles until the dizziness fades, barely a second later. My vision clears. Ugh, I need to be more careful. Backing into the room, I shut the doors to the balcony, which immediately seals the heat within. Spongy wood springs back up in the shape of my retreating feet, letting out a phlegmy squeak.

When the room closes behind me, I swear I hear the balcony doors swing open again. Đà Lạt is breezy, so it's easy to lose things, even from your head, even from a house's grip.

kidney

FLESH PASSES THROUGH AGAIN. The way it is meant to be. A house's lifeblood.

Invitations were delivered. The rugs beaten. Too many years passed in disrepair.

Welcome, this house creaks. *Silence* for the long-term guests. Do not be scared yet.

Hands reinforce its foundation, spackle its walls, and connect new tendons. *Stay.*

They do not notice it.

This house will remember them, in the end.

3

A HOUSE SETTLES OVER time. Soil shifts, then shifts again, and the wood must learn the place on which it rests.

That's what Ba told me when I asked about the creaking floorboards and the soft thumping somewhere in the attic. *One of the first villas the French built here. 1920. It's old.* The Little Paris of Vietnam, the city of eternal spring, is how this place is advertised. The longer I stay, the more convinced I am it should be renamed the Land of Noisy Houses.

I spent all yesterday and this morning drafting more house descriptions for the website before sharing the document with Florence. Her reply comes fast: *ok chi*.

Chị is an honorific for older sister and sometimes used as an endearment, like *em* or *anh*. I've never even heard how my parents regarded each other, or I don't remember. Brendan and Lily don't call me chị, but that's because we use English at home, even though it drives Mom up the wall. Vietnamese has so many ways to hint at closeness that I'm still learning. This is not the case here.

Florence is mocking me. We don't text in Vietnamese because I'm bad at it, somehow worse than when my mouth tries it. I shouldn't take the bait. She knows I'm not here to make friends. Even if we end up in the same city later, she's too close. Her family knows mine, and I'm not ready for further complication. The screen blinks to black.

I take the fucking bait.

Graced overnight by more underboob sweat (*ugh*), I rise from bed for the desk by the unfixed window. Lip balm's smudged on—because my lips are chapped, no other reason— before I take a photo, angled collarbone up for white space and to avoid particular attention on my soaked grungy T-shirt. In it, I'm holding my middle finger up, which obscures half my face. Light sears the other half, where shadows of petals stuck on the window track down my cheek like artful teardrops. I caption the selfie "*Regards*" before sending.

She, in a mutually shameless attachment to her phone, hearts it a minute later.

My skin prickles under the sensation of being watched. The house breathes heat down my neck, even though no breeze can be found within these closed-off rooms. Trespasser. I'm ridiculous, obviously, and getting laughably worked up over regular old texting.

"Time to call Mom," I say out loud, desperate for cool air. Putting off conversations with her would make it more suspicious. I don't want her coming to Đà Lạt. In the safe place of my mind, I file away Florence and the house's general creepiness and step into the hallway. Four days in, the soles of my feet have already memorized every rasping spot in the floorboards, so I walk closer to the banister where it's harder to hear me. Somehow, it's more claustrophobic when it's only me in the house.

Outside, the wind teases my hair into a riotous fluff. Anxiety boils within my stomach, then simmers slowly. The phone's lock screen flashes with a photo of me and Halle working on a ridiculous chemistry experiment in twin goggles. We were smiling. She was wearing her new hijab, the cheetah-printed one Mom got her for Christmas. Halle loved it. I used to call her before talking to anyone I needed to feign happiness around or sweet-talk, because it was easy to smile with her, to be known by someone so well.

We haven't spoken since graduation. I should change the picture already, but I like seeing it. I just never know whether the memory will warm me up or break me in two.

Her dark brown skin shone with sweat under the afternoon sun, and her nose was slightly runny from allergies. Halle hated being outside when yellow pollen covered everything, but we liked hanging out somewhere that wasn't our houses. The sports field was as good as any place, wide enough that no one bothered us.

It was several weeks before the end of the school year, and

24

Halle said to me and not for the first time: "You love checking out lacrosse players."

"I appreciate their sportsmanship, athletic abilities, and"—number five Warner intercepted the ball from Alisa, number twenty-two—"aggressive legs, yes." I glanced over at her.

"Then why do you look like you sold your soul and I'm the one living her best life?" Halle wore her judgmental face, which she didn't know was exactly as scary as her mom's.

"I'm not selling my soul though, just my presence." I showed her the itinerary the airline had emailed me. "Final now. Nonrefundable tickets. One week with my mom in Saigon, then five with dear daddy in Đà Lạt." I kept saying the names like they were places I have been, so they couldn't scare me back to pronouncing it the American way.

"He really set you up," she said. "It's crap you're going away for our last summer. We can't even finish our Before We Get Old list together." She waved the to-do list with checkboxes underneath our names for things such as binge-watch *She-Ra*, confess to our crushes, and road-trip to a non–New Jerseyan beach.

The word *last* had me stuck. She was due for Berkeley in the fall, but that shouldn't mean forever. Her mom would never let that happen. *She doesn't mean it like that, anyway.*

"You sure this is what you want?" Halle asked, *this* being the lie. All my lies and secrets, knotted together like toys in a box once made for shoes.

"I don't have time to not know what I want." I wasn't going to fuss over shit in life and go in undeclared for college, racking

25

up useless credits. I wasn't going to reassess my dating life, or lack thereof. I wasn't going to keep wondering what spaces were open to me. There was no time for more self-discovery.

"That doesn't mean you actually know, Jade." Her face softened along with her voice. She was kind, which I liked most of all. "You decided, that's all. And you can change your mind."

Smiling, I leaned into my best friend's shoulder. She always smelled like vanilla and blackberries. Even in a city, far away. I answered, "I might diversify to volleyball players."

Branches break underfoot, bringing me back to Vietnam. I'm already in the woods, walking without really thinking about it. On the line, Brendan's face appears too close to the camera, yelling for Mom from the other room. It's 2:00 p.m., but the karaoke machine blasts a heartfelt ballad. He had escaped to the bedroom with the AC unit. Smart kid.

"Bored yet?"

Bren shakes his head and waves around his game. His brows stick together in concentration. A second later, Mom settles beside him. Her cheeks are pink from laughing, her skin radiant. Amazing what not working twelve-hour days under a nail technician's light does for her health. The first thing she says is, "Jade, you eating okay?"

I've walked farther than I meant to. The house is a sliver among the towering pines. Their white barks line up like packed cigarettes. Gooseflesh pricks my legs.

I tell her I'm fine, Lily's fine. Lily spends all her time in the garden or on whatever task Ba needs labor for (because at thirteen, she's still an awful judge of character), but I see him mostly at the 6:00 p.m. dinners he insists on. I withhold that it's always hit or miss, with wholesome Vietnamese cuisine or dry cereal because the milk's gone bad again.

"Good." A smile crosses her face. "We go on temple tour next week. Con muốn đi không?"

"No, I'm staying here," I say before tacking on a lie. "It's easier to work on the website with Florence—Ông Sáu's niece—in person." She doesn't push the issue since she thinks I'm helping Ba out of kindness. Money aside, spending several days in a van and hotel to see temples that are basically carbon copies sounds incredibly boring.

Her smile lingers too long. "How's your dad?" Four years absent, and the question is still gentle. I remember the way she said his name on the phone, when we made plans to come here. *Cường*, like she'd never get to say it again. *Cường*. She probably doesn't even remember that time we came home to Lily building castles out of his empty beer cans while tiny Bren sat beside her.

He doesn't deserve any of them. Sometimes, I don't feel I do either.

Does your mom ever say she loves you is—apparently—my favorite question to ask when I'm drunk and sappy. I always need to relive the ways my family is different. Why it's harder for me to ask or tell what would be normal updates in other households. It is a justification when someone, usually Halle, says yes.

Something had changed when I got older. Not the favorite for anyone, just the oldest. I'm too big for kisses, or hugs, and

Mom doesn't say the three words. I'm supposed to feel them. And I do, she works very hard, often seven days a week. Her hours off should be for relaxing, so I don't ask for more or worry her about my baby crushes and bigger mistakes.

"Dad's busy with his own stuff, as usual." I shrug, going deeper into the trees. For now, a lie has to be enough. "I have to ask you something." I pace in a circle. Ba has suspected from the beginning that I'll run if he gives tuition money before the whole five weeks pass. It's exhausting to plan around, even if he's not exactly wrong. "My scholarship doesn't get released until the semester starts, but the first payment is due in two days. Is it okay if I use your credit card? I'll pay it right back next month when the scholarship kicks in."

Barely a moment passes before she waves her hand. "Yeah, that's okay."

The tension doesn't immediately fade from my shoulders. Leaves fall in blustery wind, willing me to take a leap.

There's still a chance to tell Mom everything, instead of leaving home and not letting her know the real me. How I part my hair in the middle because I can't stand asymmetry, how I like the color of leaves best when they're golden just beyond the cusp of fall, or how secure I feel the tighter my clothes are. But what does it mean when I sometimes don't know the real me? When I don't know what I want her to say to me in return? Is there a word in Vietnamese for someone like me? *Stubborn overachiever. A stereotype.* There's one in English, but it catches on my tongue. *Bisexual. Needy.* Neither of us has the language or time to figure

28

it out yet, and there's a power in never being known because no one can use you against you.

What I do know: I'm good at lying, even when I hate it.

"Thanks, Mom." Ahead, an ant colony looms from a hollow and fallen log, so large that the bark appears to shift and knit together. "Let me talk to Bren." I flip the camera around so he can see. Brown ants scurry along the screen in a blur of movement. Tiny holes become tunnels that run through the whole colony. Bren talks excitedly into the phone, his voice scattering the birds above. His hobby's mildly more interesting than the rocks I collected at his age.

The air is thick with damp moss, tangy and earthy. Moving closer gives us a better view, but what I thought were clusters of mushrooms nearby are actually dead ants. Their round heads are all wrong.

Quickly, I change the camera angle so Brendan can only see me and the colony's edge.

"It's huge! Those are carpenter ants," he says, face smashed against the camera for a closer look. "There's probably two, maybe even three, queens in it. Whoa."

My eyes dart from the still-living ants to their unmoving mates. My gut screams at me to look away, but I don't. Long, yellow stems erupt from their heads, the tops capped like the enoki mushrooms Ba steeped in yesterday's hot pot. The stems pin them tight onto the branches above the colony. The unnatural appendages vary in length, so they must've died at different times from the same disease. Maybe they wanted to be close to home, accidentally damning their entire colony with infected dust or microbes—whatever ants become after dying. In a squat, I lean closer. Some ants have multiple stems, and I can't tell whether the sickness lurched up from within or erupted on the outside.

"Jade?" Bren's tone is hesitating but enough to make me fall on my ass.

I blink. A hair closer and a stem could've reached inside my nostril. The woods snap into focus. Paranoia tickles the back of my neck. I look over my shoulder for Ba, Lily, a bird, or a worker on their smoke break, but it's only pine. Always pine, leading back to the house where hydrangeas sneak color onto its muted palette.

Nothing is there. No one but me and the ants I feel crawling on my skin.

Morbid curiosity has made a complete pussy out of me. Shaking my head, I stand and brush dirt from my shorts. "All right, so tell me more about these queens," I say to my brother. This time, I don't turn my back in the house's direction. My body is tilted, so I can always see Nhà Hoa through the leaves and ants on my other side, marching, marching, with only the little ones wearing their skulls like question marks.

4

WHEN NIGHT COMES AT Nhà Hoa, it's as though dark walls have dropped around the house, closing us in. I've abandoned blankets and other comforts that make a bed less lonely to deal with the heat. The ants are fresh on my mind again, so it takes a while to drift away. Even when I'm asleep, it's as though a part of me remains in my body, ready to yawn awake.

I am in the forest, and so is my father. Glittery shoes shine from my feet, the same ones he gave me when I was six. Pine needles rest on his shoulders, thick as armor. I know this is a dream because I am not afraid of my father.

In his hands, the ax catches sun. The pines topple with each swing. They're not so big fallen. Pine needles land on my shoulders and grow into my hair. Petals as delicate as fingerprints blow in the wind, loosened from wild hydrangeas. I can scream and wake up and remember how they make the air sharp and sweet, but I don't because *I am here with you.*

Other words for you: *Cha, Dad, Ba*. The needles root into my scalp.

Something crawls at the back of my throat: *Is it flowers?*

My eyes jolt open, seeing black before blue settles into the crevices of the molding. In the night, it resembles an impossibly long vertebrae or the back of an unending dragon.

I can't move.

My hands, my feet, my body, they're all there, where the mattress and soft sheets press against me. I want to move but I cannot move. Nothing but my heart does, thumping with the attic noise. This has never happened before.

I am conscious but drowning in my own body.

Eyes bulge, testing the limits of their sockets. They're dry and they hurt.

The bedroom door is open, though I always sleep with it closed. A draft rocks it on the hinges, but Ba didn't fix the windows. They are still shut, and yet the door moves where the light doesn't touch.

But I can't worry about what is at the door when there's something between my teeth.

A thing moves and squirms in the tight space of my anxious mouth. I'm used to the grinding of enamel, my teeth put to useless work, but this is something else. It could be my tongue, but there's no pain. Saliva pools at the back of my throat.

I dreamed before this: flowers and the shine of new shoes. Ba's hand before he lets go. I try to move my fingers next, but they remain limp and stubborn.

I imagine the hydrangea blooms under a bright moon, passing the house's eyes and spying on me. Mistaking my silent mouth as a pot to fill, reaching in and planting another friend.

Flowers grow. Little by little.

I wonder if I'm growing when kept still.

I make no sense at all.

Move.

The door shifts again, maybe an inch. My eyes are so dry. My mind muddles through a haze. I was sleeping, and now I'm meant to be awake. I am awake, and I'm meant to be getting up, complaining about the heat, but everything is a betrayal.

Move.

There's something foreign in me, an animal at high stress. I'm beating against my rib cage to be let out.

The pressure releases suddenly, and I bolt forward, hair sticky on my temples and neck. I spit into the blue-black. I scramble from the bed, *thud thud thud* on creaking wood, and into the bathroom. The faucet sloshes water in my mouth, and I retch. Sometimes I bleed from a slip of my cheek between teeth, but the sink is clear of blood.

I grip the cold porcelain, knuckles white, and heave close. Clear water, except for a single insect leg in the basin. Bent, with spurs.

The birds seem to squawk along the wallpaper, green with envy.

What did I just eat?

———

I don't sleep again. By 11:00 a.m., I'm still curled up near the headboard with my phone stuck on a thousand tabs about sleep paralysis and the average number of spiders the typical human swallows in their lifetime. (Eight. *Eight.*)

The astringent smell of Listerine cool mint and original wafts from my mouth, still dry and feeling full of splinters or legs of unknown origin. I've already gone through two travel-sized bottles of mouthwash, so retching again isn't going to help.

Sleep paralysis, my brain repeats, groggy, as if that is a better worry. It can be caused by any number of reasons, such as a poor sleep schedule, not actually sleeping, stress, and sleeping on your back.

I am a high-achieving teenager whose ex–best friend is the only person who knows she's bisexual and dealing with the return of family shit; a recent high school graduate hustling for money so she doesn't have to burden her hard-working refugee mother; and someone who has reliably slept on her back since infancy.

"Thank you, internet. Very helpful." I aggressively clear the browser history.

I require sustenance, even if my mouth doesn't want it. If I did swallow a bug, it must be dead. Not waiting in my gut to be nourished. There are insect carcasses on the sill again, but my focus turns to Marie Antoinette's dresser, where I'd tucked the insect leg between two pieces of paper like a pressed flower. I should've washed it away, but I didn't. I have to know what it came from.

Food first though.

Nhà Hoa has been awake for some time with hammering and sawing and digging. No neighbors live close enough to complain about noise, and the reno workers need every minute to stay on Ba's relentless schedule. Opening my bedroom door, I smell it—fingernail dust, that particular scent from nail salons.

One summer I told Mom I wanted to become a nail technician, so she made me tag along to work. She cleaned people's hands and feet, scrubbing away their calluses, and got shit tips half the time. The air was always full of polish and fine dust from sharpened nails. *You don't want to do this*, Mom said after, exhausted, when all I had wanted was to be like her. Soft. Likable.

It's the type of disappointment that clogs your lungs, and it's here.

I sniff the air again. My attention shoots immediately to the master bedroom, where there's a shuffling. I step into the shaft of light by its door and sneak a glance inside.

"Dad?"

There is only the furniture and a crowbar on the ground, half the soggy floorboards pulled up. Bits of tan-colored dust pile along the seams. That must be the smell.

Trespasser. My shoulders tighten. Another rude intrusive thought, as usual.

Turning away, I pass Lily's room and go downstairs. On the right, two statuesque figures flank the fireplace in the sitting room, boxed in by newly delivered chaise lounges and armchairs. The white woman holds the largest photograph of us from the mantelpiece.

She glances up, a bright greeting ready. "Hello, Sleeping Beauty!"

What the shit.

"You must be Jade," says her partner, a smiling man with sunglasses pushed into broom-colored hair. "Your dad said that both his girls are visiting for the summer."

The term *his girls* would make me vomit, if not for the fact that there is an ongoing intrusion happening in front of me. The potted hydrangeas seem to suck up all the sunlight in this house, leaving these rooms dim.

"This is my husband, Thomas, and you can call me Alma." She places the frame back on the mantel while Thomas keeps smiling. "We're staying down the road."

The other investors, right. Ba had mentioned them during one of those hazy dinners. I switch to a Very Pleasant veneer in response. "It's so nice to meet you."

In quick steps, Alma crosses the room and grasps my hands. Cigarette smoke wafts from her clothes in a noxious cloud. "Likewise." Her eyes are a murky hazel, paint water that can't decide between brown or green or blue. They stare at me too closely. "Your eyes are a gorgeous shape," she adds. "Like your dad's, but thicker lashes."

Your hands are exquisitely cold and knobby, I'm tempted to say. I'm laid bare otherwise, in my ratty tank top and shorts sticky with sweat. Instead a laugh escapes my smiling mouth. "And where is he?"

Weird, as Ba never leaves anything related to the house unfinished and he never lets anyone other than us inside alone.

"He had to step out," Alma says, letting go. "Will you join us?" She settles in a tufted armchair, the center seat, across from the fireplace.

I lift my chin. "No, I'm good here." Near the exit, thanks.

Walking as if he can't keep still, Thomas regards me. "How are you liking it here?"

Having practiced this song and dance with teachers and guidance counselors in high school, I know to go for the blandest, most neutral answers. "It's very beautiful. And the food is great."

Thomas beams. "The weather is fantastic up here. It's no wonder why the French made this their resort home. It's a dream, like Europe." Thomas says something about them vacationing here often.

My smile tightens. My teeth might actually break. They don't hear themselves at all. Or maybe it's my opinion that they don't care about.

"Are you comfortable here?" the woman asks. "We haven't been able to tour the whole place!"

"Very," is my riveting reply. It's none of her business how I feel here.

Ba comes from the kitchen, wringing a towel in his hands. His attention darts from me to his guests. "Sorry about that."

"Everything okay?" Alma asks as she hops back on her Birkenstock sandals.

"Yes." He pauses. She looks expectantly. "The contractors found more roots leading up to the house, closer to the water pipes this time, so we have to dig them up before pouring concrete in the patio. It'll be fine."

"Ah good, you caught it," Thomas says. "Less likely to break the concrete. Nice, thorough work."

Footsteps bounce down the stairs as Lily makes an appearance. "I've got the invites! Well, the test ones." She strides by to give Alma and Thomas a copy. Lily didn't tell me about this. I'm putting together a website as part of a deal for college money. She's doing it for free. I give our dad the stink eye.

Alma fusses with the paper. "Are you really keeping the name? It's so hard to say. The French is more romantic. *Maison Fleurie* or even *Maison de l'Hortensia*."

"We are in Vietnam," I say happily. "Everyone would call it *Hor* House if we named it that." I say the explosive word slowly and with a smile.

My sister's Authentically Pleasant face wavers. Ba might actually murder me.

"Well," Alma says stiffly. "There'll be time to discuss. If we want it to be a house of importance, that's *memorable*, and fitting, it should have a name that appeals and reflects its storied history."

"Oh boy," Thomas says. "Don't get my wife started, or we'll be answering to Dr. Alma!" His blue eyes are set adoringly on his wife.

"Don't be silly, honey," she says. "I much prefer Alma." A singular glance is placed on me. "I did my dissertation on the founding of French Indochina. This was the first home of a very high-ranking officer, Roger Dumont. I was charmed by the letters his wife, Marion, sent to her sister about Đà Lạt and especially this house." Her expression softens. "*So beautiful, it belongs in one of Papa's snow globes.*" She sighs. "Madame Dumont became a bit of an agoraphobe, so many important meetings happened right here. Of course, I want to honor it in the right way."

This woman has her PhD in colonization, and I'm supposed to mindlessly defer to her?

Thomas claps his hands together. "We'll figure out something that makes us all happy, I'm sure! Alma, we should get going for our date."

Ba clears his throat. "Well, I also need to get back outside. Will you two still join us for dinner next weekend?"

"Yes, we'll be back from Bangkok then." Thomas inclines his head at Ba while leading his wife toward the door. I shuffle aside. "Jade should be awake by dinner, I hope." He winks.

I want to die where I stand.

"We'll be up and ready, say six thirty?" Ba's hand touches my shoulder, which is the first time in two years we've interacted this close at all. In fact, two-years-ago us stares from the mantel: Ba with his arms spread around us while Brendan blows out the number six candle on his ice cream cake. Ironically, Mom's the one who isn't in the picture because she's busy behind the camera capturing this memory of Ba passing through our life the one weekend until now. His hold traps me still, as it did then.

"Perfect. We'll be absolutely starved," Alma replies, stepping onto the porch where her hair is thick linen white rather than the sad gray from the sitting room.

"See you then, Cường," her husband says, pronouncing Ba's name as *Kong*. Waving, they head toward the parked SUV.

"They're tourists," Ba says after they're gone, as if expecting questions. I have none. I don't care. His hands have smudged dirt on my shoulder. *I don't care.* "They bring a lot of money in."

My sister frowns. "Is that why you're friends?"

"It's business. Alma, Thomas, and their friends spend all their money on vacation, so why not here?" Ba shrugs, finally releasing me. "We're the same to locals. Việt Kiều." He says the last two words lightly, as if they don't hurt him. Việt Kiều are Vietnamese people who live overseas. They send money to family, they bring gifts, they visit, and they go on tours around Vietnam. They don't belong in the same way. Even Ba who was born here is seen as different by those who stayed.

"But we're not," Lily says before I can. I don't look at Đà Lạt, at Vietnam, and think Europe. What I see is a version of the place Mom and Ba left behind, and also where I could've grown up, with a language that I would know fluently, paternal family to possibly love me, and a history that would finally be known. All these things were taken from me, before I was even born. "Anyway, she has bad taste." My sister lifts a half-empty drink labeled HAPPY TEA SERVE from the coffee table. "She said grass jelly feels like worms."

Dusty footprints layer the floor, tracking toward the potted hydrangeas, around the edges of the room, and the fireplace. I'm not dealing with their mess on top of the horrible night I had.

"Jade," Ba says, stopping me before I can get away. Weary lines gather underneath his eyes. "On Saturday, we go out."

"I don't need anything," I reply. The last time we went shopping, I definitely overpaid a grocer speaking in a Northern accent to get the interaction over with. I truly would sell my soul to ascend, or descend, at this precise moment.

Ba shakes his head. "Fishing. That's what I mean. All three of us."

We used to do this every other weekend.

The nostalgia is desperate to entrap me with hope. Maybe this is the strategy he's going for: pretend as though he never left us in the first place and that this is a special summer for father and daughters to bond. "Fine."

My steps finally slow halfway through the dining room, where I can hear the workers' muffled conversation and the roar of a saw from outside. Like the upstairs bathroom, the dining room has wallpaper on the top half featuring a painted view of the pines. It's too much for me, but it makes sense that a lady who was scared of going out in the world would invite more trees in from the mountains.

The branches are flat and lifeless under my touch. Not comforting at all. Déjà vu sneaks up on me, and I let go, shoving all thoughts of forests away—real, imagined. Instead, I think of everything I've seen in Vietnam so far: square houses with dark mushroom caps out in the country, narrow colorful buildings in the city, and miles and miles of terraced rice paddies. History has left its mark among these sights, and erased others.

There are streets here named in French; there are universities built by Vietnamese people by the French who commanded them. They're named in someone else's honor. Of course, Alma's drawn here, where the past seems rosy and romantic.

But who am I to say? I wasn't colonized. I'm not Vietnamese enough to have an opinion on anything other than what makes a good bánh mì (the baguette) or phở broth (how long it's been simmering and which bones used). I close my eyes, the hunger gone.

Here I'm cut too sharp. Here I'm a wound.

5

THAT WEEKEND, MY MOUTH is barbed wire: knotted and bleeding where I bit too hard, the color of rust staining the tissue I dab over lip balm. I'd slept and woken again, frozen in the space of my own bed.

It's no big deal, I tell myself. It's actually hardly a worry at all, though I've watched the clock from 4:00 a.m. until now. Almost time for us to go fishing. The sound of beds and floors creaking indicates no one's forgotten about the family activity today. Against all odds, Lily was the first to wake and hop into the shower.

In daylight, a house is meant to be less menacing, but these walls are tall and patient, seemingly in want of a good dusting. It grows unease.

Lily shouts from down the hall. Ba and I nearly run into each other as we rush for the bathroom. His brown skin is flushed pale, worried for the first time since our arrival. I knock loudly. "Lil? You okay?" If she's fallen, if Lily doesn't answer, I'm going to kick this door down. Ba can obsess over another repair.

"Make Dad go away first," says Lily, voice muffled on the other side.

He looks neither wounded nor relieved. A jolt of satisfaction passes through me when I shoo him and he listens, backing into his room. "Done." When she opens the door, steam hits in one sudden blow. The mirror's completely hazed over; we're wisps in self-created fog. "It's already hot as hell. Do you like getting cooked?" I ask.

Lily waves the question off, though her shoulders are still pink from scalding water. She grips the towel around her body and points down. Drops of blood on tile, then the trail that ends at her heel. "It started. Out of nowhere." Her brows are squeezed together.

Wordlessly, I grab supplies from my room and return. "Here." I hold out a handful of tampons and a stack of overnight pads. "You choose what you want to try first. We can always go out and grab some regular. Also some tampons have different sizes."

Lily snatches and clutches everything to her chest. "Oh my god, Jade, I know! All my friends got theirs already."

"Okay," I say. "I'll be right outside if you have questions." The door slams shut. Her embarrassment is something I wouldn't have guessed. I thought she'd want to catch up to her friends. Puberty is a race as a teen. Everyone trades notes on what's happening and who's done what. I'd gotten mine at ten, way before most of my classmates, and paraded around our house like a princess sizing up her crown. I didn't know then that I was signing up for two weeks of pain every month. Menstruation *and* PMS.

"This stinks" is her first declaration when she lets me in again. Lily's the smarter one, I guess, but I don't tell her that. She blows a raspberry as she wraps a towel around her hair. Using one of the fancy hand cloths intended for future guests, I wipe up blood from the floor. "Don't we need bleach or something?" she asks.

"It's from your crotch. Not a murder. Soap's fine."

Lily clutches her stomach. "My crotch feels like a murder."

"Well, we'll check if Dad has any ibuprofen or Tylenol," I say. "It helps a lot. I swear you bleed less on it."

She uncrosses and recrosses her legs. "This is the worst."

Raising a brow, I let the towel dangle from a finger. "I've got it worse, Lil." Laughing together, I show her how to wring it out with cold water and let it soak before laundry. I tell her all the things I learned from the internet or people with a uterus, and nothing that Mom had told me about when I got my period.

A girl's body is like a jar, Jade. Once you open it, the inside's spoiled.

Us, lying in the dark. Me, wishing she'd tell me the pain will go away. Her, telling me I'm grown in ways that need to be guarded. It doesn't matter, in the end, who's opened who—just that you're a girl and no one should touch you. I want my sister to stay unafraid of herself and savor the power in that. "Come on, then. Get ready."

"I really don't want to go," Lily says, holding her stomach tight. She'd been lukewarm on the fishing part of our family bonding endeavor to begin with.

"Then don't. I'll stay with you," I say. It would be for her as much as it would be for me. "We can stay in bed and watch Asian dramas all day. I'll even translate for you." As much as I can anyway. My Vietnamese is marginally better than hers.

She shakes her head. "He's working really hard. I don't want to mess up his break, and . . ." She pins me with a stare. "Why is it so weird with you and Dad?"

"It's not weird," I say.

"Oh right, it's *super* weird, since you wanted to come here in the first place," she says. It really pisses me off sometimes how observant she is at thirteen. She thinks if I were nicer, Ba would keep us around more often. Ignoring Lily is a short-term solution, but I can't muster the energy to correct her. She's old enough to realize it's his decision to stay or go.

I sigh. "I am doing my best."

"Do even better," she says. "Mindset is everything."

I snort. "You're taking Mom's inspirational decals way too seriously."

"Everything might go back to normal, you know." Lily twirls a loose tendril of wet hair. "It's what I want."

The wistful tone pinches my insides. Barely nine when he left, Lily hasn't had as many opportunities to be thoroughly disappointed. I change the subject. "Can you check my throat for

46

me? The heat's making it so sore." She doesn't need to know about the sleep paralysis.

We situate ourselves, her perched on the seat and me squatting with my head tilted back. My jaw lolls wide as she shines the phone's flashlight inside. "Aaaaah." Each breath sears my throat.

Lily narrows her eyes. *Nothing's in there.* I hold on to that mantra when she takes even longer. "It looks really irritated but not strep, probably. Take a spoonful of honey and lemon before you go." Mom's favorite solution. "Are you trying to get out of it? Do you have plans with Florence or something?"

"What." I put on the best neutrally confused expression I can manage, which should be easier than this, since I definitely do not have or want plans with Florence. "No."

"Uh-huh."

"What if something happens?" I ask. "We're in a foreign country."

"We're in Mom and Dad's country. We belong half here, you know? Nothing's going to happen. Besides, Alma and Thomas are down the road and if anyone knows the number to the Vietnamese cops, it's them." Lily Nguyen: the dear optimist who tells it like it is, sometimes. "The outside air will be good for your throat anyway. You've been holed up in that room for too long."

I don't see it that way at all. I have been getting to know this house, as ordered for the website, which is easier than getting to know our dad. Somehow, Lily has reversed the roles of older and younger sister. I'm usually the one dragging her from her online role-playing forums. It would not shock me if this is an inspired

47

setup involving a small, nonlethal cut so Ba and I have to spend time together.

But Lily looks me in the eyes and says, "Jade, *please*."

———

Every good thing happens in a flash. Ba holding my hand at the park. Me carrying Bren for the first time. Mom singing a lullaby to Lily in the hammock while I watch, my head on her lap. My brain's wired this way—fleeting happiness and snagging anxiety.

We're driving to the lake now, Ba and me. It's early enough in the morning, when fog rises and falls with the wind encircling the mountains. I'm wearing a pair of his boots, because the ones he got me were too small. We left the pink rubber boots at the house, lined up on the doormat and out of place.

He doesn't remember that I've grown, or maybe he had actually bought them for Lily, even though I'm the one who likes to fish. Liked to fish.

"You remember how to knot the line?" Ba asks when we're at the lake.

My fingers are cold as I search through the tackle box. "Loop it like a shoelace."

When I look back up, my dad is smiling at me. The day is so bright it burns my eyes. When did I see that last?

I remember, even if he doesn't. The last time we stood by a body of water, on Penn's Landing. He was already planning on leaving us. I know because the next day he wasn't there anymore. Shoes gone. Abandoned clothes molding inside the hamper.

Mom cried into a stained shirt while I walked Lily to school and missed my bus. I promised myself to never let us feel his absence more than necessary. Four years since then.

Doing my exact *not best*, I finally say, "You don't get a chance to try again. You failed, and left." The words echo over still water. Our eyes meet. My heart beats furiously as I move farther from him. Whatever he has to say will hurt me less with distance. My boots sink into mud, and I pry under a rock for worms. I slide an unlucky one on my hook. Impaled, it squirms. I cast the line.

"Everything will be perfect by the end of the month," Ba says, not engaging with my verdict. I prepare to issue it more forcefully, but he continues, "As perfect as when my bà ngoại lived in the house."

A slow "what?" slips from me. During all the times he watched me light incense for Bà Nội, he never once said her mom lived in that very space we walked. Anytime we asked about his family, he recited information as if reading from an obituary in a newspaper people saved to pick up dog poop. Ba never tells us anything that really matters.

Is this why you're here? Back and forth to a country he's not allowed in without a visa, fixing a house that means something more than money. My lips stay shut. We aren't a sharing family, but Ba is telling me now. My chest caves in.

I should've lain out in the back of the truck and counted clouds or marigold petals swirling through the air, filling my lungs with something less humid than the insides of Nhà Hoa, less toxic than the stench of a bribe from his mouth.

Caught, I give. "I thought they were from the country area outside Hanoi."

"My bà ngoại worked at the house with her family when she was little. They moved eventually, but she told my mom a lot about it," says Ba. I imagine them on their phone calls, trading a history I can never grasp. "You know the back room behind the kitchen? They fit five on a mat on the floor, and they could've fit more. A lot more."

"Biết rồi." *I know.* "We have it good. Bà Nội had the six of you squeezed in a straw hut. Mom had all eight of her siblings in one room."

Both my parents reminded us of such hardships often, as though too much time swathed in polyester-blend sheets in our own beds would make us ungrateful, which, I guess, I can be. He doesn't mean it this way for once, but the anger in my gut wants to lash out. It'd be depressing as hell if the one fact my nonexistent descendants know about me is that I once worked at Walmart. That you slept near a stove to keep it warm for others. I'm not ashamed. I just want more for the family that came before me. "They worked for those people Alma mentioned?" I ask. "The Durands, or whatever."

"Yeah, the Dumonts," he says, expression unreadable. "Since the very beginning of the house. The flowers, my mom talked about them like they were my bà ngoại's old friends. She always loved the idea of growing some for her mom, but our garden only had vegetables. Had to." *For food.* He's different away from Nhà Hoa, without the mile-long to-repair list hanging from a tool belt. Face softened, he is looking at me too. "The hydrangeas

50

outside were still thriving when I first got here. How lucky is that?"

"Lucky," I whisper. We're not sentimental, but sometimes we believe in fate. Vietnam saved this gift for us alone. Is this the same thrill people get when their ancestry dot com results show 4 percent some country they couldn't locate on a map? "They're really nice. Pretty." A black-winged bird swoops and snatches a fish too close to the water's surface. My mind draws a blank when I try imagining a little me or Lily running around the hydrangeas. "How old was she?"

Ba considers the question carefully. "Things were complicated then, so they didn't keep great records, but she was born at Nhà Hoa. I think they left when she was six or seven."

Are those cuts on the door frame hers? I want to ask next, but the answer is obvious. That wasn't her room; no one was measuring her height. It's kinder to think of flowers and how her green thumbs might have tended the seeds to live this long. Hydrangeas no one else dares to prune, and so they grow wild in your absence. How does it feel to leave the things you love behind? Mom knows. Ba knows. My great-grandmother knows. It's not like I want to go through this terrible thing, but I'll never fully understand the intimacy of a home rooted in soil.

"There's more to Nhà Hoa than what Alma preaches," says Ba as he adjusts his fishing line. "Look what happened to the house when our family wasn't there. I will make it better than it was, like it's been ours all along. And your aunts and uncles will see it for the first time at the grand opening. Maybe after, your mom . . ."

He can't finish the sentence. I won't be responsible for their relationship, not again. I'm done with this bittersweet bribe. Pretending there's a strong tug on the pole, I skitter farther into the lake and let the cold shock me awake. If he's disappointed, I don't see.

Our moods flow with the tide all day, shifting between the now and the time lost. Back at the house, he shows me how to gut a fish and drag her insides out, roe and all. The way to descale and make the flesh smooth. Only the sound of Lily's feet is above us. I try to hold on to a pit of anger, but he laughs when I have to look up a recipe for nước mắm.

It's always water, sugar, lime, garlic, chili peppers, and fish sauce, but in what order? What amounts? How do I make it perfect the first time?

He shows me how Bà Nội liked it: extra garlic and sugar. The air's sour and sweet as I slide unripe mangoes through a mandoline and Ba fries up the fish.

Lily won't eat this. The fridge smells like rot again, most vegetables already gone off. With a clean knife, I slice tofu into thick blocks and run the blade in a crisscross pattern on one side. I tuck lemongrass and salt deep into the cuts and fry them in a nonstick pan. I'm not as good as Mom or Ba at cooking, so bits of tofu crumble away; still, the smell's good enough to bring Lily down.

The unbearable routine of shared dinner becomes a parade, where Ba leads with a fish platter and I follow with browned soy. Lily carries two portions of mango salad, one poisoned with fish sauce and one not.

The ten-person dining table, left within Nhà Hoa, extends over half the room. Something tells me our family never sat here to eat, but we are, and that is what matters: this place as ours, this place as healing. I know no other word to describe it.

We're so happy it hurts our cheeks to smile. The clock strikes six, and we dig in.

6

THE NIGHT IS LONG and hot. Acid burps upward the length of my esophagus, putting a fist-sized weight in the middle of my chest. The mango doesn't agree with me. Hair itches at my collarbones while I sweat right onto the bedding.

Sleep paralysis has happened three nights in a row now, and I dread waking up to that helpless stillness so much I can't relax. Scrolling through Florence's website code, I lose track of time. She's brilliant, and I'm kind of mad about it, as well as all the comments she keeps leaving for me in the CSS style sheet.

/* u into hover animation? no kinkshame in this house just ur house */

/* if u were an airhead what flavor would u be */

/* me id choose strawberry does that make me basic bitch */

/* ok what do you think of putting some 300x300 pics here */

/* WAIT I FORGOT GRAPE IM GRAPE you're green apple so sour */

I bite back a grin. I'm in the middle of texting her, since it's widely available and not obscured by a thousand syntax lines, when the hallway squeaks under the weight of small feet. Rats, maybe. My theory is that they come out to eat the wires. Ba had to reconnect the Wi-Fi again before breakfast. None show in the day, but they could hide in the walls. Like some insects, they might prefer the dark.

At least a rat would choose a better place to die than my mouth—which is enough of a reminder that my mortal, closeted body exists and I should not be flirting.

With heat burning my throat, I need to hydrate in other ways. Water bottle's empty, so I have to check downstairs. I don't bother being quiet when I pass Ba's room. He hasn't fixed the windows, so this is partly his fault. I get it more now though, how stressed he must be with Alma and Thomas over his shoulder.

The fan whirs on the other side of his door, left open a crack. Of course, he sleeps fine in this house. Clothed in night, Nhà Hoa is a different animal. Every shadow is one that shifts, and air caresses the back of my neck—a dancer moving their partner along.

It's not easy to follow someone in this house without being noticed, I think.

My steps take me through the sitting room, where the fireplace's black insides menace me by snapping unlit logs. Sleep deprivation's running my imagination wild, but that isn't

55

comforting. Large potted hydrangeas stand guard on either side, their blooms swaying in a breeze I no longer sense.

I rush toward the kitchen's artificial glow. Maybe Lily is awake and needs a snack. I should've told her earlier about how a warm water bottle can ease some of the cramps. I can bring one to her, I can—

The cold stops me, since this house has only ever been hot.

The refrigerator door is open, a woman's slim hand on its edge. Her flowery robe is thin enough that her body's dark lines can be seen through it. Hair cut from midnight falls in a sheet, in the space of her leaning down to look inside the refrigerator.

He's bringing people home. The hallway noise, the random thumping, the evasiveness, it makes more sense. My jaw tightens. *When does he have the time?*

"Hi," I say because I have to. I can't believe I'm meeting more of his guests in my pajamas. "I'm getting water."

She doesn't reply. I reach for the carton on the counter. The bottle's warm, but I don't really want to reach around Ba's date (girlfriend? sleep buddy?) for cold water. At least it isn't Alma.

Drink aside, I ask, "You need help?" I peek at the fingers pressed so hard on the metal that they are grayish white. At this point of rudeness, it's tempting to be a little shit and offer an iron supplement. I wait a beat, then another.

I'm kind of freaked out now and about to leave when her spine stiffens. She abandons all stillness, reassembling straight and tall in sharp motions. Her body makes me think of a wire hanger—long, thin lines and easy to twist. She turns around slowly.

Above eyes that aren't surprised to see me, blunt bangs slash a forehead in half. Her robe has slipped open, revealing a stretch of smooth skin. She's not much older than me. Her face doesn't shift in embarrassment or apology. We stare at each other, and it's like she's drinking me in.

This is a dream.

I must've fallen asleep after all, to absurd fantasies about noble houses and beautiful girls, where anything is possible. I really, really need to stop texting Florence before bed. Lust is an unfortunate human condition, directly after (1) caring about other people and (2) indigestion. I don't fight my nature; I surrender.

The tiles are fiercely cold on my feet when I step closer. Light wavers as she lets the door go. Heavy rhinestones gleam from her delicate ears. An utter absence of smell clouds my senses. Strange how it cloaks the oil that had seeped into everything, the curry we simmered right into the walls, and the spices dusted on the cabinets, but what I'm really wondering is what *she* smells like.

The beautiful girl offers me her hands. In her fine palms are maggots squirming in a bed of thick white noodles. The writhing sets them apart in the dim lighting. I stumble back, tailbone knocked against marble countertop. *What the fuck.*

She touches her pale chest, smearing their guts downward. "Đừng ăn," she says.

This is actually a nightmare. Okay. *Okay.* I pinch myself on the arm.

She smashes the maggots and noodles harder on her porcelain skin. "Đừng ăn." *Don't eat*, she says, when any thought of a meal has long fled my mind.

"Wake up," I command myself, pinching harder and willing my voice to find its way back to the real world. I can sometimes escape a dream when I know it's false, but I remain stubbornly here, where she moves close. Fingers claw toward her belly button, leaving a procession of dead white things.

There's no scent of decay at all, only nothingness, a void ready to swallow me whole. I can't escape. My nightmare should put on more clothes because maybe I've reached some depraved state where I can't look away from a face that promises sweet pain.

On her next step, instincts drag me back into the darkness. It could be real, but no, no, no, this is a nightmare, the stuff that almost makes sense until it doesn't. The few details that stray out of place, such as a person I can touch but she's not what she seems. Like the cliché, she's different from other girls. She'll change me. She'll make me brave. She's dead.

This is a nightmare.

Humidity makes the hardwood floors sticky under my feet. My room is a shelter with a door that locks. I rush back into it, my nails pinched on the handle.

Wake up wake up wake up.

The floorboards squeak outside my door, and I imagine soft feet on them, risen on the slight hill from the house settling. I know exactly where you should walk to not make noise, but the nightmare does not.

Nothing else moves. Blood thrums too wildly in my skin. I am hot and sweaty and dizzy.

I listen at the door, ear pressed to wood. There's a noise like pincers clicking.

Wake up.

There are moments between dreaming and waking that blur together in bright flashes. They are the source of déjà vu for me. I often open my eyes when my body is still heavy with sleep and wonder: Had I really seen that?

This morning is no different. Bone-tired weariness rather than sleep paralysis slows my movements down. I'm so tired of being afraid of myself. The monsters I create. The anxieties I conjure. If I could reason with myself, maybe I can feel better.

I slip downstairs, searching for the same cold from last night. Rain beats on the house's roof, sliding off in rivers right outside the windows. In the kitchen, it's Ba who stands by the refrigerator, swiping the shelf with a rag.

"Damn thing," he curses. Under the bleach, there's that rotting smell again.

The floor glistens as if he'd just cleaned that too.

Did you see maggots?

The words never taste air. The day before, we'd caught fish together at the lake. Now he doesn't even look at me. There's too much in this house to fix.

"Morning!" Lily has overturned a can of condensed milk in a small bowl. She watches the slow dripping in complete devotion. Dessert-aligned food's the only thing she breaks her vegan diet for.

Our stomachs growl at the same time.

I don't have much of a sweet tooth, but I do have a penchant for sweet people. It's a little bit like: Halle was the pastry to my black coffee or Lily is a butter cookie to my matcha. Yin and yang, or some other Asian shit people would read too much into. Condensed milk reminds me of Mom and the spare loaves of bread she toasts on lazy mornings. Even when she isn't here, it's comforting. From the cabinet, I pick the least stale baguette before joining Lily at the breakfast table.

I sneak a glance at our dad. "Did it ever work?" The question comes off judgmental, because there must be a rational explanation for the rotting food. My subconscious has internalized the uselessness of our electrical appliances since Ba and Lily are determined to downplay the house's flaws, that's all.

I do not question from which mental depths my perfect girl emerged.

Ba sighs and throws the rag aside, grabbing his phone from a shirt pocket. "We need to replace the fridge, again," Ba says. "Yeah, I know it's new." Ông Sáu's voice booms from the other end, blending in with the workers' conversation as Ba disappears out back.

My bread dings against the table surface as Lily drags her bowl away, asking, "What's that about?" Her giddiness over yesterday's progress has dimmed.

It's my turn to sigh. The fridge hums innocently. "Lil, it's all right. Everyone has cranky days." Reaching across the table, I dunk the bread into the condensed milk.

Her eyes narrow in suspicion before she pulls on the bowl.

"And I like to antagonize Dad when he's wrong," I admit, swirling some condensed milk on top. "It's my weakness." I bite into the loaf.

The bread forms a sticky lump in my throat as a thought slips into my mind. *Don't eat.* Led astray by my own lust-induced stupidity, I'd forgotten the nightmarish warning altogether. Anything can rot with enough time. There's no fuzzy mold, but I've lost all appetite. It had been hard to pay attention to the girl's words, with everything else going on.

"He's been having major headaches over this reno," says Lily, "so go easy on him."

I abandon my bitten-into breakfast on her plate, guilt rising over how I haven't noticed his weariness goes beyond just tired muscles. "I'll work on it."

"You better," she grumbles.

I stop by the altar, a haven where my worries can be put aside or, rather, put forward. I speak my mind and throw anxieties to one place. Incense calms me in a way smoking doesn't; I've tried a few times. It isn't spiritual, not in the same way other people burn incense for the dead to feed them or to honor their religion. Standing there I can suspend the belief that no one is listening. It's probably selfish to use the altar as therapy, but I pretend incense can burn unwanted thoughts down.

Dad told me your mom lived here. Did you ever get to see this place? Something's wrong here, and I don't know what. Sleep is terrible, I had a bad dream, I can't wait to leave. Keep us safe, and healthy. Watch over us, Bà Nội.

Then, I remember the moment I stepped closer, hoping to catch a scent on the girl's skin, and add: *Not too closely though.* That part of the story is for me.

This is the sort of thing I'd share with Halle. Instead, I return through the dining room and click on my chat with Florence, someone I'll leave behind at the end of all this. I scroll past our recent messages on how to set up a reservation system on the site. It is decidedly less spicy than her asking me what Airhead flavor I would be.

SUNDAY 9:50 a.m.

Me: do you believe in ghosts

9:53 a.m.

Florence Ngo: aliens are real, y not ghost? see one?

Me: Maybe. But probably not. This house is creepy af.

9:57 a.m.

Florence Ngo: a house needs a ghost plan like a fire plan ok

Me: What the hell is a ghost plan

9:58 a.m.

Florence Ngo: Step 1. See ghost

Florence Ngo: Step 2. Confirm location

Florence Ngo: Step 3. Run the other way and always DOWN the steps!!

It's hard to decide in a dream what the right thing to do is. Still, with all the horror and true crime Halle and I watched, I shouldn't have lost my shit as I did.

10:00 a.m.

Me: strawberry 100% makes you basic

Florence Ngo: I said IM GRAPE NOW

I'm wearing that silly smile again, so I put my phone away. Without a distraction, that distinct feeling of being watched returns. No specters or hidden eyes are among the pines on the surrounding wallpaper. Why am I so paranoid?

Dreams are private, unknowable to others. The girl in mine didn't do anything to me. Her heart-shaped face had tilted curiously as her hands smeared insects over delicate ribs. Alone, I can unspool the dream as memory. Erase away those rotted parts until only her motions remain. She had the graceful showmanship of someone who knew my deepest secrets. I'd been scared, but enthralled too.

7

THE RAIN POURS ON Đà Lạt, a slow storm that turns into sheets. Still, heat chokes the house, and me in it, the last of the shower water beading into sweat. Perched on a chair by the desk, I pick dead bugs one by one with tweezers and compare its shape to the insect leg I've pressed in paper. Mosquitoes are easy to rule out with too-thin legs, but spiders are harder. Many kinds have come to die on my windowsill. I collect them all in a mason jar to prove they exist and that they keep sneaking in when I'm not looking.

The sleep paralysis has come back, and every time I'm idle for too long I remember the girl in the kitchen from two nights ago.

The voice sneaks back into my head. The shape of her mouth when she spoke. *Đừng ăn.* Was any of it real?

I press a knuckle to the headache that has started between my brows. It comes away sweaty.

Enough. Screw waiting for Ba to fix this mess.

The voice was a dream, as was the girl, all brought on by heat deliriousness.

After shelving away the unidentified insect leg, I head downstairs with the conviction that there is nothing to be afraid of. I avoid no mirrors or corners, eyes sweeping every inch of the house.

There's a loud clanging beyond the kitchen in the old chamber that doubled as servants' quarters years before, where his bà ngoại and her family stayed. Ba curses over old cast-iron pipes, down on his luck. The box cutter is probably in there, but I don't want to explain why I need it.

The knife drawer contains exactly three choices: a large cleaver perfect for smashing garlic, a smaller knife that easily pierces meat and vegetables, and a fillet knife for descaling and gutting fish. That last one is long and skinny, shark nosed.

I take it with me upstairs. The grip is surprisingly rough. Rain sloshes against the windowpanes, but I'm past caring. This heat is choking me, and I will take the heady scent of the hydrangeas over it. The knife, unsheathed, blinks light back at me.

Steeling one hand on it, I run the fillet knife between the window and the inner wood. Spiderwebs catch on its blade, which cuts so sharply that paint and wood flick onto the ledge. Taking charge is what I do at home, but all I've felt here is small. The work is slow, snagging on thick globs of paint. When I pull the knife harder, something else moves too.

The sill groans with scraped wood, and the window shows a

smudge behind me. Blurry with rain and glittering in a sweeping dress, it smiles with a mouth as dark as frostbite.

The knife slices into my hand, and I scream. Blood slicks my bare feet. I turn from the bloodied sill, staring into the bedroom's vast emptiness. No shadows, no woman, no smiles.

Footsteps thunder up the stairs. "Jade!" Ba yells, louder and more urgent than I expect from him. "Jade?" Lily arrives first from her room and gasps before running off and yelling about a towel.

At my doorway, Ba stands disheveled, shirt spotted with water. I glance at the window, where his reflection has replaced the menacing shadow. My eyes are hot as my hand throbs. My imagination runs wild with theories: the smudge was the girl, my grandmother, every missing person presumed dead I've ever seen on TV. It *is* someone.

"Are you going to stand there and cry?" Ba asks, the question blasting away my bewilderment. Urgency has faded to exasperation. Those large eyes are a stranger's again. "I told you I was doing it."

"And you didn't," I say as my hand bleeds from the tension I can't let go. "For over a week."

His head shakes. "Come on. First-aid kit's in the bathroom." He cleans the gash roughly, the only way he knows how. This is the second time we've touched here. We haven't even hugged hello yet.

Are you going to stand there and cry, says the cruel thing that torments me by replaying moments that hurt. I'll grind my teeth into dust before I give either the satisfaction.

Lily waits, anxiously watching Ba tighten the bandage over my open palm.

"Why this house?" I ask. "Your grandma worked here when she was little, but it was never hers, right?" Most of these villas belonged to French officers when first built in the early 1900s, and Alma had already told us who owned this one. On the wallpaper, another bird has been eaten by silverfish, giving it the texture of crushed tissue. Outside the rain lulls as if to leave us space to shout.

"This is a good house." Ba's eyes level mine. "Good location."

The many abandoned houses on this hill say he's lying. There are even more in Đà Lạt, built in the European style tourists love so much. "Why not a new one, then?" I ask.

"What's this about?" He lets my hand go. Lily sucks in her cheeks, nervous. My sister knows how an impending fight sounds in my voice. On those rare occasions I laid it out with Mom, the whole town house trembled.

My mouth is as parched as the night something crawled into it. I stop myself from reaching in and grabbing whatever's behind my tongue, at the cobblestones of my blood-red throat.

Way too much to admit. I stick to the facts instead, not holding back. "The nasty bugs, the rats that keep eating the wires, the brand-new fridge that apparently never works." *The windows you screwed up.* "This is a shit house. Who's gonna stay here?"

"Don't say shit," Ba says. "Alma and Thomas có nhiều bạn." He's switched to Vietnamese, which I have a much smaller catalog of bad words in. It's a shame because I want to ask what racist retiree friends do they have to invite but in a much more colorful palette.

His reasoning isn't baseless though. This house and its French architecture, the soaring flowers, the tiniest details that are both French and a little "exotic." As Florence had said, people eat that—poop emoji—up.

The thing about fighting is, it's easy to let something true slip when your emotions run so close to the surface, the vessels loose in your skin. Holding his stare, I say, "I saw something in that window, where you were standing when you came in." I want my dad to believe me. I need him to.

"Jade," he says.

"And the other night, downstairs—"

"You think too much." He gets up. Lily moves out of the door frame.

"No, it's, *ma*." I say the word *ghost* in Vietnamese, but it sounds a little bit like I'm saying mom. The pronunciation is similar.

"You watch too many scary movies." The first-aid kit snaps shut, but I'm already bleeding through the bandage. "Bad for you." He taps a finger against his head.

"No." I grit my teeth, searching for the words *I saw*. "Con thấy ma." *Con*, your child, a semblance of closeness that I'm trying. *Please recognize me.*

"You saw nothing," Ba says. "You don't want to stay here, but that's the deal, Jade."

Anger explodes at my pulse points. "It's not about that."

"Stop." He waves a hand in dismissal. "Nothing bad happened

until you got here. You want to leave early and still win. No. Stay four more weeks."

He sees me as a liar, but how can I lie to him when we don't talk? The me in the mirror is flushed red. I want to put her to rest. I wish this was a ruse. I wish I could sleep for four weeks and walk away.

"Why am I even here?" My voice comes out small, and I hate it.

Shoving past him is easy since he doesn't try stopping me. Passing by Lily's stressed, questioning face is harder. *I can't talk to you right now*, is the look I channel. I will never cry in front of her.

My door slams shut, and I throw the window open, a guillotine in reverse. Cool air rushes in, drying my skin and cooling me down, but I am a flame. Rain splashes on the sill and mixes with blood. There's iron, then flowers, the hydrangeas in Đà Lạt fresh cold, finally let in.

I throw open my suitcase and toss clothes inside, ignoring the shocks of pain from my left hand. Ba is useless. None of this is worth it. I should be back in Philadelphia, making up with Halle, crossing off items on our Before We Get Old list. I should be somewhere I can understand almost every voice around me. In a place where I am enough of everything I dare to be.

Everyone graduates with debts. To their parents, or siblings, the school, or the government. My debt will just be more than I planned because I never want to owe anything to my dad.

Blood slides from the sill and onto the wall, where it inches toward the floor. I'll let it stain, because it's exactly what he wants: a mark on Vietnam.

```
appendix
```

THIS HOUSE IS TICKLED whenever a body's split between rooms, quartered or halved in easy numbers to keep track of. A thousand births here but never quite like this.

Her head enters the parlor, then the first third of her neck. Her middle slides in after, and finally the part that latches to the torso. She walks this way after a feeding.

It took years, but she finally brought ones who will stay. Pliable meat and soft minds, tucked safely in its hold. Eardrums are too easily ruptured, and so this house must be patient. The two young ones won't die for a while yet.

She is tedious work, but necessary.

It is becoming more beautiful, after all, and a house must be clever when it has no feet or hands of its own.

8

SILENCE IS THE ABSENCE of sound other than itself—penetrating, filling, clawing its way through your ears. Silence is the worst sound of all, I'm beginning to realize. Nhà Hoa is silent in the mornings. No birds, no honking cars, no construction or neighbors, like back in our Philly suburb.

Just itself, wrapped around me.

I'm sitting on my bed, with fingers numb over the laptop. The flight itinerary I spent all night on is toggled next to the list of potential summer jobs. The spreadsheet calculates the cost on early travel home, as well as likely earnings if I'm hired and started in the next week. Very few digits would remain in my savings, far less than what I need on August 5th to pay Mom back and the next tuition installment. Especially because I'd be taking Lily with me.

I've wasted enough time in Đà Lạt.

As soon as it's 7:30 a.m., I balance the computer on my forearm and hug the phone against my body to take outside. Barely down three steps, and Lily peeps out of her room. "I knew you were going to do something," she whispers in an accusatory tone.

"No time to mess with you," I say, barging on outside.

Equally stubborn, she trails after and plants herself right on the porch beside me. Her ankle bracelet glints over one fuzzy sock. "You're going to call Mom and make us leave." She doesn't believe me, or worse, she does but cares more about pleasing Ba. I don't ask which it is.

"You're a genius," I say, then press Call while Lily tries diving for my phone. It takes ten seconds for Mom to answer and immediately raise the camera above the length of a table, at which my aunts and uncles and cousins shout greetings over steaming soup bowls.

"Mom" is all I manage, exhausted by the sheer effort to not burst into tears. She reorients the phone so it's facing her alone.

"Ăn gì chưa?" she asks, plucking the beansprouts' spring-green ends before throwing them into her bowl.

I hadn't. "Yeah." I'd skipped dinner, and I'm too moody for breakfast. My injured hand settles over the keyboard so she can't see. The spreadsheet flashes with a series of *eeeeeee*'s.

"Hi, Mom!" Lily shoves her way into view.

"Oh my god, you're awake?" Mom teases before her voice dips, clearly suspicious. "Everything okay?"

When my face does stuff (aka show emotion), it sure is a pain. My youngest uncle, Cậu Nhỏ, tells a filthy joke in the background, and Mom stifles a laugh because she's worried about me. I had let my feelings slip. Nothing is more real than the cadence of her laughter—not the creaking floorboards outside my bedroom, whoever or whatever I think is watching me, the bugs twitching on my sill.

This woman—who doesn't even know how to swim—crossed an *ocean* in a rickety boat to escape persecution, and I'm scared of a reflection. A dream. My reasons for running away seem ridiculous now.

I look up to Mom, but I'm not like her. She wears glittery tees, embellished jeans, and a smile, for anyone. At home, inspirational decals, throw pillows, mugs, and all kinds of décor and comforts shout at us.

Believe in YOURSELF.

Live. Laugh. Love.

Be your own kind of beautiful.

Sometimes, she brings them home without knowing their meaning. *"Jade, what's this?"*

"'Carpe diem,' Mom, for live in the present."

And in this moment, she is happy. Somewhere deep inside I've always known that money was only one factor in her not going back to Vietnam sooner. It was always me.

"I still have school in February."

"Next summer."

"I don't want to leave Halle."

The excuses rewind in my mind. I'd never wanted to come here because of the reality I would have to confront: this is not my home. I do not belong here. I am not Vietnamese enough, and everyone knows it—the lady selling gourds, the kid taking my tea order, my own dad. I stumble through the wrong tones and words, so I rarely speak it at all. Worst of all, I may be more like Alma and Thomas: an American.

This entire time, Mom didn't want to leave me behind. She missed years with her siblings because of me. Even the money was me, for college.

She wouldn't want to leave me behind now. She'd take Brendan and pack to meet up with us. It's one of many reasons I love her so much.

I can be brave too in my own way. For her. I shut the laptop. "I don't wanna get into it, but Dad's being extra annoying." Since that's partly true, playing the role of disgruntled teen is easy.

Lily lets out a long sigh of relief that can be mistaken for exasperation and then, with an off-camera wink at me, groans. "Seriously."

Our aunt slides into the frame to tell us that's nothing new. She nudges Mom until they both burst into laughter. I smile. Adding "maybe ghosts exist" to the list of things I can't tell Mom lightens my shoulders. When I shut off possibilities, I am also less likely to act on them.

For instance: I like girls. I like boys. Still sometimes more girls than boys. I like people who aren't either.

The thing is, I'm 95 percent sure she'd love me no matter what. Yet, that 5 percent of the unknown can be anything from disappointment to too many questions. I don't have all the words to answer them. I don't have all of myself figured out to answer them. That's what college is for. I need that space. That, and her peace of mind, is the prize.

"We getting ready to go another temple. Your brother is very bored." Mom turns the camera to Bren, who skewers a beef meatball with his chopstick. Scowling, he mutters that it's too early. He doesn't seem to feel anything for our dad at all, and I envy him. He's safe from Ba's shortcomings. The screen returns to its makeshift stand. Mom slurps up her noodles. "You call Halle?"

My stomach drops. I can't do this right now too.

Then she adds, "I asked her to watch Meow-a-Lot."

"You what?" I say, my voice coming out low.

Mom scrutinizes my digital face. "I pay her. You don't know?"

"We don't talk about everything," which is a lie and a truth in one. "I gotta go, Mom. Lily will call you on her phone." My sister's too excited by my lack of fortitude to question the retreat back into the house. She stays behind, dialing Mom's number.

Of course, Halle wouldn't have told her about our friendship blowing up. Mom would ask why, and Halle can't answer that. We might not be gentle with each other anymore, but she adores Sir Meow-a-Lot. At least someone is in safe care.

I lift my bandaged hand, blocking out the sun rising over pine. It was an accident, that's all. If I go home now, after spending almost two weeks here already, Ba wouldn't have to give me anything. It'll have been for nothing, and then I'd have to work my ass off to make up a tiny portion of what was promised. Or I'd have to defer for a year.

Nothing can hurt me here. Not more than I expected, anyway. I'll walk away winning in three and a half weeks, money in hand without bothering Mom. My petty side, however, demands satisfaction. I'm on schedule to finish the website, and he already thinks I'm a liar. There's nothing wrong with playing into a trope. I've always been good at that.

Ba will deal with the consequences of not believing me. Regretting that I haven't been nicer, I scroll through my phone and hit Florence's name.

TUESDAY 8:34 a.m.

Me: how about meeting up for that coffee?

Plea sent, I return to my bedroom. The knife, caked with blood, beckons from the floor. *Finish what you started*. I pick it up and work its blade into every other closed window while a plan draws out in my mind. Ba has to see it, experience it enough to admit that I am right.

Rather than an exorcism in this house, there will be a haunting.

9

FLORENCE IS TEN MINUTES late, so of course I've gone through three outfit changes. Shorts and tank tops lay haphazardly throughout the room. I hadn't listened to Mom when she said Đà Lạt gets cold, so nothing I packed is warm or attractive enough to make up for my shit first impression. I'm tying my top when I hear a motorbike revving down the road.

Carefully, I crane my head out a window to make sure it isn't one of the renovation crew, avoiding the dead bugs I haven't had a chance to clean up. Sure enough, I recognize the bomber jacket. I duck back in and check my lip balm in the mirror, as a thread of dark humor surfaces: this is the Marie Antoinette room. It's easy to put your head where it shouldn't be.

Florence is parked out front, where her conversation with Ba stops when she sees me. He watches me too, by the pile of bricks from a local masonry, made specifically to match the house's original brickwork.

"Hey," she says. She reaches back for a spare helmet, about to throw it when her eyes narrow on my hand, rebandaged after the call with Mom earlier. Her palm opens instead, helmet dangling from her fingers. Blue-black paint shimmers on her nails.

"Đi đâu?" Ba asks.

I give him one look and one word: "Out." The scars on my knee from crashing my bike into a ditch at nine tingle, but I take the helmet anyway. I'm short on trust for two-wheeled vehicles, but there's no better option. Florence knows this city and all the places where I can find the information and supplies needed for my plan. Plus, she saw me at my most unprepared self last time, and I am not about that.

I settle in behind Florence, hands around her waist, before she leads us away. As we reach the winding paved road, she speaks. "Lean with me on the turns, 'kay?" I wonder how she knows I haven't been on a motorbike before, if she notices the trembling of my hands. "Don't fight it, or we, uh, die or whatever."

I laugh against her shoulder, my heart dragged at the motorbike's speed. I'm being rescued, however stereotypical. *You're calling the shots*, I remind myself, *you're in control*. Still, whenever I feel Florence's lithe body tilt, I close my eyes and follow.

The café is a lot more posh than I expected. Plants hang at the entrance, the wisteria cut short enough for us to pass under. Chalkboard makes up the back of the register, lit by various neon signs. Thank god Mom isn't here or else we'd be walking out with a *Life happens. Coffee helps.* sign.

We order separately at the register. My stomach grumbles as I consider the limited baked goods. A pastry almost half the size of my face becomes my victim, and a second one is saved for Lily. When I turn around, Florence is standing by the entrance with her frothy beverage, head tilted toward the outside.

Bright, sun-filled slopes divide Đà Lạt, and she leads us down a narrow path away from her motorbike. I should be concerned about where we're going, but instead I obsess over the several terrible ways this talk can pan out. I need Florence's help, but the truth—*ghosts*—is too much to admit.

And here in the sun, the airiness can deceive anyone, even me, that houses like Nhà Hoa are charming and historied rather than creepy and ruined. Not rushing from stand to stand at a crowded market, avoiding conversation, I see clearly how Đà Lạt intends to be different from Saigon's skyscrapers. I'd never taken the time to appreciate its softness. We work our way down moss-eaten stone steps, the gray walls on either side dotted with damp.

Florence stops on the step ahead, turning around with a lift of her drink. "Here, taste this."

"What?"

"It tastes exactly like the milk after Lucky Charms," she says, smiling as if that explains everything about this request.

"If you wanted to trade spit," I say, the remark loose before I can shut my brain off, "there are better ways to ask."

Laughing, she shakes the cup in my face. "This is how I do business."

She knows, or suspects, I'm not here for fun.

Sharing drinks is on my "no" list, but given my impending appeal for help, I glance from my drink in one hand and pastries in the other. I nod in consent. She grins and tips her cup near my lips. The sweet and milky taste rolls over my tongue. "Is there even any coffee in this?" I complain. "Isn't Đà Lạt famous for coffee?"

"Famous for too many things," she says, pulling away. "Doesn't make it good. Coffee's bleh, anyway. I come here for the cereal milk."

People pass quickly on the steps, absorbed by their phones.

I shake my head. "How can someone with such bad taste come up with those A-plus themes for the rooms?"

Ahead, Florence waves a hand lazily. "My boarding school was in Connecticut, so I know all about fancy."

So boarding school is an actual thing. Florence in a plaid skirt and tucked-in white button-up? I can't imagine it or why she would go. I wash down the cereal flavor with some strong coffee. "You miss it?" I ask. "My dad mentioned you'll be at Temple next year."

"I do and I don't." Her shoulders rise and fall. "I have a cousin in Philly. You want to be somewhere else? You looked miserable coming in."

"It's fine," I say, a lie I can't dedicate more energy to. I try steering the conversation back to what I need. "I want to do more research on the house for the historical flair, and I need help translating it, getting it from the library."

"You called me out for a library card?" Florence laughs, then switches to a hardened tone. "Okay, chị." Chị denotes a level of respect, but the way she says it sounds like *okay, bitch* and right now, I'm not in the mood.

"Why do you call me that?" I ask.

Florence stands aside, feet on separate steps. Black fishnet stockings fill in the rip in her jeans. "You've refused to meet for over a week, and you seem like you have it all figured it out, but maybe not? You also assume everyone around you is an idiot, and you just happen to not be one." Her eyes are dark and challenging. "Plus, it sounds like a lie. Or do you really need my Vietnamese tongue too?"

"I have a Vietnamese tongue," I snap, catching up to her on the steps. Technically, Florence is right. I can't read Vietnamese, despite Mom's efforts over the tonal rises and falls for each accent mark. It was always easier speaking English like everyone else. That I was capable of learning it, like calculus, and chose not to, is a regret that's too deep for psychoanalyzing at the moment. "I don't think you're an idiot, actually," I say. "Almost the opposite." Her programming is *everything*.

"So you aren't denying it," Florence says, the corners of her mouth turned up, pleased. "What's up with your hand?"

I hold the pastry bag tighter in my bandaged hand. For most of my life, I have been lucky. I've avoided breaking any limbs. I've never gotten in a major accident. The few scars I have are tiny marks where I scraped my knees in the bike fall. Even sweet, careful Halle has broken four toes in a mistimed door slam.

This wound is a first. All the bad luck in the world is spilling from it raw and unfiltered.

That's the only way to explain how Florence figured me out so easily and forced my perfectly laid-out scheme to escalate too fast.

"I cut it opening a window," I say. She waits for more. "The house is haunted."

I do not use "I think" or "probably" or "maybe." Those words grow doubt. Her eyes don't leave mine as she reads me. Maybe she perceives me as Ba does—paranoid, imaginative, a liar. I'm at least two of those things on most occasions, but this isn't one of them. My jaw aches from the tension of grinding teeth.

Behind me, someone utters an annoyed "move!" We shuffle aside, with Florence flashing her middle finger at the passerby.

"So you really did see a ghost," Florence says when our backs are turned against the stone wall. "When you very randomly texted me that time with such charm." Her sarcasm is an arrow to my ego. I'd blame the insomnia and sleep paralysis for my poor performance if it wasn't for the fact that I had simply wanted to talk to someone. Her.

"I'm not completely sure what I saw, but it isn't a normal place." I sigh. The story unravels from my mouth at a steady pace, covering the apparition in the kitchen (redacted to be clothed), creaking noises, disrupted sleep, and the reflection of a grinning woman. I hadn't realized how much of it lived in me, without my mom or sister sharing in its burden. Florence listened, intently, until the end.

Her expression is thoughtful. "No wonder you look like shit," she says.

I stare, deadpan.

"Beautiful shit. Glorious shit." Florence claps her hands together, spilling a bit of frothy drink. "Shit." She licks the back of her hand. "Better?"

I hold the stare for a little longer. "As long as you don't tell me I smell too."

"You don't," she answers, then more quietly, "Just kidding, anyway." The bar is low when someone tells you they're kidding about you looking like shit and smelling, and your stomach does a flop. "That house does have terrible feng shui."

"It's not feng shui," I say.

"Yeah, I know," says Florence. "I believe that you believe ghosts are real."

What the hell is that supposed to mean? "Do *you* believe it?"

"Aliens are real," she counters. "So why not ghosts?"

Same nonanswer as before. She'd obviously been in the house enough to choose themes for the rooms. For whatever reason, it hasn't triggered her fears in the same way. Still, this almost-stranger hadn't implied I was imagining it as Ba had claimed. Her openness is frustratingly comforting.

Florence sips her drink. "Đà Lạt has a lot of ghost stories, and stories start from somewhere."

"Like what?"

"There's the girl who was murdered and thrown down the well. That happened on the same road your house is on. People say they hear her down there. Or there's that girl who crosses the road at night and makes people crash. The hitchhiker or ride-taker who disappears from the car before she reaches her destination."

Leaning against stone, I ask, "Are they always girls?"

Always in movies, shows, and based-on-true-events stories, the ghost is a girl or woman whose virginity or lack thereof is a moral lesson and whose mental state has grown fragile. Sometimes, the fight is not only for her own life but also for her born or unborn children. She torments the next female in line.

"Seems like it, huh?" Florence says. "Even dead, we're the scariest thing."

I remember my ghost in the kitchen. Beautiful, sharp, and absolutely terrifying—I would've run from her in life too.

Whether to reassure Florence or myself more, I say, "Nothing can actually hurt me, but I need help." It can't touch me. The ghost wouldn't have waited outside my door otherwise. Or maybe, I dreamed it and I saw wrong. It doesn't matter; I've already made up my mind. "Will you help me?"

Her glance is inquisitive, questioning. "Why don't you leave?"

The question strikes me wrong. My impulse is to argue. *I belong here. It is my house too.* But those are lies, or truths I don't believe in. At least in the States, I can use the factual *I was born here, asshole.* But Florence doesn't mean it that way. I think, I think, I think.

"Because I need money." The pastry's cellophane bag crinkles in my hand. "Parents are separated. I have to stay this summer." There's a stone lodged in my flip-flop that I work deeper into the rubber.

"And does your dad know about any of this?" Florence asks.

I see his broad shoulders strained while replacing the stonework in the house or laboring over a meal to be served at six every evening, though Lily can't eat most of it and I'm the one who cooks for her. "He knows and doesn't care. Doesn't believe me, at least, so I need to convince him that the haunting is real and that staying there was always a bad idea. I have a plan."

Her brows rise. It's risky since she might tell her uncle, but there's no luxury of waiting. Less than four weeks left to extract a sorry from Ba for at least this fuckup.

"It involves research, but also pranks," I say lightly. "Maybe fake blood? Undecided."

"You want to haunt a haunted house." Florence's exact summary uncovers the plan's sheer lunacy. April Fools' Day was always my least favorite official day of the year since people would bring whoopee cushions and other ridiculous prank items into school. But I don't want to be funny. I want to be terrifying, so much of a terror that Ba can't close his eyes. I want to be a shadow larger than the thing that cast it, but it can't be done alone. I've watched enough *Scooby-Doo*. Everyone knows the person who isn't there is likely the one under the mask.

"Pretty much," I say.

"Okay, then. I'm in."

I finally focus on her again. Her body's turned toward me now. "Why?" I ask, even when this is the answer I want. The one I ended up telling the truth for instead of a practiced lie.

"I'm bored. I have time to kill until freshman orientation." Florence shrugs, her dark hair shiny in the light. Then, smiling wickedly, she adds, "You're going to need better ghost hunting and ghost haunting tricks though. Lucky for you, you scored a boarding school delinquent."

10

IMPULSIVE ISN'T A WORD I associate with myself, and yet it's all I've been in the past twenty-four hours. At least I'd possessed the wherewithal to shoot down Florence's idea of smuggling a jar with a printout of someone's head into the fridge, but was standing in front of the bathroom mirror at 4:00 a.m. with vinegar and Q-tips actually better? As I wrote, the usually ominous words *GET OUT* had seemed as childish as a kid's crayon sign warning adults from their bedrooms. Then, I waited all morning for Ba to take his early shower, when the steam would reveal my handiwork.

He didn't scream. He didn't run away. His steady footfalls carried him downstairs to the day's work.

Checking after, I saw the clear arc of a palm smearing through the writing. My face had looked wrong and blurry in the mirror: not myself, this foolish girl.

"Next time try, '*I vill suck your blood!*'" Florence says now, lips puckered. "Or '*you're next.*' Something threatening."

"Right," I reply. "Adding vampire and ax murderer vibes would've made it less of a flop." My whole body is tense from riding behind Florence on her motorbike and the last dregs of embarrassment over how horribly the first trick failed. "I'll keep it up to be consistent, but we need better ideas after tonight."

We're parked outside a squat library building, where light rain darkens the pavement in uneven patches. Droplets catch on her glossy hair as she grins. "We'll go more high tech. It'll take another day to wrangle the parts." My gut instinct is that we'd be better off spending time on research, but I want a reaction, *any* reaction, from Ba.

I nod, heart's pace increasing as I stare at the building behind my accomplice. What if we find something definitive on Nhà Hoa? Or if there's nothing at all to this strange house and the things that happen inside it? I hand over an index card with a short list of topics to search for.

Florence twirls it. "Wanna come with me, chị?"

"As a tourist, you know I can't, *em*." I smile, saccharine sweet. She's cute, but like my anxiety, she's a distraction. She knows it too. Florence might not take any of this seriously, but at least I'm not alone.

She cackles. "Knew you're in it for the library card." She heads inside, yelling that she'll be right back. I'm not allowed in, so I wait in the drizzle, out of place as usual here. My jaw is unstressed for once, since I woke up on my own time without paralysis weighing me down. I have to actively stop myself from grinding teeth as five minutes turn into ten, twenty, then thirty.

Florence emerges from the library doors, arms empty, and runs. "Get on the bike!" she yells.

"What?"

She nearly slams into me before pulling me on the motorbike. With my helmet barely on and arm around her waist, we're off. Pain shoots through my injured hand as I shout a muffled "*where are the books?*" Laughing, she speeds us through the streets of her city, then outward where pine rules. My stomach sinks when Nhà Hoa throws its shadow over us again. "We could've gone anywhere else."

"I have to see the source of our investigations, don't ya think?" Florence says as she reaches into the rip in her jeans. With the flourish of a game show host, she unveils an assortment of rough-edged paper from the fishnet.

"You said you had a library card," I deadpan, standing now near the porch.

"I do." Florence hops off the bike. "I'm overdue." A long pause. "And maybe also banned from borrowing more books since last summer." When my face doesn't change, she adds, "Seriously, I can tape it back after if you're so worried."

If *worried* represents wondering what the fuck I've gotten myself into, then I guess that's right. Mom had warned me to not talk about communism or politics in Vietnam. She didn't mention anything about desecrating and committing grand theft of library books. Common sense is easily overwritten when Florence grins at me that way. "Let's get inside first," I tell her.

As we kick off our shoes inside, she observes, "It already feels different in here."

I wave my bandaged hand. "I knifed the windows, remember?" Wind blows freely into the house, spreading dust through the rooms. It tears petals from the hydrangeas too. I shoo Florence upstairs while she mutters "okay, okay, okay." I'm not hiding Florence per se, since her busted Converses are downstairs for all to see, but I'm not advertising the fact that we're hanging out to Ba either. My sister pops out of her room as soon as we reach the landing. *Ugh.*

"Sup, Lily," Florence says before I shove her along, muttering about "website stuff." Why am I explaining to my little sister who didn't even ask?

Lily's eyes sparkle before she closes the door. "Have fun." Right. That's why.

"So, she's in the Paris at Night room, you're in Marie Antoinette," says Florence, craning her neck to study every single door and corner, as if a ghost will pop out on command.

"Yeah, and my dad's in Napoleon." We make it to my room, where someone's picked up all my clothes from the floor and folded them in neat piles on a bed that I did not leave made up like that. I frown. "Other two bedrooms are empty."

"Is it truly empty if there are ghosts in it?" she asks from a plush chair, legs thrown over the armrest.

Sitting on the bed's edge and shoving bras to the bottom of the piles, I ask a question that makes sense: "Why do you keep adding a placeholder on the website for a sixth bedroom by the way? Are you counting that one downstairs?"

Florence raises a brow. "I'm not doing that. I thought you were."

I scowl. "Does your uncle have access?"

"Does your dad?" she asks.

He's terrible at computers and the internet, hence my being assigned this work to begin with. "All right, so not important right now," I say, and draw closer to the stolen library materials in her hands. "Those come first."

Satisfied, Florence offers me the top page. "This one's about Yersin." Though I can't read it, it's nice that she gave me a chance.

"The bacteria science guy who founded this place," I say. "He's in Đà Lạt's Wikipedia page. He wanted this to be a resort town for French officers." Đà Lạt had been the perfect choice for its mild weather, never mind that people already lived there.

Florence folds the page and lays others out. "It's basically Vietnam being screwed by the French, then the Americans. Sometimes, at the same time. All the plantations you saw coming in? Coffee, rubber. They came for that, put Viet people to work. And to bring the church to us, duh." Her fingers toy with the golden cross around her neck. Another unexpected thing about her. She reaches for me next. "Give me your hand." I must look skeptical because she wiggles her fingers impatiently. "Trust me."

And I don't, but I give in, laying my right hand in hers. The touch is cool but a little sweaty. Grabbing a pen from the small

91

desk, Florence writes *1893* and draws a blob with a menacing brow that's probably meant to be bacteria.

"Okay," I say slowly, since she'd ignored the perfectly good paper on the desk. "My dad said Nhà Hoa was one of the early villas. First hotel was in 1907 and the houses came later. Maybe 1920? 1921?"

Florence obliges, adding a skull underneath those years, then the year for when the first cathedral was built. Emptiness bridges my hand to hers, which is branded with the year Ông Sáu and Ba bought this house. "Is there anything about Nhà Hoa specifically?" I lean closer in hyperfocus. "Or my dad's grandma?"

"They don't have many historical or census records from then," Florence says, deflating the pitiful hope for any connection. "Guess they didn't want to keep a record on screwing entire countries over. Can't you ask your dad?"

"I really can't." Despite her frown, the conversation is shut off. I say, "Alma and Thomas are coming over to eat with us in a few days. I'll ask more at least about that Dumont guy."

"Good idea. He's mostly in footnotes in these." Florence adds another miscellaneous note, *1954—France GTFO*, on my hand. "What about that ghost you saw at the fridge—full ball gown, disco flares?"

My mind short-circuits. *Don't even blush, you trash demon.*

"She didn't look like a plantation worker," I say. The hem of her robe had been well stitched, the floral too beautiful. "Didn't notice anything particular."

1955—US invasion is next on Florence's skin. "So this ghost could have been a person living here as early as 1920," she says, drawing a crooked line between my hand and hers. "Or as late as last year."

"That leaves a hundred or so years where anything could've happened in this house," I conclude as our eyes meet. Her brown irises are cool toned in the window's slanting light. The buzzing begins. "Back where we started."

A wasp flies above her head, but she doesn't notice. I stare at the space behind her. Like the rest of the room, the windowsill has been cleaned—nowhere are the dead bugs and container I store them in. The wasp is a perfect figure eight in ominous yellow-and-black stripes, and it drops to the sill where I normally find them lifeless and waiting to be brushed away. Its stained-glass wings twitch in the final throes of death.

Oblivious, Florence announces loudly: "Pee break! More brainstorming immediately after, promise." She bolts for the exit, winking conspiratorially, and I grimace. "I'll give a shout if a ghost peeps on me."

We should probably wait for our technologically advanced haunting plans, but I'm too impatient after today's setbacks. I need this simple thing to check off my list. Florence's text message comes around 2:00 a.m., confirming that she's parked away from the house. I've tented the covers over me.

THURSDAY 2:06 a.m.

Me: remember his window is on the house's right, count back four windows

Florence Ngo: K

A selfie then fills the screen: Florence in harsh lightning, the night sky as her backdrop, and looking stoic as she grips a tall, scaly branch like a magical staff.

Me: Please don't create your own evidence.

My smile falters.

2:09 a.m.

Me: Lily's room is at the back, far left looking at it.

Scaring my sister wasn't part of the original plan, but it's more convincing for someone other than Ba and me, apparent paranoid liar, to experience a paranormal event.

Even though I'm expecting it, my body tenses when the noise rakes across the house's seams. However tempting it is to check outside my door for whether Ba's switched his lights on, I stay put. A distant *tap tap tap* rings into the quiet night, then stops suddenly.

The hallway creaks under his feet—heavier than Lily's—as I hear someone enter the room between us, sliding more windows open to look outside. Then it's silent for many minutes.

The second time it happens, Lily texts me: *Do you hear that?*

I don't answer. This repeats two more times, the sound amplified each time, before a hallway light turns on.

2:41 a.m.

Me: Go go go!

2:43 a.m.

Florence Ngo: Im leaving! Its hard work, thx?

I watch the sliver of light under my door until Ba's satisfied with whatever he did or didn't find and goes back to his room. I lie awake until Florence makes it home.

Me: you really scared her

Florence Ngo: hahahaha cool I even spent more time on your dad's window than hers. Btw did you see the bush below yours? the leaves are turning red

She's easy to scare, I write back. Lily hates horror and even thrillers, so it's not surprising. A good sister would feel bad but no, giddy—that's the feeling I'm swimming in.

eye

GAMES WERE PLAYED IN this house, once. Full of children's laughter as they said *hide-and-seek*. *Cache-cache*, in their mother tongue. The children loved looking for the doll-like bride.

Not in the wardrobe.

Not in the fireplace.

Not in Maman's flowers.

Trốn tìm, they said. A game meant for feet, but this house has always been good at beating the rules. It's no trouble at all moving doors and shadow if it keeps them laughing.

This house won't tell, but.

She's always underneath the bed.

11

"YOU DON'T UNDERSTAND," BA says to my sister, sun illuminating his flat hair. "Storms come and go. It's the rainy season. I already told you July weather is unpredictable."

"But it *wasn't* storming last night," Lily insists, hands on her hips, as we stand beside the back patio's freshly poured concrete. "I heard a bunch of noise, like . . . trees beating the house up."

Her concerned eyes dart over to me. I didn't answer her texts, so to admit that I heard anything now is to imply I didn't care enough to answer. Even when I'm the problem, I'll always have her back. I point to the surrounding flower beds. "They're all dried out. And you'd wait to put in concrete if it rained."

Ba stoops low to the new concrete, using a trowel to smooth out its already perfect surface. "It can be windy without rain," he says. Over and over again, edge to edge, under his precise hand. "Đà Lạt's way up high in the mountains." He makes eye contact with me. "Did you hear something last night, Jade?"

Asshole, paying attention to me for once.

"I must've slept through it," I say. Lily huffs out a long sigh. Maybe, *maybe*, she finally understands my frustration over Ba and her indifference to what I've seen. Then remembering Florence's message, I gesture toward my room's general direction. "But did you notice that hydrangea bush basically bleeding under my windows?"

"Don't exaggerate," says Ba. "Leaves on hydrangea bushes turn purply red when the soil doesn't have enough phosphorus. Even stress can make it change color."

I snort, then say, "So our flowers are being sensitive?" Plants are weird as hell.

"*I* am going to turn purple from all your questions," he says, rubbing the spot between his brows as though a headache's started. "I'll look at it later." Matter settled, Ba waves us closer. "It's ready." The section nearest to the door has been primed for us. "Press your hand firm on this side."

This delights Lily. We've only ever lived in apartments or townhomes on already established streets. "Can we send a video with our handprints to Mom?" She smiles wide. Nodding, Ba reaches for his phone to record.

While my sister squashes a hand in sludge, I inch away, intent on updating Florence on our mild success. Ba's voice cuts me off. "You too."

"Pass," I say easily, raising the bandaged hand. "I don't want to."

"We're already missing Brendan's," he says. "We need you." No one has ever said they needed me, and especially not him. Against better judgment, I turn around. He scratches the back of his neck with stained fingers. "My bà ngoại couldn't leave anything behind here." Bùi Tuyết Mai: a name I'd foolishly written on the list for Florence. We didn't even find a birth certificate. "Our family should be celebrated here." His earnestness tugs at my chest until the camera's red light flashes.

"Come on!" Lily shouts over her shoulder. "I'm gonna be stuck here forever if you mess around."

A bitter laugh nearly escapes my mouth. It's always a show for Mom, or someone else. I squat next to my sister, pressing palm and fingers into the gray. He can look after these when I'm gone, an easy replacement. Ba snaps a photo next. Maybe this one will make it on the mantel—a time skip over years he's missed with us. Lily uses a twig to imprint our initials and today's date.

Cool air twines around my legs. It pulls Lily's ponytail in a flutter. Ba unwinds the hose for us, and Lily helps scrub concrete from my hand since the other's still sliced raw. Only days ago we fought. *Are you going to stand there and cry?* he had asked. I might, right now, if I think too hard about everything I can't have.

"Remember to send it to Mom," she says to our dad.

I warn her in a low voice: "Do not set them up."

"I'm not," Lily insists. "They're not divorced, so technically they're still together."

"You know exactly what I mean," I say. They've been living in separate spaces for four years; it's over. Liquid pools at our feet.

Before she can reply, Ba interrupts. "Don't forget. Alma and Thomas are coming over this Sunday. Keep your rooms clean for the tour." Cleaning is the one nemesis Lily will run from, so she vanishes into the house.

The reno workers are on their lunch break, so Ba and I are alone. He kneels by the concrete where he's left an imprint, right beside mine.

The pull returns in my chest. Hope, longing for all the things I've already sworn off. This is why I need these acts of defiance, little hauntings that echo all that's happened. *Ba can't be trusted*. My heart snaps in half, as quickly as a cheap diary lock. I dry my hand on a rag and leave, again, to prepare.

———

The sky is too light for the time of night I fell asleep, and I'm outside again. Clouds swirl like dirty sink water down a drain. *You're not supposed to be here*, my animal gut says. *Not in this dream.*

Nhà Hoa grows behind me. I hear the vines tightening as a hundred nooses, and the first word I scream is *Dad*.

He doesn't answer. He never answers in a dream, I know that, but panic sends me in a lurch, the second call for him dying on my lips under a girl's finger.

The girl.

Her eyes are the color of crushed leaves during fall, brown and golden. I hadn't been able to tell that night in the kitchen. This time she's wearing a silk áo dài in the palest yellow with roses stitched at the edges. She presses harder on my lips, turning toward the house.

My gaze follows to the attic, where a red-haired woman stares down at us. The woman flashes a knife-sharp smile; she is a nightmare wrapped in a long mauve dress. Cold rips through my spine.

A loud crack.

A body swings from the balcony. The flowery robe flaps open and closed in a lonely wind, revealing smooth torso. This time, it sickens me. The girl in the yellow áo dài stands underneath the bent iron, near her own dead body with the twin heart-shaped face. I wonder which has more heat: a ghost or its fresh corpse.

I step back, away, when I should be waking up. "Did you hang yourself here? What the hell is all of this?"

Upstairs, the red-haired woman snaps a hand to the glass as her smile cuts farther into pale cheeks. Nails curl against glass, screeching.

"Đi," the girl tells me, dragging her finger to her own lips. "Shh." Those eyes beg me to follow. "Đi."

The woman upstairs snaps another palm against the attic window, as nimble as a cat scratching after birds he cannot eat. The gaze prickles my entire body when we leave.

The pines soar even taller here. I should scream myself awake. I've done it before in a nightmare, and in what world is following a dead girl not a nightmare?

Her áo dài flutters with every muscle, but nothing else moves. The ant castle in the fallen tree is back again, the tunnels still and empty. She kneels, and though I know I shouldn't, I scan the branches and leaves above, where the ants are frozen. Dead or dying.

"Why are you doing this?" I am asking a dream why she torments me. "Who are you?" The words overflow in English, then I remember her soft voice warning me from before. Vietnamese—this girl knows Vietnamese. "Tên gì?"

She tilts her head from the colony and back to me, fingers squeezed on a dead ant. "Cam," she says.

Cam. It means orange, but she doesn't pronounce it that way. She uses a harder intonation, distinguishing it from the Vietnamese version as something that cannot be peeled and torn apart.

"Jade." The way she says my name is a sigh, the *d* barely there. "Không nên đến đây." These words don't match the shape of her mouth. They float in translation. *You shouldn't have come here.*

"I didn't want to come," I say. "I had to." I want to break things when people say I don't belong. And yet, it isn't that simple when family is involved.

Cam rises. "You shouldn't have come here."

Her reactions are designed to specifically catch my attention, but she isn't a figment of my subconscious. It's too similar to real conversation, with the anticipated pauses. The more I look at her and this off-sync place, the surer I am that it is not a dream. We are meeting somewhere between our worlds because if I am certain of anything, she is not of the living. "Tell me something helpful. Please," I say.

"We'll be noticed if we talk about them," she says.

A chill runs through me. "Who's them?"

The dead girl studies me. "She doesn't leave the house," Cam finally says, "but it doesn't mean they don't listen." Her movements are erratic and fast, too quick for me to run before fingers slide over my temples and hold me in place. "I can only show you." Her breath glides along my ear.

Suddenly, we are somewhere else. *I* am somewhere else—standing in the master bedroom at Nhà Hoa. The air vibrates with hundreds of tiny wings, but there is no other noise. The floors remain silent under my feet, as if I am nothing at all.

This Nhà Hoa is young, its furniture unscratched. An officer's uniform is crumpled next to the four-poster bed, muddy boots sprawled under an antique chair. Beyond the sleeping man is a breathing, living Cam whose body is swarmed with mosquitoes.

Her eyes are open and bulging wildly, but her body doesn't move under the writhing of countless wings and legs. Strangled cries come from her stilted throat over several minutes. I tense with anticipation, because this distress is intimately familiar. The wait for sleep paralysis to end never gets easier. Cam springs up when the pressure releases, slapping her arms and face. Blood smears all the way down her knee-length nightgown. Cam screams, "Mosquito! Mosquito!" The man—starkly white in the darkness—wakes and grabs her by the arms.

"My love, my love," he says, mouth out of sync with his deep voice. The sound travels to my ears as though through water. "You were dreaming, and—and these are insects. The usual."

Clumps of mosquitoes fall from her hands, but still he denies that it isn't natural how his skin stays unblemished while welts grow all over hers. Cam sobs uncontrollably, buried in his broad chest. "It's not. She's still here, Pierre, and she's getting me. She says I don't belong." Each syllable cleaves into another. "C'est sa maison." She breathes hard, desperate to be heard. "This is her house, and she'll never leave."

12

THE BATH WATER IS hot, scalding in the way I like, as last night's dream or limbo or whatever replays in my mind. I'm hidden behind the shower curtain where the wallpaper's glossy eyes can't watch, but I know the birds are there. I hate this strange place. If someone had asked me if I believed in spiritual shit even a month ago, I would've asked what they're smoking. Now, it's all I can think about. I've dissected the shift from what felt like a limbo space to the hazy dream after Cam's touch.

She wanted to show me what she dared not say out loud. So if it was a vision of her in this house when she was alive, that makes it a memory—not a dream. Not really. She'd been afraid of this "*them*," but living her kept saying "*she*." Did she mean the bugs or the red-haired woman? Cam had suffered from sleep paralysis and the relentless horde of insects as I do. Another Google search for Nhà Hoa's history revealed nothing but pictures of forlorn villas. The phrase "ants with sticks on their heads," however, yielded results that matched the ones I saw outside and in my sleep.

A fungus hijacks the ant's body, makes it lock on to a leaf to die, and rerelease spores to get the rest of the colony. Zombie ants, exactly the thing I do not need.

Apparently, there are other kinds of parasites you can't see, floating in contaminated water and soil, just waiting to be consumed. They might not be zombie ants, but they cause a shit ton—literally and more—of pain.

I scrub the information from my brain, using those minutes before Florence's inevitably late arrival to calm down. By the time I'm pulled close on the motorbike, I feel safe with the hum of her bike taking me away—that is, until we get to the secret meeting place.

"You brought me to another scary house?" I ask, a sharp nod at the clearly abandoned villa. It's a stained cream with a sweeping dark roof, windows punched through. A porch wraps around the whole structure, holding a rusty swing set hostage outside its entrance.

Florence grins. "It's inspirational, and you know it. This is where teens go to scheme." She leans coolly toward the house. "Final girls don't run up the stairs in crumbling houses, so we'll stay outside obviously."

"So what you're really telling me right now is you watch horror movies too," I say, checking out the villa. It must have been built around the same time as Nhà Hoa, and yet the whole place feels . . . hollow. Not nearly as interesting even in basic design.

"Very educational for this type of thing. Hold up." My accomplice retrieves a bag hanging off the bike. She places three smallish boxes on the porch railing. The words *SOUNDGOOD BLUETOOTH SPEAKER: NOW WATERPROOF* are big and bolded on each box. Florence has even chosen different colors—blue, silver, and sand. "We are leveling up," she says proudly, her beaming fading as she peers into my face. "Usually I'd have one smartass opinion from you by now. I should've gotten a green one, huh?"

"They're good," I say, even though there's no joy in tormenting Ba. Not with Cam on my mind.

"Something else happened?" Florence asks, coming close, concerned. Despite not really believing in ghosts, she's asking me as though it matters.

"The refrigerator ghost," I say after a minute, knowing it's a ridiculous moniker for Cam, whose name I want as mine for a little longer. "Saw her in a dream. Or part of it was, and the other was something else. Maybe a memory I was watching? She had sleep paralysis too. In Nhà Hoa."

Her eyes widen, and a different accusation than the one I'm overthinking comes. "Are you sure this refrigerator ghost isn't also window face?"

"No, they're different," I say with unfounded conviction. Carefully, I tell Florence about the vision and "*them*," the enigmatic entity that Cam feared. "It sounds wild," I finish, "but it's happened before. All of it. Her partner was some kind of French soldier, so it had to be 1954 before they left or earlier. She was scared of this woman, I think, who was in the earlier part of the dream or limbo too." That slow conclusion has gnawed at the back of my mind all morning and, now released, can't be reined back in.

Florence makes a small "*hmm*" noise before answering. "Tuấn—my uncle's friend—thinks houses can absorb energy like they do stains." Her heel rubs over a rickety floorboard. "A bit of fish sauce here, soy sauce there, can't ever get it out, you know? Or how days after cooking, your house can still smell like curry." She takes a big, exaggerated sniff, and I inhale with the motion of her chest. We're still in the middle of the woods, but when she's close, I don't smell the pine at all, or the flowers. There's the scent of something metallic and sharp, and gasoline, with an overlay of citrus, like a leaking car with days-old freshener. She reminds me of something real: my neighborhood's concrete-broken streets and sunlight over the dashboard. That a Vietnamese girl born and raised in Vietnam, then schooled in Connecticut, would remind me of home is weird.

I wonder what she thinks when she looks at me.

"It's not just a coat of paint," Florence continues as we walk slowly around the porch. "It's the house's vibes."

My knuckle grazes a chipped wall, so I don't do something inappropriate like step closer. The theory is odd, but Vietnamese people are superstitious. Even I hadn't escaped childhood without such teachings. I ask to be sure, "So, Amityville-level stuff? Past events screw up houses forever?"

"I haven't seen that, but no, more like . . ." Florence pauses, wrinkling brows in thought. "Okay, Tuấn says don't buy houses from ugly people, whether on the outside *or* inside. Because places learn whoever's using it." Then, she adds quickly: "He's an interior designer with a lot of opinions I don't get. Uncle was very upset when your dad decided to do all that stuff himself. But it actually doesn't look bad, really."

On the surface, I almost correct. Mortar has been chiseled and hammered away on Nhà Hoa's face, its cavities filled with new brick to look pristine. But the refrigerator rots our food, an infestation of silverfish laps the restored but still moldy walls in the bathroom, and the noise from the attic, from nowhere at all, rings in my ears.

"A ghost you can maybe ward off with some salt or spiritual shit, but when you're literally inside a house, what do you do?" I ask, rhetorically. There'd be no option other than to get out, which is impossible with all the upcoming bills, Lily, Mom, the fact that houses are not sentient, and ghosts can't actually hurt you.

She bumps her shoulder into mine. "I didn't say houses *do* anything. I'm saying, maybe that residual energy's giving you bad dreams."

"Maybe," I reply. It sounds ridiculous and yet real and threatening—every house learning as you learn to live inside it. Every house listening. If Nhà Hoa learns anything from me, it's weak mind games and bisexual panic. A nervous laugh bubbles from my throat.

We linger at the villa's mouth. "Do you still want to"— Florence tilts her head at the speakers—"*you know.*"

I roll my eyes and say, "Of course." I'm not ready to expose more of myself and how this is the one thing I can control in my life right now. "Send Tuấn a thank-you on his theory for me."

Her reply is sheepish. "I'd tell him when I get back, but he'd spill to Uncle for sure."

"You all live together?" The question is distracted and meaningless. Vietnamese families tend to live together across generations. It's only mine that's broken.

Florence eyes me curiously. "Just me, Tuấn, and Uncle, yeah." I understand, slowly, with my stomach tight that she's trying to tell if I am safe. "I'm the one kid. My parents, I guess, tried it out and. Yeah." Her shoulders move in a shrug, yet every part of her seems tense, not the loose-boned movement of a girl who doesn't care.

All this time, I had not asked about her parents because it isn't my place. I sort of get parents who are separated, but it's different entirely for them to choose to be somewhere else without you.

"They're doing business in Hanoi. My family was always a little unusual in that way," Florence says. "Could be worse. I could be in foster care or an orphanage." She smiles at me, her mouth perfectly perked up. "They got rid of me but kept our dog. At least I can piss and shit on my own."

I wonder at what age did she discover presumed idiocy as a good deflector for scrutiny.

We move out into the sun, her on the lower step and me beside the creaking swings. The corners of her eyes don't crinkle like they usually do during a smile, so I know it's fake. I deeply dislike her faceless parents. I don't smile back; I burn with an honest answer. "Just because you feel lucky to be alive and fed doesn't mean you can't be angry."

Anger is a fire. Anger is adrenaline. It's kept me going for so long, burning for so long, with ambition, with pettiness. *I'll show you* had become a mantra throughout high school. Bullies, racists, useless guidance counselors: *I'll show you.*

Anger is the thing that brought me here to Vietnam, and now to Florence.

Anger is what she deserves to hold in place of self-deprecation.

A breath is tethered between us, our chests rising and falling together, that magnetic pull I felt the first day we met and couldn't acknowledge. Lust is an unfortunate human condition, yes, as are so many other things. Understanding someone's core, or guessing at it, is a thrill. Getting it right brings you too close, and that's fucking scary. It's like cupping the only water you have in your hands in the middle of a desert. Drop it and you're done. Wait too long and it's gone.

"I am," Florence says at last. "But I'm not keen on burning myself out. Not as fast as you, Jade."

brain

INGREDIENTS:

- 0.68 kg pork flesh, ground
- 0.23 kg sea spawn, smashed
- 1 thumb of ginger
- Egg
- White pepper
- Other aromatics, diced or eyeballed

He kneads the mixture in a bowl.

Their father is a builder. This house knows hands like these, calloused and dark, always working.

He kneads until the fatty chunks blend in, a mass of grayish pink, then adds a white pinch.

He reaches for a tucked-away jar and unscrews the lid.

They pour into the blades, which mince them to itty-bitty pieces, like dust.

He mixes it all in the bowl and kneads.

He lays spoonfuls in yellow envelopes and folds them into party hats. This house is so happy it could sing.

13

THEY ARRIVE AT 6:30 on the dot—Alma adjusting the tiny floral scarf around her neck, and Thomas beside her with a bowl of greens already dressed. They have a healthy vacation glow and sunglasses-shaped tan lines around their eyes.

"Hello, girls," Alma says. "Don't you look charming!"

By accident, we're in matching smock dresses; my sister's is light blue with a watermelon print and mine fire-engine red. Mom never quite got over buying us matching clothes from when we were kids. It's the single "nice" thing we packed. Lily and I smile, together, and open the French doors for them.

"How about a tour upstairs while we wait?" I ask, with the precise enthusiasm of someone whose distant father ordained them as Guide of This Blessed Evening in a House They Still Don't Want to Be In. I'd barely had time to set up and check if

Florence's haunting trick would work. It's a gamble how outraged or frightened everyone will be by dinner's end.

"We'd love that," Thomas replies, putting the salad on a gleaming table. Alma produces a bottle of wine from her bag to rest beside it.

They marvel the entire way upstairs, fingers running along the stair rail Ba commanded Lily and I sand and then moisturize with linseed oil. Its wood grain is clearer than the lines on my palms.

Lily's room, Paris at Night, is first and perfectly made. Arcs of light bounce from the star chandelier to the walls, but what's got the couple's attention is the antique vanity table with a three-paneled mirror. "It's wonderful," Alma whispers. Her manicured nails clack against the polished surface, caressing the curve to an elaborately chiseled hairbrush. In the mirror's reflection, her face is covetous. The diamond edge of her chin is ready to cut. In this house, her cigarette stench is wrong, as out of place as soured milk or a dead rat. "I love a beautiful antique. When we saw it earlier this summer, it looked beyond repair."

"Dad has been hard at work," Lily says, beaming and lying through her teeth—about this at least. She restored this piece and its contents under YouTube's direction.

They admire similar features in other rooms, whatever is old and renewed, like the twin bed frames in French Countryside Getaway. The master bedroom's the only one they don't enter, maybe repelled by that sensation that we are trespassing. Its balcony has stayed closed since the king mattress was brought in. In

115

mine, I stand between them and my belongings, in case they're tempted to be handsy with my privacy. I'd hidden one of Florence's Bluetooth devices here.

"It's extraordinary," Thomas says after, back in the dining room. "You can feel the heft of this house's history."

There are no wineglasses, so Alma pours red wine into four regular glasses, one topped off higher.

"Thank you," Ba answers, stepping in from the kitchen. He's moussed his hair and pressed his slacks. His button-up is unstained. He's charismatic in his own way, when he wants to be, so the fact that he's carrying three bowls of hot soup doesn't detract from the image of businesslike sophistication. "All of it was waiting for a patient hand, and investors who saw its value." His large eyes follow the wine being distributed. "Three for the adults."

"Don't be silly, Cường," Alma says without proper intonation. I flinch, swallowing the right pronunciation. "A few sips never hurt a child. Italy and France, they enjoy a bit of spirits with their meals." She winks at me.

"How old are you, Jade?" Thomas asks. "Eighteen? Nineteen?"

"Seventeen," I say. "I turn eighteen in two weeks."

"Same day as the opening, then?" Alma fishes through her bag and reveals the invitation Lily prepared last time. She slides it over to Lily, and I glimpse the pen marks all over it. "I have a little feedback here."

Please join us July 28th for Nhà Hoa's opening party.

I grip my glass. "Yep." Lily should've been the one to tell me

116

first. Ba looks unbothered. Since cake's the last thing I came here for, I smile very bright and raise my wine. "May the weather be perfect, and may the house bring in beaucoup money." The liquid sloshes over my papery tongue, bittersweet, and Alma and Thomas pause before bursting into wild laughter. It echoes, though the house is full. Over the rim of his glass, Ba is bothered now.

Soon, the savory scent of wonton soup lures us in. Thomas pops a wonton in his mouth, breaking for a *mmmm*, while Alma compliments Ba on his cooking. I'm about to slurp up chewy egg noodles when I notice Lily isn't touching her food. Crap. I didn't make sure there was a vegan option. Our parents taught us to never waste anything, and Ba counts on us to never make a scene.

I slide her bowl closer to mine, but she snaps, low. "It's fine. I'll eat it." She glares at her meal as if ramping herself up to wrestle a bear.

"It's fine, *I'll* eat it," I say, even though I'm still annoyed with her. I place the entire salad in front of her instead. It's all lettuce and nuts. "Hang on."

It's a good excuse to slip away to the kitchen. The soup is still simmering on the stove, in case people want more, and packets of yellow noodles wait on the counter for boiling. I shoot a text to Florence: *eating, soon okay?*

I open the refrigerator. Whether it's the heartiest of vegetables or brand-new meat, each day we wake to the smell of something gone off. That smell lingers even after we remove the offending rot, like now. Our moods spoil or are spoiled; it's hard to tell. The tomato and cucumber inside, however, are from the garden, freshly harvested. By the time I'm done washing and slicing them in thick wedges, Florence has texted me back.

T minus 5. Dancer emoji.

The smile has to be forced from my face before I return to the dining room. My phone slips into my lap as I nudge the additional ingredients into Lily's sad salad.

After daintily swallowing a spoonful, Alma adds to the reno conversation, "I would definitely go for holly or even koa for the pergola. Both look more expensive."

At her side, Thomas gulps down some noodles and gestures with chopsticks. "I have a cousin who ships wood from all over. I can wrangle a good deal out of him."

"We'll have to rush if we wait any longer," Ba says. "It has to be perfect for opening day, so people get excited and make reservations right away."

Any second now and the noise will start, so I fixate on my wontons instead. The wrapper is not overly soft, the filling delicate with a bit of a kick. It's been so long since we had this that the flavor consumes me. Did Ba change his recipe? I chew slowly, tongue lingering over new textures. Who has he tested his meals on, if not us? Maybe I've just forgotten what this tastes like. Mom doesn't cook often with how late she works at the nail salon.

A sharp trill breaks the silence from upstairs. I jump a little in my seat, having been embarrassingly focused on my meal. It grows, full blast, in crescendo.

Alma hesitates on their next wood option and peers at the ceiling. Thomas's attention shifts as well. "Is that . . . ?"

"Music," Ba says before turning to me and Lily. "Did you leave something on upstairs?"

"No," we answer together. Wiping my chin, I add a "that's creepy."

It's the musical score for some movie. It cuts briefly to the sharp wail of a sad woman. Fucking hell, is that *Billie Eilish*? I resist the urge to rub the spot between my brows. Luckily, Florence's distant DJing ends then. For now.

"You must've," Ba says sternly.

Lily comes to the rescue with a very ironic question. "So, where are you both from?"

"Cold Spring, New York." Thomas smiles across the table at Lily. "We sold our house a while back to do some traveling, but our kids are there still."

It'd be better to work my way slowly into the topic of this house and its history, but I can't do this all night. "What brought you here?" I pause, twirling noodles innocently. "There are so many old and new villas in Đà Lạt. Why choose this one?"

"New isn't always better," says Alma. Her expression is amused, like we're sharing an inside joke. "In the States, this house would be a historic landmark. Not many people could afford the cost of upkeeping such a marvelous house."

Thomas chips in, "And it's so hard for foreigners to get any kind of footing in this country." He halts, probably realizing who he's talking to, before clarifying his point. "What I mean is, bureaucratic rules about who can own what, and travel visas. Our lawyer fussed for months over the paperwork alone. That type of thing! Thank God we found your dad and his business partner. And as for why this house . . ." He glances expectantly at his wife.

A flush almost as dark as wine colors her cheeks. "As I mentioned before, I did my dissertation on the founding of French Indochina, so my interest is both professional and personal."

"Oh my god," I say. "Right, that's so cool." The phone is hot in my lap under the table, open on a music player. "Did something special draw you to this house? From your research."

"Oh yes." Alma clasps her hands together. Obviously smitten with his wife, Thomas tucks her stray hair back into the fluffy bob.

In rising excitement and volume, Alma says, "Roger Dumont was key in establishing order in this region, but his wife, Marion, was a very accomplished linguist in her time. Latin, German, et cetera, all the great languages, and then of course she had to come here with her husband. She became quite good at Vietnamese too. It's a bit unusual for spouses to come along, but she was an absolute asset to her husband. She was known as the Lady of Many Tongues."

Here's my treasure trove of highly specific and obscure information. Ba's fist closes tightly around his chopsticks, ready to snap. Right, Roger and Marion employed our family. We were here first, and yet where are we in history books?

Alma can't be stopped now, judging by the animated look in her eyes. "Marion held many parties and meetings in this house," she says. "Entertaining officers on leave, translating documents where needed, of course. Geniuses hardly have their equals, so she never had any reason or want to actually associate outside of this house. Unfortunate though. She could've been a great teacher to the locals."

Because I need to know for myself how no one cared for the way my family tended the hydrangeas that live until this day, I ask, "Did someone else live here?"

"No, not really," she says slowly. "Roger and Marion had children, and personal attendants—a house as big as this *needs* care—but they were very much distinguished pioneers and masters of their hearth."

The woman has her PhD in colonization, but that doesn't mean I'm happy she knows more than me—however fractured that knowledge. Having perfected the art of texting with a phone in your lap, I press Play.

I'm shocked it isn't *Thriller* playing, but the beat's aggressive and jars Alma out of her reporting. I turn it louder, never once glancing down. Lily's eyes widen, torn lettuce at the corner of her mouth. Thomas places a hand over his heart, staring wildly around.

Ba has had enough. His napkin smacks against the table. "I'll check."

And this is why it's me and not Florence controlling the speakers from outside the entire time. As long as I know where Ba and everyone are, I can let the music ring out from upstairs, hand hovering over the stop key. I listen for the creaking steps and crooning floorboards beneath the sharp entanglement of spoons and forks. When I think he's too close to a speaker, I shut off the player completely.

He doesn't join us for several minutes, during which they— we—wait, tense.

"It was my computer," Ba lies, chuckling. "Left it on earlier. All off now." He scans the table, then picks up the bottle of wine. "How about another?"

It doesn't take a long time to send them off afterward, once the soup grows tepid and the conversation one-sided. The music picks up periodically, and Ba says he's got to get that computer checked. Lily and Ba are exhausted at the end of it. On our way upstairs, Lily confides in me that Ba seems to be lying. I agree, because I know. I'm not really lying *to* her by agreeing.

Later, I run the faucet in the bathroom before stepping on the toilet lid. Reaching around folded towels, I find the small hole eaten through the wall. *Rats*, I reason again, because of the droppings scattered nearby, and reach in to search along the side. The tape unsticks, and a Bluetooth speaker falls into my grip.

Buzzing with wine, I message Florence: *Mission accomplished!* Bells emoji, champagne emoji, dancer emoji.

The last thing to drift in my mind is *them*, the Dumonts, and whether the Lady of Many Tongues had red hair. If they haunted Cam in her dreams. Perhaps Marion Dumont never left, even after dying, but I have tomorrow for solving mysteries. Right now, I'm allowed to feel enough. I'm allowed to sleep, proud of what I've done.

———

I wake drowning in sweat, sloughing layers like a second skin. I forget where I am until the crown molding blinks into view. Nhà Hoa. Đà Lạt. Vietnam.

Dawn is far from my window. Invisible weight anchors my body to the bed, threatening to skewer me on its coils.

In the hallway, metal teeth grumble on wood, the sound exactly like the workers' handsaws on overgrown roots. It doesn't come closer, only moves back and forth.

My eyes strain against the paralysis, but I see nothing but the closed door. The sound repeats, grating inside my ears.

When will it be done sawing? *What* is it sawing?

My jaw is locked tight, so the heart can't escape upward in a panic.

I had developed a routine to get through this in the past few days: count, breathe, count, relax what you can. But my breath, in and out, falls in line with the saw.

Back and forth.

One, two, three, four—

Forth and back.

Five, six, seven—

Again, something is being cut; dug into; desecrated.

I burst from under the blanket and throw all the fabric to the ground, breathing unevenly and flexing fingers and toes. Mine, all mine and working. My belly's still swimming with wontons and sliced green onion. I'm a container too full of quartered party hats.

Back and forth.

Did I forget to put the speaker away? Is Florence playing a prank on me?

It's scary to think of her among the pines at night. The floor is cold under my feet; nothing's been watching me from the side of the bed.

I touch the doorknob, then twist it. It's a dark hallway except for a shock of pale flesh. I switch the light on, thankful Ba installed something useful instead of beautiful, and see.

She stands, spine toward me, outside the neighboring room. There's a red box cutter in her hand, and she cuts it deep into the door frame, white flecks gathering on a sheath of black hair. Over and over again.

It's Lily—it has to be Lily, the hair has a line crunched in from a hair tie, and yet I don't want it to be. The ridge of her working shoulder blade shows under thin lilac pajamas.

My hand is out, reaching. I touch her arm.

Nothing happens, for a second.

A force throws me halfway over the railing. My tailbone throbs as I arch over that sanded wood, one hand slack on her sleeve and another clinging to the banister. She fucking threw me. I try to make sense of it and her glazed-over eyes.

The blade on the box cutter is a shark fin of gray, drawing near to my throat. I can either fall or be cut.

"Lily!" My scream is swallowed whole in this house.

A deeper voice answers. "Lily."

My dad's reddish-brown arms encircle my sister's, pulling her away with a soft "shhh."

"Thức dậy," he orders. *Wake up.*

I'm frozen over the railing.

"She wanted to see how tall I was," Lily mutters, the box cutter dropping. "She wanted to see how tall I was."

My body unbends, listening. "Who?" I ask. She blinks rapidly.

"You were sleepwalking," Ba says, patting her head. Slivers of wood fall from her hair. Disoriented and staring at the tool on the floor, Lily begins to cry. I take her into my arms with a nod at our dad. He picks up the box cutter, closing the blade away. *I've got this.* I didn't remember that I shouldn't touch her when she's sleepwalking, that's all. It's been forever. Last time was the night before her elementary school graduation.

Although her room is fine, she insists on coming to mine after. Arms full of pillows and blankets, a misty-eyed Lily stops and glances at one wall. "You brought your night-light here?"

"If I didn't want to trip on shit in America, I also don't want to trip on shit here," I say as I unplug it from the wall, pitching us in darkness. When she goes to set up in my bed, I nudge her to the floor. She's almost fourteen, and this is our normal, and my bed is not safe. What if she wakes up paralyzed too?

It takes a long time for my heart to settle. Lily shuffles on her makeshift bed.

"Are you mad at me?"

"No."

"Okay, then why am I on the floor?"

"Because I like my space."

"Are you sure you're not mad?"

"Lil," I say, turning over though I prefer sleeping on my back. Every synapse in my brain wants a rational explanation for our experiences. "It's okay." I reach down in the dark, and a cold hand takes mine. "It's going to be okay." That I can

125

promise; us, the way I would never leave her. "I'm not mad. You were sleepwalking." Fingers squeeze tightly, our fine bones almost twins.

They hold on to me, almost hurting me, but even in sleep I don't let go.

14

NHÀ HOA IS A bride to be unearthed on her wedding day. A white veil has fallen over the house and its grounds. There is no rain, only mist—tiny little specks that I imagine taking between my fingers like snowflakes. Dispelling the mist bit by bit until I can see all of her—beyond brick and wood, and chipping paint, into her bones.

It's a morbid thought, I know. It feeds my anxiety, but that's the thing, isn't it?

Sometimes, you can't stop yourself.

Sometimes, there might actually be something for you to be worried about.

I hope not. I really, really hope not.

The rustling pines shed their sweet scent as I walk by. My feet are sure on where I need to go, the soil beneath them as familiar as the curve of the hallway outside my room.

You shouldn't have come here, she had said.

Me, alone, or does she mean Lily too? All three of us in something we don't get. But Lily wouldn't hide a real haunting, not even for love, which is why she's the perfect supporting witness. My insides churn. What if I caused the stress that led to her sleepwalking? It has to be a coincidence, or maybe it's the house's residual creepy vibes, as the theory goes.

The fallen tree lies open as before, the wood soggy with chewed-out tunnels. Carpenter ants swarm inside. I study the vegetation hanging over them. Where before there were a few ants stuck to the leaves, now there are dozens. A thin brown webbing hugs them close, but it's unneeded. Their mandibles have already attached to the green. The stalks on their heads barely a fingernail's length.

None have been pinched between a ghost's fingers.

It's all too gross. All insects are, even butterflies.

People think they're beautiful, but I see their feelers. Their black eyes. Their fuzzed skin. The faces they wear on their wings.

Yet I can't look away from the ants and how shit it is to be stuck in one place. Victims of a fungus.

The ghost wants us to leave, and I can tell Ba. Ask again to be believed.

My hand reaches out, and I smash them between thumb and pointer. Again, again, and again, my breath hitching.

Free them. That's what I'm doing, right? I am not afraid, I think, every time a head is squashed in my hand, as jammy as a Fig Newton.

I turn to go back, my heart beating fast and well. *I am not afraid.*

The mist breaks apart as the house reappears in view. On this pale morning, the hydrangeas are even more beautiful. Brightened, in contrast, to the house. My eyes drift to the attic window where the red-haired woman had been in my sleep.

Balanced at the top of a short ladder on the porch is Ba, hanging wind chimes. They sway in the breeze, a collection of chuckling metal. "Đang làm gì đấy?" he asks as I speed up the steps. We haven't talked about last night. The dinner and Lil's incident—all tucked away now. Another family secret.

"I was talking to Mom," is the lie I go with. I rub my hands across the bottom of my shirt, leaving him behind. I go to the second floor and peek through the crack of Lily's room. Napping. Good. I shut her door as quietly as I can.

No one should see me right now, looking like shit, so this plan will cost my pride. I click on Florence's name on my phone.

"This is weird," she says as soon as she picks up. "We do calls now?" Florence yawns.

"I don't have time to explain," I say. There's no rush searching for an attic revealed through supernatural means, but I have to do it while I'm not afraid. "That dream, or whatever limbo, I told you about, it gave me the idea to go into the attic."

Florence sits up quickly on the call, saying, "Uhh, Jade, no. Bad things happen in attics. Only second to basements."

If I slow down, I may not do it. Once my brain catches up, I won't. The guts on my hands prove that I am braver when

I don't think. "I require your virtual company, that's all. It'll be fast."

"At least take Lily with you."

"That would make me *more* scared," I reply, then whisper. "She's a wreck after our prank." It would make her nerves worse. We held hands almost all night.

The ceiling is a stretch of plain white. Our town house in the States doesn't have an attic, but I've seen plenty in friends' homes. Usually the hatch is right in the middle of a hall. I walk down the hallway again to make sure I didn't miss it. Nothing.

I've inspected each and every room for the website descriptions, except . . .

I shove aside hangers in the hallway closet. At the rear, sure enough, are the thin lines of a door. Smartly hidden and unobtrusive. A single brass lock hangs from it. Ba installed this one new, and there's no padlock on it yet.

"What's up?" Florence asks.

I angle the camera. "The attic entrance is through the hallway closet."

"Sounds awesome. Very normal."

Surely Ba would've told us if any part of the house was dangerous. I tilt my head back. There're no holes in the ceiling, no potentially spongy spots as with the floor in the master bedroom.

The door gives easily under my pull. A steep staircase leads to the top. I feel for a light switch, but there's nothing. Short as I am, I still have to duck to get inside. It's slightly wider than my hips, making it awkward to swivel around.

Several locks, some with the color rubbed off, are on this side of the door. These must've been with the house on purchase. "I'm going up," I report to Florence. Each step is taken carefully as I run one palm against the wall to steady myself.

Then her breath cuts out over the phone. I scowl, swiping through the screen, but I have neither data nor Wi-Fi. I'm barely at the top of the stairs. "What the hell." The smart thing would be to turn around. That's also the paranoid option, and I am not paranoid or delusional. I am simply curious.

Taking the last few steps in a hurry, I make it to the attic where drapeless windows allow plenty of gray sunshine in. The attic is large and coated in a thin layer of dust, undisturbed except for Ba's footprints, drag marks leading to several plain brown boxes, and the scuttling of furry rats.

The vaulted ceiling is a large rib cage, arching steadily and holding the body together. This is a room that really bears its age on the surface. Sections of the walls are opened, revealing yellow stuffing.

If the ghosts don't kill me first, the asbestos will.

I step farther in, skin already itching from dust. The chimney runs up through the room, all exposed brick. One wall has a number of hooks and a rack lined with velvet, once a gun display. On the opposite end is an old writing desk wedged underneath a window. It's the only thing other than the boxes that isn't covered with a sheet.

My fingers slide over the wooden top before pulling on the handles. Dust and webs break apart, spilling into the air. From the stacks of paper comes a gray thing, squeaking and baring teeth, as I shout, "Rat!" It scurries off the desk.

With one hand over my chest, I pick through the stacks. The paper feels so thin I'm afraid it's going to turn into dust. When I examine a pile, I see them: tiny pink and hairless things with black eyes. Baby rats that make no sound but curl into one another. The future source of our eaten wires.

This, I could tell Ba and he would believe. I won't though. They can't even see how close they are to death. "Why are you leaving the walls," I murmur, carefully gathering a photograph stack and avoiding where I'd disturbed a perfectly good home. Scared a parent away.

I turn one page over and suck in a breath. Photographs. Black-and-white photographs from a world not that long ago. Nothing surprises me since they're mostly nature, this house, white people in Vietnam, until I reach a formal family portrait.

The woman from the window sits at the center of this photograph, surrounded by her family. Her eyes are sharp and deep-set, the angle of her nose narrow. Her family blends into the background drapes. They'd taken it in our dining room, the hint of wooded wallpaper scratching at the edges.

Her dress is a beautiful lace and buttoned at the front with a wide sash. Her hat is even nicer, with a variety of flowers. A girl stands to her right, and the husband towers on the left, hand on their son. The kids are obviously twins, both wearing their mother's dark line for mouths and deep eyes.

My gut tells me she's the Lady of Many Tongues. Marion Dumont and her husband, Roger. The ones Alma told us about. Loopy handwriting stains the back—*1925, le sauvage l'a ruinée.* A visceral dislike rips through me.

Turning it again, I review the photograph section by section, certain that something else tugs my attention. Three-quarters of the way down, I find what must've displeased the Dumonts. A face peers from the long drapes. It's a Vietnamese girl, probably the kids' age, with round eyes. Her mouth curves in a dimpled smile. The eyes give her away. Ba's bà ngoại, my great-grandmother.

"Oh shit," I say, then cover my mouth as if she can hear me through a photo. Leaning closer, I search for other shared features, but the details haven't survived aged technology. She wasn't meant to be in this family portrait. Has Ba seen this? Did he put it back like it doesn't matter? The paper crinkles under my fingers. Maybe it hurt him to see, the same way a dull ache has started in my ribs.

I rummage through the rest, but Bà Cố is nowhere else. I place the photograph in the pouch I've made with my shirt. At the bottom of another pile, wedged under a side panel, is a picture with a face I know. In it, Cam wears a traditional bridal áo dài and a wooden smile, arm looped around a man in uniform. Standing on their other side is Roger Dumont, a near double of Cam's partner. The house looms behind them with Marion waiting at a window.

What is it like to open your eyes and see your world completely gone wrong? The invaders emerging from the mist like pale ghosts, taking and building, and taking. Latching on and draining you dry. Then calling *you* a savage. It doesn't take a genius to parse that word from the handwriting on the photograph. Bà Cố and Cam are incidental relics. The racism is not subtle once you start to look.

A loud thump from the chimney startles me into a string of curses. No one is there. I shut the drawers. The chimney thumps again. Against every instinct, I move closer to the pillar. My steps are slow, as deliberate as an animal ready to run. The thumping doesn't resume, but I don't dare check around the corner.

The exposed brick is cold and crumbly, absolutely silent. Maybe Ba had moved inside to fix the chimney, though I haven't seen it used once. It's kismet, how everything lined up. Compelled by all the puzzle pieces fitting together, I lean forward to place my ear against the surface.

"Jade!" A girl's voice, to my left. Florence quickly crosses the room and snatches my arm, pulling me back down the stairs. She slams the door to the attic, turning on me in the tight space. "What the hell?"

I blink several times before it sinks in that Florence Ngo is standing here with me. In what look like full-length plaid pajamas. As my phone gets service, several pings set off. I explain, "I had no service up there." I scroll through my messages—most from Florence and one from Mom's phone. The latter is clearly from Bren because of the caps and punctuation, and also because it says, WHY ARE YOU IGNORING MOMS CALLS???

Her nose flares. "I thought you fell and broke your neck or something!"

"Were you still lounging around in bed?" I ask, still energized by the photographs.

"Don't change the subject," she says, though she already looks less mad.

"You could've called your uncle and told him to call my dad."

"Oh yeah. Dear sir, your daughter is having prophetic dreams and went into a hole in the closet and then suddenly disappeared while on the phone with me. Can you please make sure she isn't being choked out by a ghost?" She rolls her eyes. "It sounds bananas."

My nerve is pressed, briefly. "It's not," I argue or lie. "You don't have to help me."

Florence gestures at the large pile of photos. "Yeah, I do."

"Well," I say, brain computing faster than I can follow. "It paid off. I found the sixth bedroom." When she raises a brow in confusion, I elbow the small door. "Sixth bedroom, the one that keeps being added to the website. It's the attic. It's huge." The answer to every question I have is close. It feels right that she would be here with me. "I'll explain more in my room. You can change into some of my stuff."

"Your clothes are too short. I'll freeze," Florence says, eyes flickering down my legs. A wave of satisfaction hits me. "Anyway, plaid is very in." She adjusts her collar with a jock's confidence.

"I'm just surprised you like matching pj's," I say. "So orderly, boarding school girls."

A grin lights up her face. "You think about what I sleep in a lot?"

"I am now." I don't back down. "But let's get out of the closet." After a moment, we roll in laughter, snorting and coughing dust and probably snot by the end of it all. This whole week has been ridiculous, but the photograph is something definitive that I found all on my own.

And Florence, well. I really look at her. Her hair is windswept and wild, shining down her back. The cold has lashed her cheeks red during the drive to me. I can't help but smile. When those clever eyes brighten, I know that she's noticed.

15

WE'RE BOTH DRESSED PROPER today, me in the fire-engine red dress again and Florence in her usual ripped jeans, fishnet, and faded tee. Our impromptu meeting after the attic adventure yesterday had been interrupted by her uncle calling about a late lunch appointment and Ba tasking me and Lily with rooting out "irregularities" (aka small chewed-out holes) in the house.

Today though, Florence and I have time to lounge outside, the photographs and backpack with our next prank between us.

"*The savage ruined it*," says Florence, repeating the translated phrase from the family portrait.

"One of those," I say. Of course we would find a racist's cache here. Hardly anything else is ever preserved in history. Even this single photograph of my great-grandmother as a child hiding in the curtains was branded.

"All of those," Florence replies as she thumbs through more.

"This Lady of Many Tongues and her hubs threw parties after every war crime, look." In countless images, officers carried guns on their hip and drinks in their hands. These people existed in the same time and place as my great-grandmother and our family. No wonder Ba never shared his reasons with Alma for choosing this place. She is fascinated by the wrong things.

When Florence reaches the photograph with the Vietnamese bride, my chest twinges with an urge to snatch it away. "That's Cam. The girl at the fridge," I say, glad I'm lying flat on the ground rather than facing her, even though the people pressure-washing the house probably have a full view of my ass.

"I see why you were being secretive," Florence says in a teasing tone. When I look over my shoulder, she's up close to the photo. "She is hot."

"And dead," I remind us both, lightly but helpfully. "Alma claimed no one else important lived here, but it's obvious." I shuffle through the pile. "These two." I point from the white dude in the family portrait to the one next to Cam. "Twins, yeah? So Cam must be Marion's sister-in-law." Because of how anxiety colors my perceptions, I rarely trust my gut instincts, but the answers are slotting into place. Only some, but there's time for more.

"They love erasing that kind of stuff. We were either the servants or, well." Her hand forms an O, followed by a crude motion. "My grandmother was with a French dude. Never hear the end of it from *either* side when it actually comes up."

I never knew to ask how her family survived. Our parents save such stories for the most random and disorienting moments to share, like while peeling hột vịt lộn. You learn to eat the whole fertilized egg that way. I'm lost for words over the million little ways we can still hurt for family we hardly know.

"It would make sense if Marion's the one haunting Cam," I say. "I'll ask when I see her again."

"You sure that's smart?" Florence asks. "We still don't know who's adding the placeholder for the sixth bedroom on the site."

The question grates on my nerves. "She's the one warning me. I don't think"—a pause—"a ghost is doing HTML coding."

She flicks a dandelion near my shoulder, replying in a cool tone, "Okay, *bluefiyahangel.*"

I flinch.

A wicked grin graces her face. "Wasn't my haunting playlist good? It even has a follower."

Groaning, I smack my head into grass. "Oh my god, I was definitely eleven when I made the account, okay? I never bothered to change it." Everything was always private, and I friended no one. Even Halle, who begged to collaborate on playlists, since I knew it'd end up 90 percent movie scores.

I'm still searching for a witty retort when a car starts. Our eyes flit toward the sound of a motor coming alive. I'd almost forgotten this was a stakeout. Ba climbs in the truck. *Finally.* First trip out of the house he's made in two days. Lily joins him and waves out the window when they drive past us.

"Let's go," I say, gathering the photographs and my pride from the ground. "They're shopping for more décor, but who knows if my dad can resist coming home to micromanage everyone."

Back inside, Florence unslings her backpack and takes out packages of smart Wi-Fi-controlled light bulbs. "Thank you, Reddit," she says dramatically. "Home of assholes and delinquents alike." I could only afford five, but that's better—it needs to appear random enough that Ba's first instinct isn't to check them. Florence will handle the circuit breaker, manually, for additional flavor.

The three installations downstairs are a breeze, and as we hurry upstairs, a thought strikes me. "Maybe we can talk to some old people instead and see if they remember who lived here last and what happened."

"They'd have to be extra elderly," Florence says as she pauses on the landing, ripping cardboard from another bulb. "My uncle says the house was empty before '75. Like way before the other people in other villas left."

She'd told her uncle about this. I linger by Lily's room. "Why?"

"He doesn't know," she says. "Can't you ask your dad straight up? About the history here."

"No." My jaw is tight. "His family moved to Saigon later. If anyone knows, it should be your uncle. You guys are local."

It sounds like an accusation: *You told someone else. You asked.*

"We're not the ones with secrets," says Florence.

I want to tear every useless sheet of library book into tiny pieces. I want to ask her what she means and hear the full truth. I want to draw closer. I want to not feel my throat closing up, as if stung by a wasp.

The air has become claustrophobic, so we replace the

remaining bulbs separately. But she doesn't leave, not until dinnertime when they're back, so she can be seen departing on her motorbike. We joke and we laugh, pretending that the pranks are practice for college life, even if it feels forever away. Anytime we get too close, it's too much—that desire to dig beneath each other's skin.

Tomorrow, she promised. *We'll scare them then.*

It's quiet when I settle in, exhausted, that night. Lily's back in her room again, so I keep our great-grandmother's photograph on the nightstand and scatter others around me, searching line by line in each for any small clue. When I fall asleep, without her hand squeezing mine, it is a wandering darkness.

It lasts, and lasts, until a curved moon throws its light on a fluttering canopy. The master bedroom should be empty, but there are two bodies like before. No mosquitoes buzz this time before the smaller form rises. Cam looks much more gaunt and blank-eyed, body swallowed whole by an ivory nightgown.

"What's this?" My voice floats in water, unheard. This must be memory, then, or a vision she wants me to see. But what I want is to speak to her.

In impossibly slow steps, she glides into the hallway, taking the exact pattern to avoid creaking wood. Cam stops once, outside the bathroom, where she mumbles breathlessly to the observant birds, *Don't let her take me.* Conviction seizes her gait again, and she continues downstairs through the pale room and into the kitchen by the same drawer where we store our knives in real life. I flex my hand, fully healed here. Shears glint in her grasp, opening and closing.

The shears are lost in the folds of the nightgown as she goes outside, sure-footed, to the climbing hydrangeas. Cam snips one, then another, until she carries an armful. She does this again, and again, until hydrangeas cover the mantelpiece, until they adorn both kitchen and dining table. The house is untidy with dishes and unfolded linen, full of drifting dust.

Her voice echoes, muffled but intent. "Pretty little heads." She doesn't clip the hydrangea bushes bare, except for one: a sick bush with fanning leaves fading to red. Even in the past, this plant had been stressed or lacking phosphorus as Ba said. She steals all its flowers, some the size of fists and others buds that measure to a pinky. Fresh blooms smile from every surface. She places them in bowls and cups of tea, and the petals overflow in a steady stream.

In these memories that are not mine, I smell newly turned earth and sweet flowers.

A thick centipede crawls from the last hydrangea bouquet in Cam's hands. Hundreds of brown legs scutter quickly over broken branches for an escape, but it runs over skin. Sitting by the fireplace, the canvas of bone white behind her, Cam dangles it over her mouth by one end.

"Fuck no," I say, recoiling despite this not being real. Like a rearing snake, the centipede's long front pincers snap into her slender cheek.

She shoves its middle, legs and all, between her teeth in a sickening crunch.

Between one blink and the next, Marion is there, arm draped over her shoulders. One hand rakes through Cam's blunt bangs.

The centipede has finally stopped struggling as Cam drives both halves inside the dark hole of her mouth.

Marion whispers into the girl's ear, then those forest green eyes sharpen on me.

———

I jolt awake, frozen in bed. My lashes are stuck to the thin skin under eyes that won't open. I need to wait for the minutes to pass, for the paralysis to fade. It always does. Emotions muted in the dream flood over me now, disgust bleeding to confusion. *Why did she show me that?* The door hinges whine, a surprising shriek that raises my hair on end. Is it Lily? Ba? Breathing, I count.

One.

Two.

Fingers touch my chest. *No.*

Three.

No.

Four.

No.

The pressure increases to a full hand, solid and strong. Paralyzed muscles refuse to release the scream building inside my trachea, but my eyes are allowed to see.

Attached to the hand is a pale woman whose forehead stretches like the white of a malleable egg, deep-set eyes pressed in the shape of thumbs. I choke on pooled spit.

Marion Dumont smiles. Desperately, I try to claw back

control, but my body has betrayed me in its stillness. She pushes me into the mattress, head dipping close.

You can't touch me. You're not supposed to be able to touch me.

An utter lack of smell makes her unreal, yet I can feel her. I see it all. A skeletal nose, the width and length between a person's knuckles, pins her face together. Her expression drips with cruel amusement.

"Mon cœur est ici," she says. A laugh stirs the air. Nails dig into my skin, and she repeats herself, laughing. "Mon cœur est ici."

A hush in the night, her skirts brush over the floor. Her body begins moving backward, but the head stays in place. My bulging eyes can't stop watching this terrible, unnatural thing. Retreating, the hand keeps reaching for me. The beige on her sleeve twinkles with glittering thread. Her head hovers above my bed as her neck extends in the texture of saltwater taffy between me and the doorway.

She speaks again, the tongue French accented: "My heart is here, little rat." The floors creak under a body's weight.

Her head is the last thing to leave, slinking through the threshold with a wild, stunning grin. When all of her vanishes, my lungs are loosened.

Body springing upward, I cry out. Move too fast, peeling my tank top down, checking my flesh where nails have left indents. Photographs slip from sweat-ridden covers to the floor. Not once did Cam touch me that night in the kitchen, however close we stood. Not once in those memories, in which I'm nothing but an observer, did she turn her gaze toward me.

Marion had done both, effortlessly. Each finger could've punctured my skin, if she truly wanted.

Cam had warned me that talking makes them notice. I didn't listen, and her neck, *god*, her neck—

The house cradles me so I don't scream.

16

ALL NIGHT AND MORNING, I watch my door for every hiss and bump. My fingers worry the edges of the photographs until there're almost holes in them, and that's when I stuff them all underneath my mattress. They can't watch from there.

I keep only the family portrait out, proof that my great-grandmother lived and survived. Things had once been good in this house. She remembered flowers, but not their beheading or intoxicating perfume. She'd been fine in this house, so why can't I? I must be different, or fragile, or—"*No*," I exhale. It isn't about me. Like people, places change over time, desperate to stay relevant.

I inspect my teeth for spare legs, then get dressed methodically in my favorite shorts and crop top. The expanse under my collarbones is unmarked. No one will believe me when I hardly believe it myself.

The portrait peeks up from my front jean pocket, creased directly on the Lady of Many Tongues's face. It's easier to think of her cleaved in two, but even then she'd probably sprout another head, another neck—"*No.*" My tone cuts through the heavy sleepiness threatening to bowl me over.

The past can't take more than what it already has.

Alma would pay a lot for these photographs, Ba might be scared after finding them beneath his pillow, but this belongs to me. It should be Lily's too. I push myself to go downstairs. The sweetly sour aroma of canh chua wafts from the kitchen, and despite everything, my mouth waters for its stewed pineapple slices and flaky white fish ladled over warm rice. Comfort food.

Ignoring that deep hunger, I find Lily hunched over the dining table, surrounded by bright paper. "Hey," I say, giving her a quick side hug before settling in the next seat. "What you up to?"

"Work," Lily says slowly, folding a sheet of paper before flashing its cover to me. *Join us for a spectacular grand opening at Nhà Hoa on July 28th,* screams the bolded font. Then in smaller print: *Celebrate Jade Nguyen's Birthday.* The invites boast a photograph of Nhà Hoa, soft yellow with bone-colored brick exposed in the most artistic of ways—peeking through the clusters of hydrangea, beside newly painted shutters, and covered in vines. The sensation that the house smiles, with teeth, overwhelms me.

No way Ba approved my name to be near it.

I shake my head, telling her, "It's really not a big deal." The ten days until then, however, strikes me with cold dread.

"You say that every year," Lily argues. "I'm making a fuss about your happy eighteen." She meets my eye. "There's going to be cake, I made sure. Child labor pays in chocolate."

"You don't have to do everything he asks," I say. "Even for me. I hate cake."

"I have to help! Dad's so stressed out that his eye and mouth's been twitching," she says, expression soft. I've barely interacted with him the past few days, but I trust Lily's observation. She loves Ba so much it's unbearable to witness. "Anyway, you hate fun," she continues. "So what exactly are you and Florence doing?"

Because it's the exact thing she wants to needle out of me, I say in a deadpan: "Each other." She squeals, which is an easier reaction to parse out than if I shared the truth about this house that they care so much about. "Learning bad jokes is a hazard of being her friend."

"Ooh, friend." Lily smirks. "Okay, okay." Her hands rise in surrender. "I'll mind my business, but you're being sus." She crosses her arms.

I sigh. "Remind me to never, ever hug you again." Gingerly, I lay the family portrait in front of her. "Check this out."

Her gaze sweeps over the photograph, not reacting to the family sitting prominently at its center. She doesn't recognize Marion, thank god, and zeroes in on the other figure. This small, joyous thing can be ours. Lily holds it next to my face. "Is that Dad's grandma in the curtains? Bà Cố?"

"I think so," I say. "I found it in a desk."

"It really could be," Lily says, glancing back and forth. I'd always looked like Ba's side while Lily and Bren favored Mom's kinder eyes and round face. "Bà Cố wouldn't haunt us, right?"

My insides clench. "Did something happen?"

"Well, um, maybe you're right about the haunting stuff. I found a message on the mirror," she explains. "Oh, I guess it was in English . . ."

Shit. Those were meant for Ba to round out our haunting, but with all that's gone wrong in the past week, I can't even remember when I last wrote on the mirror. It would help my case if Lily believes in the haunting, but she looks small and less herself, as if standing in the real woods rather than in our dining room with the false wallpaper.

"It said, 'I see you.'" Lily sits up straighter to look me in the eye. "Did you write it, Jade?"

Did I write it? I search my brain through all my and Florence's schemes. All that repeats, however, is Marion's head hovering over me. In this quiet, I can still hear Cam munching on the centipede. It's why I can't sleep yet. Each memory raises more questions. "No," I say. "Maybe Ba meant it as a joke."

Lily's skeptical. Not my best work, but it's harmless since she's still safe. "Keep it," I say, tapping the photograph. "Light incense for Bà Cố. Tell her to watch over us."

"Are you sure?"

"I made a copy on my phone," I say, withholding that I blacked out the Dumonts' faces.

Then Lily asks the one question I should've expected. "Did you show Dad?"

"No, that's . . ." My voice trails off. I fold one of the

invitations. "Không muốn." *Don't want*, because maybe the language barrier will soften the blow. Silver linings are her favorite to tuck away in that big heart of hers. She, like Ba, wants this house to masquerade as a home lovingly passed down generations. "I wanted to share with you. You can do whatever with it."

Shattering that hope will only hurt her. They must realize it for themselves. Fake paranormal activity to get out of a real one, that's what I'm doing. I briefly glance at the sconce with a smart bulb, then back at Lily. Only ten days left until this house opens. I am reliable, good Jade, the person who always sees things through.

The next haunting is ready.

In high school, I never once sneaked anyone inside the house, but tonight after washing the pot I stewed Lily's tofu and peanut curry in, I left the back door unlocked. I'm not this indecisive once I go all in, but a million anxious thoughts surge. What if Ba finds the light bulbs before then? Am I doing the right thing? Will Lily actually believe me after this? What does Marion want? Is Cam my friend?

"Why can't you be more straightforward?" I say under my breath in the bathroom that night, staring at my reflection. I'm not sure who I want to be listening.

I'm so sleepy and tired that every shitty event blurs together. The birds on the wallpaper don't help; they make me dizzy from their perches, sitting there. The birds, Cam had pleaded. Mumbled so low her mouth barely moved . . .

A notification flashes on my phone with Florence's name. *In.*

Cold water drips from my chin onto the screen. How does one day feel as though it's hours and years at the same time? Since my accomplice is setting up, I should be at my inconspicuous post too. Lily's and Ba's doors remain closed and ajar, respectively. The fan whirs on in his room, sending tepid air outward.

I slip inside my room, avoiding the bed where the faintest blot of my body is still immortalized in the covers. I haven't been back all day. Perhaps it's animal instinct, that hardwired drive to survive when your brain is working, but I freeze.

The photographs—of Đà Lạt, of the parties thrown here— are lined up neatly on my windowsill, nestled in a garland of dead ants. Black-and-white faces stare at me. I'd left them under the mattress. *Who moved them?* It doesn't matter, because for once, I'm going to heed the warning. Cursing, I fumble for my phone.

WEDNESDAY 11:37 p.m.

Me: cancel

11:38 p.m.

Florence Ngo: omg but I am already here

Florence Ngo: fine

As soon as the text loads, Lily shouts from her room, "Oh my god. Jade!" I throw my door open and rush down the hall, any hint of relief gone. "Daaaad!" She's pulled the comforter to her chin, sitting on the bed's far edge. The lamp in her room blazes red, melts into blue, and shifts into purple, exhibiting the full spectrum of color as advertised.

Only I don't have the app controlling the smart light bulbs open. I'm not the one doing it.

My sister scrambles from the bed, crying. "It switched on suddenly." She runs past me. I turn enough to see that Ba's room glows red too, haloing him with murderous light as she meets him in the hallway. His expression is tight and grim.

As we crowd together, as my brain struggles to explain this away, all the lights flicker in no discernible pattern. Color splatters across our faces, on and off, on and off. We're stuck at a rave no one wants a part in. Lily clings to Ba's arm. My phone vibrates.

11:49 p.m.

Florence Ngo: S O S I'M TRAPPED

What does she mean by trapped? "I'll check downstairs," I say to my family before I hurl myself into the blinking darkness. Anything can be done before the fear sets in.

Ten seconds later, another message: *Jade the doors locked*

I rush through the house for the back room. This door, painted white, encloses the circuit breakers. The old servants' quarters. The door should be jammed, but it opens on the first twist. I step inside, where she's a shadow in the moonlit room. It takes a moment for my sight to adjust. "Come on," I say to Florence's surprised face, but now the doorknob is stuck. "What the shit."

Ba will be down here any minute now.

In a bare whisper, Florence says, "It moved on its own. The circuit box, it . . ." Under the door, the gleaming strip of light dies, wakes, and dies once more.

"Florence," I say. Her speechlessness has my heart hammering. "Flo! Over here. Come to the window." A small rectangle hangs high on the wall, out of reach. She snaps out of it when I touch her elbow.

My hands fold together as a makeshift step. Her weight sinks onto me as I support her against the wall. She undoes the latch and pulls herself up. The scab on my left hand tears on that last scramble, and I grit my teeth. Her body lands with a gentle thump on the other side. Blood dots my bandage, forming a macabre constellation that foretells misfortune.

It sure as hell foretold a lot of pain. My palm closes as the door bangs against the wall. Ba's shoulders tremble, almost too subtle for eyes, when he looks at me. "Everything's normal," I say, as if I'd know what a normal circuit breaker is. His expression doesn't change. Is he worried or scared? Is he looking at me in this room where our ancestors slept and wondering if we too could fit as a family?

He doesn't read my mind, so there's no answer. The lights behave as Ba and I check entrances and exits, going upstairs after locking ourselves in. The stairs unbend with each step. Everything has returned to normal, except for Lily, silent Lily. She stands in her room, illuminated by the hallway light, hands splayed in shock. A figure to pray to.

Glass shards glitter from my little sister's hair, shoulders, and feet. The chandelier above shakes with broken bulbs, roiled by some unseen force. Fresh tears wet her cheeks. My instinct, again, is to run to her, but the chandelier swings back and forth, as if scolding me:

No more.

17

MY SISTER AND I set up on twin beds within the French countryside–themed room. "Trust me," I had said when she asked why we couldn't stay in mine. Maybe our Lady of Many Tongues will take it easy on us in her children's old room. At least it's free of bugs and glass. Traumatized, Lily falls asleep, body furling to a question mark. Although I'm exhausted, I ply myself with herbal teas and melatonin and clean sheets—just in case.

The last night and day have been one unending nightmare. And yet my greatest wish now is to commune with a ghost. I will myself to dream furiously, and purposely. To Florence's "WTF" texts, I leave one message, the most important one of all: *helping sis feel safe, talk later.* A dead girl's name is the last word my lips whisper.

In this limbo world that isn't quite dream or memory—I know this since nothing compels me in any direction—the light bulbs are still whole. My bare feet lie on dust, then rock, and grass, out to the woods where she will be. If a pale face gazes at my back, I do not perceive it.

Pine needles around and above stir in droves. I am a visitor, and yet I feel safe. I am more awake here, ironically. Aware. Cam's áo dài flutters as fast as hummingbird wings around the white pines. "Đừng làm nữa," she says, but the sounds jumble, mismatched. *Don't do that anymore.* She touches a tree trunk. "Don't eat." *Đừng ăn.*

It's always *don't*, it's always *no*.

"Don't eat what?" I ask, echoing far and loud. "We can be less vague now. She's already noticed. She visited me. She came from the dream or memory, whatever it was you showed me." Twigs crunch underfoot as I cut Cam off. My fingers rest over the precise spot Marion's nails dug into. "You're her sister-in-law." Though there have been days to process the photographs from the attic, it comes out as an accusation.

Those eyes waver on me, ashamed, embarrassed, almost enough to make me regret it. "My husband, he arranged for it with my parents," Cam says. "Pierre was . . . nice. Not like his brother or her."

I've no plans to get married, and least of which to someone I can only describe as nice—especially when they brush off their partner's fears as nonsense. The one married couple I know to be remotely happy is Halle's parents. It had been difficult to tell in that first dream-memory with all the mosquitoes, but the pictures weren't altered. His hair was silver threaded, eyes fine lined. Older; it's not that unusual in arranged marriages.

"They said yes," she says. "But they wouldn't see me afterward. Not one time."

Her voice grows ragged with unquantifiable grief, a reminder that she was real once. Her bony hands twist together. It must've been lonely and terrifying being abandoned that way—deemed uncivilized by your new family and considered a traitor by your old. I don't have the words to comfort her. Softly, I say, "You deserved better than that."

Cam lifts her chin. "Your family was kind to me too." It's the first time she's mentioned them at all.

"Are they here?" I ask, heart close to stuck in my throat.

She turns toward the house. "No."

Briefly, I close my eyes. Some small part had hoped that they were really there, devising ways to save us, that I might eventually see them in a dream or in this limbo space. "Can you really show up in person?" I ask finally, turning the conversation around to things that will help me survive this.

She plays with the stitching on her tunic. Her consideration is slow and careful, then spoken as if it takes all her strength to share. "Easier . . . but never long." My cheeks suddenly burn. That means she'd been real and almost naked at the fridge. Both Marion and Cam had appeared on different occasions, blocking out all sense of smell.

"We are so alike, Jade," Cam says. Again, my name said with the *d* barely there while her attention burrows into me. "Girls

156

who don't get what they want. I am less angry, but"—Cam smiles, because she made a joke, so similar to what Florence said about my burning out—"I don't want you to hurt as I did."

Anger, confusion, and short-lived amusement turn to shame as heat floods my head. Cam's only thinking about me. Not everything else that's going on. Somewhere in the waking world, I am lying in bed across from my sister because she is afraid. I'm not made for multitasking emotionally.

"So the lights exploding over my sister," I grit out, drawing near since bravery costs nothing in this in-between space. "Did you do that or her?"

In the terrible, silent moment that follows, Cam breathes in a rhythm that matches mine. But my chest thrums with anger, not some misguided attempt to fake live. "Them," she whispers. "They listen, always."

"You keep saying that, but I've only seen her and you," I say. "And you're both dead." She flinches. "What can she possibly want from us? Why do any of this, instead of resting in peace?" Whatever higher being is out there surely knows that when I die, I'm staying dead.

Her bangs flutter side to side. Cam works something inside her mouth, vigorously as though the centipede's crawled back up. I can't even begin to ask about that because the fragile world around us shakes with every furious motion of her head. There's no time to run or wake before she grabs me, wind curling her long dark hair into a net. "You need to listen too," Cam says. One touch to my temple, and I'm gone.

The sensation, briefly, is of drowning, where every sound is muddled, as I fall into her memory, or her re-creation of it. Resurfacing, I stand at a doorway within Nhà Hoa. Its wood is still fresh and full of children's laughter. From a distance, their voices echo, completely uninterpretable. Cam pulls a silver brush through her hair, sitting in front of the three-mirror vanity my sister restored in present day.

In each reflection, she's distracted by her dead ends while the floorboards creak closer. I freeze.

The acrid tang of vinegar and gas station bathroom assaults my nostrils as a hot breath blows on the back of my neck. Slowly, a hand grips either side of the door frame, enveloping me from behind. It lingers, uncut nails and all, reeking and hateful, until Cam notices, tufted seat clanging to the floor.

"You should be in be—"

Brass haired and impossibly thin, Marion Dumont ambles straight through me, launching herself at Cam. "Don't you dare tell me what to do," she snarls. "You're no madame of this house, little rat."

Cam catches her, pleading, "Let me help you, please." This memory is different from the last—more volatile, earlier than anything she shared before. Their voices are distorted in my ears.

"Help me?" Marion laughs, the corners of her mouth cutting into sunken cheeks. "Parasites, all of you good-for-nothing servants, *poisoning* me." She throws Cam off. "I go where I please."

Cam watches, stunned, as the red-haired woman spins about the room. "Oh, my precious little house," Marion says, her too-big dress slumped against the wall. "I will take care of you always."

She sings off-key until she's gray all over, limbs as stiff as a marionette doll's. Exhausted, she doesn't push her sister-in-law away the next time help comes.

All the while her feverish head never stops whispering. "*I* am the madame of this house, and it knows, it knows, my dear little rat." Her fingers trace figure eights over the walls before being dragged away. "It knows."

———

Funny how a house can be more than just four walls: the center of the universe, the one place your father is happy, an obsession. The edge of the world is at Nhà Hoa. Fog draws close, swallowing garden and patio whole. My, Lily's, and Ba's handprints are the only things I can really see, cloaked in morning. The real world.

She was sick. Marion suffering and making Cam suffer too, draining what paltry fat she had and addling her mind. *Why else would Marion talk to this house?* Houses don't have histories or souls, or I would've been haunted my entire life.

Normally, I thrive on spreadsheets, on order and organization, but too much has happened in a week—hell, over one night from those malfunctioning lights to Cam's tragic past. I turn my back on the fog to look through the kitchen window. I don't know what should be in this script for Mom anymore. Swiping over to the long list of missed calls, I hit her contact info.

It rings, and rings, and the first thing Mom does when she picks up is scold me. "You have not been picking up my calls or calling back, but you wake me up at 6:00 a.m.?"

I smile and say, "Sorry, sorry." One decline had become two, and soon missed calls piled up more than I can keep track of. Now, I've waited long enough to hear her voice. *Mom.* I look at the sky, then back at her when my heart finds a steady beat. "Tell me about ghosts."

She turns on the lamp at her bedside table. She doesn't look happy to hear from this daughter, and about this. "Are you eating? You look tired. Maybe Bren and I should come up."

"Mom, it's okay," I say, "I made xôi for breakfast." Unable to sleep, I had devoted all my attention to perfectly making sticky rice with coconut. "You know Lily will inhale it when she's up. And we already have tickets to meet you back in Saigon in two weeks."

Her soft brows crease in worry, but she doesn't insist on it. She never does. Even when I need her to. "Tại sao con hỏi?"

Because I'm being haunted. I can't sleep. Ba won't believe me.

"I want to know more, that's all," I say. "Florence tells me a lot of ghost stories." Not a complete lie. She'd told me plenty about girls drowned in wells, girls on highways, girls caught between identities. I have a girls' story of my own too now: girl caught in an unwanted marriage, then haunted by the woman who prevails over a stolen house.

"No one can be sure they're real," Mom says finally. "Some people are not buried right. Then some don't go when chết oan." The phrase rings in my ear. Unjust death. "Ghosts can be hungry for different reasons. They die young or they get killed."

How many scary movies did Halle and I watch with a secret burial ground underneath some creepy house? Or about hospitals where a lot of people died? Revenge has always been easy to understand, but hunger implies that something can be filled. What is a ghost's limit when they have no real body?

"Tiếng Việt, ghost gọi là ma," says Mom. "Bad ghost is ma quỉ." Under her scrutiny, I stop rubbing at my stiff jaw. "Not really good to talk about. They're stories."

"I know," is my answer. A story is what holds me hostage during sleep. The half-built pergola surrounds me, a golden cage to contain all my anxiety. "Is that why after someone dies, you go to the temple? So they move on?" When Mom's dad died, she wore a white sash over her forehead and went to the temple every Sunday for seven weeks to kneel and bow under a monk's direction. With her kneecaps red and aching, Mom completed the ritual.

"Yes," she says. "To help them transition to the afterlife." She straightens up against the headboard, fully scowling now.

"We have an altar set up here, you know," I say, hopefully enough to distract her. "For Bà Nội and Quan Âm. He really wants to make this place home."

"It's important to him." The way she says it is wistful, as though they didn't spend the year before he left arguing about money and how every paycheck he earned he sent to his siblings back in Vietnam while she racked up credit card bills to pay for our necessities. Mom loves too easily. She forgives too easily. Had Ba sent her flowers, she would take him back. I know she would, as if we aren't enough—and I hate that I think this. Mom deserves to be happy. He isn't the one to do it.

"We stopped back in the rural area where my family lived when we were kids," Mom says, her voice low. "Even that place

161

is different. There are roads now, and more houses. I didn't recognize anything." I hadn't realized they planned detours from their temple visits. She glances off-camera, to the hotel room she and her sisters are surely sharing. "You want to hold on to the things that are the same. Maybe your dad is like that."

One day, I'll buy you a house in Vietnam, is the promise younger Jade made. Mom might have forgotten or took it as childish nonsense, but I meant every word. I grinded it out in school, in extracurriculars, and at jobs, so that we would be worth that first step into the rickety boat that took her to the States. All that work, only for me to screw it up in a deal with Ba.

I have it wrong, anyway. Mom doesn't want a new house. She wants the one she left behind as an eight-year-old girl. She wants nostalgia. In my family, I'm not the only one chasing after ghosts.

dermis

SOMETIMES ALL THIS HOUSE feels is death. Birds caught in metal and broken glass. Nails rusting half in, half out. Mold brings color to the rooms but slowly kills everything else.

It's much more fun these days to be lived in.

But she is naughty. Bad. *Vilaine*, as she might say in her tongue. She lacks a soft touch. This house is its own, cracking open for visitors, and bathing in old damage. It needs more time. It needs forever, in fact. She must learn that or she is no use at all.

The world would spit her back even if this house slams a wall into her neck.

Tedious thing.

18

Đà Lạt's night market sparkles under fluorescent bulbs. Fish scales are at their iridescent best, flashing and intriguing passersby, and clothes with glitter and sequins catch light like diamonds. Steam rises from hot pots, beer spills and pools under small plastic seats, and laughter rips through the crowd, an off-key symphony.

I could spend my entire night here, away from that oppressive house and what I saw. What is allowed to touch me. It'd been a long day pretending with Lily that all is well.

"Want a souvenir?" Florence asks when we near the clothing stalls, her hair shining over a shoulder, as if I want anything but her. "You look cold."

"Nah." I hug my elbows as we pass a stand with Disney-themed sweaters. Everything inside stills again, a snow globe turned briefly upright. I don't need more baggage leaving

Vietnam than I had coming in. I've capped it on the metaphysical already.

I should've listened to Mom about packing warm clothes. It reminds me of how every winter she wrestles progressively thicker jackets on us. I'm a bit too old and tall for wrestling now. Mom trusts me, anyway, to make my own decisions. That's her mistake.

Call on me tonight, I had texted Florence. It reeked of desperation and tongue-in-cheek, but she came anyway: on her motorbike, helmet outstretched, and grinning. For a second, and now, those lips are all the baggage I want leaving Vietnam.

As though she understands, we lay our mistakes aside, and she pulls me closer to her jacket. I'm thankful for an excuse to finally share heat. We blend in, two girl friends chilling barely centimeters apart, and it's some Lara Jean shit, which is to say: fucking adorable. We can be the stars in this romantic comedy while the inevitable waits.

"How can you be bored here?" I ask, near her cheek so she can hear me.

Her face breaks in fake surprise. "How can you be bored in Philadelphia with the Liberty Bell?"

"I've never even seen the bell." I snort. Most things get dull after a while, even if you've been away. But in the fall, this could be real—walking with her in the city, on campus, in our respective dormitories, through new places we discover together. Living a closet-free life was always part of the plan, but the people existed as hypotheticals before.

Florence is not hypothetical.

165

Case in point: she steers us toward the food stalls. "I have friends here. They're fine, but they're not my best friend," she says. "Don't you want to go home?" Her clever gaze settles over me.

The question is fair, hinting at all that's gone wrong with our prank, but didn't I say the inevitable should wait? Once I speak the truth, I won't be able to stop.

My heart is here, the Lady of Many Tongues had said days before. Here, where I see how beautiful Đà Lạt is. I had thought the same of Saigon, despite the smoke and lights and buildings— how it could've been mine in another life. A different one, not necessarily better or worse. We could've been friends in less screwed-up circumstances.

Shrugging, I choose the three easiest facts to share. "I miss Halle. I miss burgers. And fries." Halle's name hangs suspended in the air, a puff of white, then dissipates.

Florence's hip grazes mine, grounding me as we walk through a throng of people. She plays along, more patient than I give her credit for. "We have the last two here. Halle is . . . ?"

No lies tonight, I remind myself. "Ex–best friend. Complicated. Now cat sitter," I say casually. "And I mean *really* bad burgers and greasy fries, McDonald's style, not that farm-fresh shit. I should've gotten it in Saigon when I was there. I didn't realize Đà Lạt was so cultured."

She laughs. "Very American of you."

I feign offense. "I shared my deepest secret with you!"

By the time we leave the next stand with two orders of silken tofu in ginger syrup, I'm full-on shivering. "Okay, *now* I need more clothes," I say. A hawk-eyed vendor watches us, focusing on our food with laser precision. One drop, and we'll have to buy it all.

I snatch up a Nike long sleeve that really isn't Nike. The motto *Just do it* seems like something Mom would pick, and that's the fourth truth tonight. I miss her. I miss Bren. Calling her this morning had been a risk, and being out of that house allows those vulnerabilities too close to the surface. When I'm scared, my mom is still the person I want in the corner with me.

"That's way too much," Florence cuts in, before I can pay the older woman at the stand. Her loud voice shifts into perfect Vietnamese as they haggle over prices. I'd never heard her speak in full Vietnamese before, because planning was easier in a language we both have proficiency in. I'm taken by her mouth—how it moves, each intonation perfect. "Have you been paying the full price on everything at these markets?" she asks after I fork over the negotiated sum.

"So? It's hard keeping up when they talk fast and talking is exhausting in general," I say. Her mouth quirks in a way that highlights the tiny dimple on her cheek. There hasn't been much occasion to notice before now. Smirking, I add, "Seriously, teach me how to say 'take all my money and don't talk to me anymore.'"

"That's ridiculous," Florence says, taking the bags with our treats so I can pull on the new sweatshirt.

It falls unceremoniously over my shorts.

Her cackle increases in volume. "You look like a middle schooler, which fits with that attitude."

"I'm a whole seventeen," I say. "I skipped a grade even."

"A hoe seventeen underneath," she replies with the conviction of someone who didn't just make the worst pun ever. "Smart ass."

"Don't slut or brain shame me," I say as we reach the wide, open steps that slope into the market. Our knees bump together when we sit, the space between us almost closed.

Unwrapping the food, she stirs silken tofu into the thick syrup and breaks it into a thousand pieces. After taking a spoonful, she blows steam into the air. I should be hungry, but all I remember are ghosts.

"What's it like going to boarding school?" I ask before the dream's muffled sounds can cloud my head. "Internationally too. Thought that only happened in movies, or for rich white people."

"Eh." Florence smacks her lips together. "One looooong sleepover with some people you like and some people you don't. I met my best friend there though. Gemma. I got the nickname from her."

Right, she had interrupted when her uncle introduced her three weeks ago on our doorstep. With uncharacteristic mischief, I demand, "You have to spill the original name."

Her spoon thrusts toward me in challenge, sending an arc of syrup over my knuckles. "Bích," she answers. My stomach does an odd leap. *Ngọc bích* is another word for jade. "Never really felt like me." We shared the same name once, translations for each other from different parts of the world, but mine has always felt right. Each letter is hard, impenetrable, something strong. My mom named me well.

"I'm sure your classmates always very respectfully pronounced your name too," I say with a roll of my eyes.

"They're shits about everything. Stuck together all the time, you know?" she says. "Some of them started calling me Big Flow 'cause my periods were such a pain, messing up the bed. Then Gem said Flo, for Florence. It fit and still does." Chin tucked, she leans on her knees, the dessert container abandoned at our feet.

"Florence," I say, the name quiet and more intimate now for myself and for her, appreciating every moment I am not alone in this place. "It's perfect." I lick the syrup from my knuckles. Spicy and sweet, it's what she'd taste like in this moment. She's watching me so closely. Surrounded by fleece, our thighs lined together, and pressed in all sides by market goers, I am sure my cheeks are flushed.

I set my container down. A fly twitches and drowns in the golden pool of her dessert. Our hands find their way to the same place between us, where she traces around the gash on my palm. It hurts a little, but I like it. "It reopened when you gave me a boost, huh?" she says. We've danced on the edge of the truth long enough.

Before I can convince myself otherwise, I tell her, "I'm going to leave." She doesn't appear surprised. I tell her everything, from the afternoon we spent deciphering photographs to after last night's escape through the window, to the things that make sense and heaps that don't. She breaks her silence periodically with an appropriate "oh shit" that draws my laughter, despite the topic. "I talked to my mom this morning about hungry ghosts," I say. "So she probably thinks I'm close to a break-down." It's so strange sharing with someone that I sit, minutes later, dazed and terrified that I'd shown a modicum of human emotion in a very public space. On *hauntings*.

Her skin is still warm, which is how I realize she hasn't moved away. "I believe you, Jade," says Florence.

I look up as my rib cage loosens, allowing long drawn breaths in and out that do nothing for my rapidly beating heart.

Her voice is solid as she presses on, "House this old, it could've been an electrical issue, but . . . I believe you. You're petty as hell, have bananas ideas, but you'd do anything to protect your sister. Even if it hurts her and you a bit. You see a problem as it is."

The words sink in deep, more intimate than a knife. I hardly recover before an awkward laugh rises out of my chest. "So yeah, our haunting is off." Truthfully, I'd forgotten why I wanted to over time. Pissing your dad off is great until the universe's super-natural forces answer your prank instead. "I'll call my mom tomorrow and make up some bullshit reason." I'll try a version that isn't: *I'm sorry, but Vietnam can never be my home. Ba can never be ours.* College can wait. I can live another year in my false self. I can wait to date a boy, or a girl, or anyone. I've lived almost eighteen years this way, so what's one more.

"You can tell her you're craving McDonald's," Florence offers as an explanation. Her awful joke releases the stubborn tension in my neck. "So no partying it up at UPenn," she adds, though my plan had been to study exhaustingly long hours with a make-out session here and there.

"I'll work the year off and go to college after."

"There are a lot of fast-food options in Philly," she says, pausing, then starting again only to stop before a syllable comes loose. A wry smile replaces what she would've said.

I hold her gaze in that tight space. "Something like that, yeah." Under the fluorescent lights, her eyes shine. Brown, and lit from within. That inner beauty shit is actually real. Nonhypothetical Florence is going to kill it at college barely fifteen miles from my house, but she's probably under the impression right now that all my time will be spent working fast-food establishments.

"I don't know why I thought you were smart," she teases. "You're double the idiot. Ghost hunter. Ghost haunter. Now, I have way too many Bluetooth speakers and I already started getting a white sheet fitted." She raises her brow, as if to say *get it?* "What am I gonna do without your mess?"

Good question. I also want to know. I trace the rings on her hand.

Ask me if I like you. Ask if you can kiss me. Ask me for more.
Because tonight it's yes, yes, and *yes*.

When I am dreaming, I walk Nhà Hoa's halls. It's not from our time because a carpet runs the hallway's full length, plush and patterned in what one might determine as *oriental* or *exotic*.

I aim for the exit into the woods where the hungry ghost can't see us. Cam should be waiting for me, but the only flutter of clothing is on a small girl scurrying from kitchen to sitting room. No, this isn't a dream. I missed it: the invisible plugs in my ears. I'm visiting a dead bride's memory.

Laughter rings out from that room—from more than one person, nothing I've heard yet in the restored Nhà Hoa. Once, my whole family laughed together. It was never at dinner, since Mom worked such long hours, but on those Saturday nights when we gathered with their old friends, the ones they met at refugee camps in the Philippines. There was a lot of laughter. Then of course, separated, people picked sides—even the children.

Lily is the only one who can't.

The small girl, I remember, realizing then that it might be my great-grandmother. I move quickly around the corner. I have to see her face in motion. Maybe her brows are perpetually raised as Bren's are, or she— Marion Dumont walks straight through me. Her body is fuller than in Cam's last memory. Rouge colors her cheeks, her scent nothing but crushed flowers. That neck is set normally. She isn't dead or sick yet.

She shouts at the staff in the kitchen. French, broken Vietnamese, fast and demanding. My—I turn back around—great-great-grandparents, all white fog seeping in from the windows, meaningless to her except for the production of food. Her guests smoke and clink glasses together. The small girl refreshes their drinks, oblivious to my presence.

All around me are officers who undoubtedly keep Vietnam in check and profitable, their starched uniforms muddied at the hem. One other person stands out. Her heart-shaped face is turned down, and she speaks to no one. So many mouths move, but here they're not translated. Fast French. Nothing I understand.

172

My great-grandmother smiles when she reaches Cam, who smiles back. Cam sneaks a candy into her pocket, her eyes mysterious under straight-cut bangs.

"Camilla," Marion says. The words and the mouth do not match up. The wrong record, mislaid audio. "Will you please help set the food, dear sister?" Only *dear sister* doesn't sound like its meaning at all. It slips in the teeth: broken floss, chicken skin, something for your tongue to consider removing.

Her husband places a hand on her knee, as if to say no, but Cam excuses herself anyway. A squeeze on his hand, as quick as the candy for my great-grandmother, now hidden in drifting fog. The faces blurry.

"Ce sont tous des parasites," goes the French from Marion's mouth. *They are all parasites.* She picks a fresh oyster from the platter Cam carries back. "If they're not working, they're scheming. Should we not keep them busy, then?" Her thin mouth turns upward in a grin as she demands everyone's attention, lemon sluicing from the gray shell in her palm to hardwood.

The fireplace seems to shake.

Thump. Thump. Thump.

Softly enough that no one stares at it for long.

They don't appear worried at all, should anything fall from within, because its mouth is in flames, crackling yellow and orange in a country they already own.

I wake, and the fireplace is dark and wide. I am in the sitting room, alone and cold. I don't remember coming here. I don't

173

remember how I said goodbye to Florence. And though I want to crawl back into bed, I stay still and do not move, because if the house settles, I do not want it to know that I can see it. That I am waking up.

19

MY BODY IS RUN-DOWN from being on a chair all night, so I do nothing more than lie in bed until noon. In the twin across from mine, Lily sleeps soundly—unaware that as soon as Mom's done touring the pagoda in Đà Nẵng today, I'm going to get us out. I have our flights picked.

A sharp knock shakes our door, and Ba lets himself in barely a moment after. The skin below his eyes is dark, smudgy, as if he hadn't slept. I remember Lily saying that he's so stressed his eye twitches. I wish he'd give up on this house and leave with us. "Come down," he says.

"I'm not hungry," I reply. Outside, the sun shines even as the sky pours rain. Somewhere, there's a rainbow. I imagine it arched perfectly over the lake we visited once and not again. Was that the last time we talked alone?

"Come down," he says again, brown fingers on the door

frame, feeling for more scratches, something to prove that I've damaged this place as much as Lily and the box cutter. After all, I'm the one who's always guilty. "Đi xuống." He pays no attention to Lily's drooling face. "We need to talk."

His voice is tight and angry, a rare thing these days, so I go. The bed creaks under my weight. The hallway is filled with the smell of braised pork. Salty and savory, another thing my sister cannot eat. "Lily needs actual food," I say, though we won't be his problem for much longer. "She can't live off rice."

"She'll eat if she's hungry," Ba says, which is the same ridiculous thing he's insisted on for the past three weeks.

"Then I'll go pick up more food." And see Florence one last time. How did we say goodbye?

Ba looks over his shoulder. "You aren't going anywhere."

The remark slows my stride inside the kitchen, where a big pot simmers with thịt kho. A layer of seasoning browns the eggs. In Cam's memory, my family had been cooking a French dish. The thought dissipates when Ba stops at the corner by the altar. It looks cold. Days have passed since I last lit incense. Maybe that's why my head feels too full and heavy.

"It isn't funny," he says, staring at me.

"I wasn't laughing."

Ba gestures toward the teacups lined up for Bà Nội and the Quan Âm statue. Propped up are us—me, Lily, Mom, Bren, him—smiling from old photographs, all free from the frames on the mantelpiece. It takes a second for me to understand what he means.

"I didn't do this," I say. The altar is for the dead. It is for the bodhisattvas we pray to, the worries I can leave nowhere else. The altar is not a place for the living. "I didn't put them there."

"Then who?" Ba asks. He removes the pictures from the altar and closes his hand over them. "No more tricks." Conviction laces every word. "You will finish the website like we talked about for the opening party. You will stop all the unnecessary shit you've been doing."

The stove is too hot. Steam rises from the caramelized pork, sucked away by the fan. This house feels too tight, too small, like the rib cage holding in my heart. Too much.

"I told you this house is haunted," I say, low. "It's not the first time pictures up and moved."

"I don't believe in ghosts," Ba says.

"No," I say. "You just don't believe in me." I squeeze all the emotions that are too big in a box, because he can't see any tears. His words have followed me since the day I cut my hand. *Are you going to stand there and cry?* Never again.

With his fingers drumming close to the gas burner, Ba says, "I installed a camera after the dinner party."

Each tap sends a sick lurch through me. "You did what?"

"I hid them in the wind chimes out front and back. Florence came in before the power went haywire," he says. It surfaces with ease through my archives of memory: he'd been right in front of me hanging them up while I was busy with ant guts on my hands. "You and Florence have been staging the haunting."

"Because you aren't paying attention to the actual haunting!" The anger bursts. Every trick we did, the house—Marion— subverted it. Made it bigger. Made it real. How to explain—this

177

entire room feels like a pus-filled eardrum, an infection burning me up and clouding the words between us. Each line is worse than the last. "Did you know that someone died in this house?" I ask. Marion, who was horrible long before sickness. Our personal ma quỉ.

This, he answers with quiet resolve. "All places have death in them, Jade, with enough time." Talking to me as if I am a kid afraid of shadows and mist and noises of the night.

"But murder?" This is my guess, the conclusion I've been coming to all along for why Nhà Hoa has been empty for a hundred years, why Cam lingers with her abusive sister-in-law instead of moving on.

"Who says there was a murder?" Ba asks. He turns the stove off, but the thịt kho keeps boiling. "Your next tuition payment is due August fifth. If you want it and the back payment for your mom, this ends today. A summer is a summer. A deal is a deal. You can't leave before and still walk away with the money."

There's a creak behind me, and I hope, I wish, for something that will prove I am right. A ghost, a specter, many-legged insects ready for martyrdom. What I get instead is my teary-eyed sister. "You came here for *money?*" She hadn't missed a single word, judging by the fury in her tone.

Only one of us ever wanted to play family. My promises that everything would be okay blow away in one instance. "Hold on, Lil. That's too simple, and I'll explain everything, but you know this house is actually messed up and haunted. I was planning on calling Mom and—"

"Dad just said it was you and Florence!" she shouts. Her

round face is blotched with red, an open book detailing the pain I've caused her. "So you wanted us to bond with sleepovers while I'm scared, so I'll trust you more than Dad. *Against* Dad, and we can all be as hateful as you."

"How can you think that?" I whisper. *Hate* is too simple a word; what I've always felt is pain. From how that still wasn't enough for him to stay. From how white people treat us when they think we don't speak English. From how Vietnamese people treat us when we don't speak well. From what others say when you try to protect yourself. "I wanted to keep us safe."

Her bitterness congeals at the surface, sagging her mouth in a frown, and she doesn't stop. "I shouldn't even be surprised about this," my sister says. "I'm not going anywhere with you. Are you listening, Jade? Nowhere." Resolute, Lily storms off in her pajamas, hair thrown loose from a ponytail.

The refrigerator hums, my insides stunned and ice cold. I look at our father, whose expression is blank and unopinionated now that he's through with me. As long as he gets what he wants, Ba has never cared about collateral damage. I am so tired. None of it matters to me anymore.

———

This house. The ghosts. Who is eating whom?

I sit cross-legged back in the Marie Antoinette room, three walls of pillows around me, and pretend that it makes me safer, that it doesn't matter, because we are leaving. Even if the only thing Lily said to me for the rest of the day is, *why don't you haunt me for my attention?*

179

Fog kisses my window in a shroud of white. Underneath it all, a shovel sharpens into the dirt, as steady as a knife on whetstone. Ba is still working outside. *2:07 a.m.*, my phone flashes before the battery dwindles.

The hydrangeas have gone wild. They must be upending themselves and running inside, over the place they keep guard to finally claim it as their own. Vines must be breaking into the house, and Ba is fighting back.

I tiptoe across the room and crouch low next to the window, eye-level with the sill. A moth convulses in front of me, in the last throes of death, and outside the earth is pierced again.

My head rises above the sill, searching the ground below for my dad. A cellphone's light captures his outline. A dying hydrangea bush and its bloodred leaves have been overturned.

Ba's thin hair flops every time his foot slams down on the shovel. He's entirely focused. Does he even know the time?

Quietly, I sneak into the hallway. The bed in his room has not been slept in. His notebooks reign there, laid out on every surface. Lily's back in her own room with the door shut since she blames me for all weird occurrences. I keep the lights switched off. On the lower floor, I fumble for a candle and lighter from the entryway chest.

I worry the inside of my cheek, not caring if it bleeds. My screaming gut instinct is louder than usual. *This is all wrong.* Door hinges chuckle with every close. Everything is misty and white and could be day rather than the black sky I know to be above us. The candle lights my way forward. Down the steps and to the right, bending around the house to the spot where Ba digs.

The dirt pile grows. I don't think he's noticed me, but he says, "Đi ngủ đi."

"Sleeping is the last thing I want to do," I say. Watching Lily drift off had been one way to distract myself from overwhelming fear, but now I'm left alone again in the room where Marion held me down. I'll sleep when I'm close to dead. And Ba, he lost the right to tell me what to do. "It's 2:00 a.m. What are you doing?"

He doesn't stop digging, and his voice emerges, gravelly. "Fixing these flowers."

I stare at the fallen hydrangea bush, our poor stressed-out plant. It is luscious and tragic, a set piece belonging in a fairy tale or play. Ba must be working on the roots.

Yet the sound that comes from the hole in the earth is unnatural. It reminds me of wisdom teeth and fading under laughing gas in the dentist's chair. Sleepy drunk, no pain, but the excavation of each deeply grown molar.

As he kneels, he reaches bare hands into the soil. The skull is pale and dirt stained, larger than his palm.

I stumble back.

"There you are," he says, setting it aside as daintily as he would a porcelain cup.

"What the actual fuck," I say. "Did you, *did you*—"

He hooks another skull by the nostril. "I saw in a dream that they were here," Ba says, jaw twitching.

My body is bloodless and reptilian cold. The faces are long gone, having fed the hydrangeas Bà Cố loved so much, and their names, we will never know them. No dead are honored here.

Ba's tone is emotionless. "The house has to be perfect for the opening."

"Who cares," I snap, stepping closer. "That is a body part." Bile burns my throat as my brain fires off plans. "We should leave. Call the police or whatever. You *know* this place isn't right now." Thoughts scatter in my mind as I try to make sense of the scene. *You made me feel insane. You said I was lying but you see. YOU SEE. You dream.*

His brown eyes turn to mine, equally big. "You're always telling me to go," he says. For so many weeks, I've avoided conversation and bonding, and finally we stand close enough for me to see what should have been obvious. Veins move underneath the whites of his eyes. They writhe with hidden tendrils that etch them pink, irritated.

Every noise is blocked out as I wish, for once, that this is a nightmare. I pinch myself. *Please let it not be real. Please.* I twist my own soft skin.

"You said it's fine to go when you're unhappy," he continues, laying bare our past.

I was a child. I *am* still a child until the house's unveiling, my birthday.

"Don't forget who told me to go four years ago." His words cleave into me, prying my other buried secret. "If you say anything, I will tell your mom, sister, and brother that you told me to leave."

The years Mom had to work as a single parent is my fault. The judgment from teachers when they found out I signed report cards for all three of us. The made-up reasons for why we lacked a dad. No matter how much I tried to lessen the burden, those and other hardships are on me. "It wasn't like that," I say. "You chose to go. You chose to listen."

"You didn't need a dad anymore," says Ba. I mistake him for a crying man before he yanks at the end of a thin wiggling worm.

My breathing stills, but every cell in my body screams to run away.

The worm dislodges from the eye duct, glistening as it falls into the grass. Tears blur the edges to everything, all my nightmares made into reality. The next worm he feeds back into his gaping mouth, as the bride had done with a centipede. All at once, it makes sense.

As Marion likes to say: *They are all parasites.*

Ba insisted on our six o'clock dinners, piling food into my bowl and refusing to make vegan options for Lily.

Đừng ăn, Cam had first warned with palmfuls of maggot-infested noodles. The refrigerator was never broken. It was her trying to save us, rotting every food so we wouldn't eat any hidden eggs. Unlike the fungus overtaking the ants' bodies, some parasites are not easily seen at all.

Ba dreams with Marion. She's hooked into him as she was in Cam, making her de-head hydrangeas in the night, shoving spindly legged bugs down her throat. And he wants to control us too.

I want to throw up.

"This house will be perfect," he says again. "I'll finish up that sixth room very soon, and you will finish the website properly." He looks up at the attic, which shies away under mist.

Slowly, the question that hurts least surfaces in my mouth: "The placeholder on the website. That was you?"

"I can't be responsible for everything around here," Ba answers with a smile. My eyes itch, desperate for a scratch, any scratch, and my long fingernails can fulfill that urge and dig until a culprit is found. Unweigh myself with whatever lurks in the corners of my eyes. Ba hasn't stopped talking. "The more, the merrier, so we need every room, she said. More money too, and popular. My brothers and sisters will see what I've done with it for our family. Your mom will understand what I had to do."

Ce sont tous des parasites.

"Pick it up," Ba orders as his foot nudges a skull. I flinch. "Remember: we're in this together." He cradles the other skulls in his arms like newborns. He always held Bren and Lily so closely then, enveloping them in safety. But now I'm not jealous. I'm afraid.

"Is this really you?" I ask, my voice finally breaking. "Or Marion?"

He smiles. "Of course I'm your dad."

I can't tell at all, I realize, who he is or what she might do. I grind my teeth. "I'm not touching a skull."

"Fine, then," Ba says, studying me and their handiwork. "You bring the shovel."

We bury the heads in the woods, all together. If someone finds one, they will find the rest turning the earth up so why bother with three burials. It's logical, and it saves us time. The spot's not far from the fallen carpenter ant colony. I don't even search for them because I know they're there, growing, spreading. We don't say anything else on our way back to the house, where I rinse my hands at the hose and let water numb me down to the bone.

liver

THIS IS A STORY một người mẹ once told her children:

A boy lived in a poor village by the river. His family were farmers, but what they farmed was not theirs.

Each night they had rice and canh rau má. The boy would save two grains of rice in his sleeve while his parents and siblings licked their bowls clean.

The next day, he would feed the baby bird that had fallen into their fields. Some days, the bird ate one. Others, two.

When his mother found him one morning, with the baby bird and its nest of dried rice, she cried, *"For each grain of rice you do not eat, it's one maggot in the afterlife."*

But as good mothers do, she told no one else and he kept feeding the bird. One day, the bird was not there—only blood and feathers.

Years later, when the boy-turned-old-man died, he arrived to a bowl of maggots in the underworld. Eating, but never full like his mother, father, and siblings.

There might not be a hell for houses, but this house never lets a scrap go to waste.

20

PARASITES LIVE ON OR in other organisms, eating from their hosts. They're so small that you'll never see them. And they can be anywhere.

Cyst-growing tapeworm from pork.

Brain-swelling virus left by a mosquito bite.

Intestine-burrowing amoeba hidden in salads.

Flesh-eating bacteria slipped inside an oyster.

The internet is a portal to hell, full of illustrations that capture their monstrosity. Parasites have evolved to relentlessly feed off others. Some relationships are symbiotic—both sides benefit. In others, the host dies.

And Marion, overwhelmed by whatever made a home of her body, died.

Could there be a breed of the zombie ant fungus that infects humans? Or maybe it's some supernatural parasite latching on, holding on to the horrors in this house.

After last night's terror, Ba is certain about my compliance. He doesn't monitor my behavior. It's Lily who brings up food, judging by the creaks in the floorboards outside my room. She's mad at me, but I'm a living thing she won't let starve. Maybe there's hope for us. The dishes are untouched. Instead I gnaw on my lip, both sweet and salty because of the Pocky sticks and shrimp-flavored chips I smuggled into my room. I don't have an appetite for anything real. How can anyone, if they know what I know?

My text to Lily—*Don't eat anything Dad gives you*—is left on Read all day. I send others too, instructing her on how to bake the tofu I marinated yesterday or stir-fry the safely packaged noodles. My options are awful, no matter how I spin it: (1) Call Mom and tell her every wrong decision I ever made and why. (2) Report Ba to his business partners, who for sure care more about money and prestige than his well-being. (3) Pretend I didn't witness anything.

The last one is especially impossible. My entire body reacts to every sound resembling the chatter of a loose jaw, every movement that might be attached to an insect wing or feeler. Anything close to a shovel's weight gets dropped from my guilty fingers.

There's something I'm missing. It scratches at my brain.

Under my windows, the house's side is scratched too. I look.

A reno worker sets a new hydrangea bush down. Its leaves

are a healthy green, to be rooted from soil rather than flesh. Lily hovers behind him, directing to the right spot.

Someone tried to tell you this. The red leaves of the plant Ba uprooted.

The night Marion Dumont held me in my own bed was the same night Cam cut flowers in that dream-memory. Those blood-red leaves had peered back at me under moonlight. It's not just that. My fingers are white as I scroll through my messages with Florence, the last few asking about whether I talked to my mom left unanswered. It's all the way back, the message I barely paid attention to.

Btw did you see the bush below yours? the leaves are turning red

The things you get used to in order to survive. The logic you rely on. I have to let them go. Ba claimed before that stress or phosphorus deficiency causes changes in color, but nothing is that simple at Nhà Hoa. I pull the photographs from underneath the mattress. All this time, there have been warnings. It's about time I acted on one.

I open the door. At my feet is a bowl of bánh canh. Fat white noodles swim in a rich brown broth, the orange-pink shrimp floating like Christmas ornaments. I step over the tray and into the dark hallway, where everything is shut tight. Ba must've gotten another headache. That's probably Marion digging in too deep. Even when he hides her secrets, she won't let go.

Perfect was the word he used. The house is almost perfect and ready for guests. Ba's rummaging around the attic, fixing the sixth room as promised. Downstairs in the foyer, a painting of the Lady of Many Tongues has been hung since Ba's abandoned all pretense. It is grand and nestled in a gilded frame, a commissioned piece weeks in the making. Marion will work him to the marrow, then drink him dry. She watches me leave.

My steps are hidden under the noise of hydrangeas being packed back in and the patio being fitted with lights. The photographs are crushed in my hands as I trudge through the woods, the air so dense it could be a second body closing in for an embrace.

"I'm so tired." The words empty, drifting for the pines to hear. Nothing stirs while I walk toward Alma and Thomas's vacation house. I don't know the number for the police in Vietnam, but they will. A laugh rattles out of me.

Fifteen minutes later, I'm at the hedge surrounding their French-style villa. This one's been built completely new. Its edges line together in perfect unison. It doesn't loom over me. The windows are large and clear, as much light in the house as outside. They must be home.

Rather than going around, I squeeze through and over the hedge, sharp pinpricks of branches stabbing all sides. I tumble onto grass. From the veranda, Alma shouts, "Jade, dear!" Smiling wide, she takes one long drag from a cigarette before flicking it aside. Her head bobbles in good cheer, entirely too quaint over the silk scarf tied around her neck. "Come in. You look cold." People keep telling me that. Pine needles and leaves cling to the tightness of my tank top and polka-dot shorts. Underneath, I'm wearing a layer of gooseflesh that I don't feel.

I hurry and join her stride into a modern, all-silver-appliances kitchen. "Tommy, fix some tea, please," she says. Her husband gets up from the breakfast nook, greeting me before he fusses over an electric kettle. Alma, looking as respectable as a high school guidance counselor, leads me to another sitting area full of beige plush. She picks up a spare cardigan and flattens it on a large armchair. She pats the seat, indicating that it's ready for my dirt-stained ass. I hate guidance counselors. "Is everything okay?" She glances at the rolled photographs in my hands and then back up.

This is my moment.

No, it's not okay at all. Six words to set us free. To get help, the thing I should've done after the slipped knife. Yet I'm frozen, still as I am during an episode of sleep paralysis. As routine and as familiar. I'm not even surprised by my utter uselessness.

"I . . ." My voice trails off. Looking people directly in the eye is a particular gift of mine, but I'm feeling neither gifted nor talented at the moment. I take in the room, and how different the atmosphere is here, and how it tastes—inedible, all new fabric and metal, Đà Lạt's nature slamming against well-insulated walls. It's a very stale house.

Abundant sun bounces off the many entertainment screens. A glowing star of light beams from one spot: a hairbrush in silver, with wings curving along the grooves.

"Beep, beep!" Thomas chuckles as he slides a teacup in front of my face. "It's hot."

I take it without an immediate answer, probably scaring the boredom out of these folks by now. "Isn't that brush Lily's?" I ask. The saucer warms my lap, but my thighs itch against the wool sweater. Now, I stare at Alma with earnest intensity. That brush belongs with the antique vanity my sister restored in her room. In Cam's old room.

"Ah," her husband interrupts, so I stare at him too, not drinking the flowery tea he prepared for me. His ears are pink. "I happened to stop by the house and spoke with Lily. She understood my anniversary with Alma's coming up, and. Well, Lily was very kind in parting with it."

What the shit.

Alma's head bobbles again. "You paid her for it, didn't you, dear?" He nods, standing at her side, hand cupping her shoulder. She adds, "It's not worth much actually in the vintage market, it's very replicable, but sentimentally, it means very much to me."

"Right, of course, Dr. Alma," I say. I crush the photographs even more before sticking them in my waistband like some cowboy about to shoot his own privates off. Which, at least, seems more productive than the sudden anger thrumming through me. Help, from these people? I chuckle, belatedly. "My sister is thirteen. She's old enough to know the value of stuff. Did you talk to my dad at all?"

"Um, no," Thomas says. "Not lately."

The woman with her spry white hair says, "Your dad's made so much progress on the house." Cheerfully missing the point.

"I can't believe the party's only a week away!" Thomas continues. "We put the word out among the expat community. It'll be a full house, how exciting."

Coming here has been my most ludicrous decision, including when I decided to haunt a haunted house. I had actually considered letting *them* pass judgment on Ba. Thomas looks at me as someone to pity. "Well, better get back to it. I needed a break from all the construction," I say with false cheer. The brush will have to stay, though it might help my standing with Lily to get it back.

We rise, them reaching for my untouched teacup, which falls shy of their fingertips. It crashes and breaks, scalding the floor. "Whoops," I say. "I'm so sorry."

"Totally fine," she tells me in a tight voice that indicates she wants me to get the hell out.

When I'm finally outside, I head back into the woods with another laugh. I need another plan that doesn't run the risk of becoming an academic paper. I can't believe they're the second couple I know to be happy together; Thomas's willful adoration for his wife sickens me. I hold the photographs close so they can't fly away.

Ce sont tous des parasites. If Marion and this house are in a symbiotic relationship, who is eating whom? The ghost obviously believes she's in charge, but I'm not sure. I can't worry about the ghosts' affairs when my own is a match short of fire.

Ba's gone off the rails. I'm short 38K. Mom thinks I'll only ever bring a boy home. Halle doesn't want to talk to me. Lily's beyond pissed at me. Only I can change the answer. Is this how it feels to be a parent? Making impossible choices or avoiding them to survive yourself. I learned the hard way how you can't rely on anyone else, and now Ba's using it against me. Shame burns through my skin, no longer contained. Lily wouldn't have said the things I did. Lily wouldn't do the things I've done or will do.

The fish was in a tank: swimming, swimming. There was only a circle for a path. Its tail was fantastic: a paintbrush dipped in clementine orange. Nothing like the fish we hook in the river or pond. Mom had gotten it for us.

"It's not very happy," I said, watching it swim and swim.

Ba looked at me, his eyes flat stones. *So, let's make it happy.*

We buckled ourselves in the car and drove into the city. The tank sat in my lap, under clumsy cling wrap. I was happy to be with him. It was so rare—the two of us—because that's what happened when you're not the favorite. When you are the oldest.

At Penn's Landing, we walked to the pier side by side, my arms around the absurd tank and Ba's around himself. I should've known a lot of things by then, but I thought we'd grab some water ice together, then sit and watch boats pass.

Ba started crying. Right at the railing, both of us with wind-whipped hair and the fish sloshing in its hell. Bà Nội had died seven months before this; the heavy drinking began less than a month after that. Bác Sang, Ba's oldest brother, had called from Vietnam, his voice carrying on speakerphone. "Why didn't you pick up? Mom asked for you. She wanted to talk to you."

My hand closed over his. Pulling away I knew it would smell like metal, from the railing and from his work. He never stopped crying. It's scary to watch a parent cry. Ba said *I failed. I should've been there. Má. Má.* In Vietnamese, there's so many words to convey closeness, but why did no one teach me to say I love you when it's hard?

Ba was the youngest. His mom put him on a boat with her dreams. He came here and lived with his uncle. He was hers, but she wasn't his, an ocean stretched between them. Not enough. There were nieces and nephews he never held, cousins I barely knew. So many things drowned between us.

Ba took his hand from mine. He felt the tank's side, then tapped it. *Do you think it's okay for it to leave, Jade?*

And I knew. I was only thirteen, but I knew what he was asking me, from me.

"Go, then." I was so loud the pigeons scattered. I was so loud as I let the fish die, its water joining the Delaware's gray green. "Just go." I was as loud as my beating heart.

His eyes—my eyes—said it all. Okay. Okay.

I couldn't love Ba in his grief, and I made him leave.

21

"THIS IS A TERRIBLE idea," Florence says as we walk side by side in the woods. Coming from her, it confirms that this is, indeed, a terrible no-good idea. But I've no other choice; I haven't had a dream for two days. I haven't even had sleep paralysis since Ba dug up the skulls. Maybe Marion thinks I'm tame now. She's wrong. I'll do anything to exorcise her from our lives. Even when every dream raises a question, Cam is the only person I can ask. She lived and died in this house.

In my hand is a bundle of incense pilfered from the altar. Maybe she'll answer me away from Marion's domain. Ba can't realize what I'm doing either. My shoulder brushes against Florence's, warm through our clothes. Since there's no delicate way to put it, I ask calmly, "Do you believe in possession?"

Her brows raise impressively high. "Like . . . *Exorcist* style?"

"Less Catholic," I say. "I'm thinking about all those ants I found outside Nhà Hoa."

"The zombie ones?" Florence clarifies, eyes shielded from the sun. "Because that was an awesome 4:00 a.m. read. Thank you." Although humor laces her tone, she's been glancing at me more than usual, waiting for me to say more about my fight with Lily. The words are too raw to repeat, even without Ba's secrets, but she knows I'm determined to set things right. I am here to stay, for now.

"Marion was sick before she died," I say, sharing the facts I bombarded her phone with. "What if she's trying something like that with people staying in the house? Messing with our food, or it's like that first memory Cam showed me. She got bitten up by mosquitoes."

Florence holds her hand up in objection. "But she's not staked through the head by a fungus and spreading nasty spores, right? Parasitic ant activity doesn't mean *paranormal* ant activity."

"It doesn't have to be ants," I say. "There's rat lungworm." Found in rodents but also snails, shrimp, frogs, and crabs. "Round-worms." Plentiful in soil and plants. "Blood flukes." Helpfully occupying water. "This *other* fungus that's fucking up cicadas' seventeen-year reunions, and mosquitoes, which probably carry the original sin, on top of worms that swell up body parts."

She snorts. For a moment, I'm sure she will turn around and leave—the magic from the market outing long gone. Last nights are ripe for sharing because the promise of it being the *last* makes us all braver. You don't usually text your crush afterward with

198

gross and terrifying theories. Florence takes half the incense from me as we reach a clearing. "And that's why you want to talk to Cam," she says. "In person. See what made this house empty for so long."

"Yes." The heat in my throat doesn't subside. Worms are lurking in Ba's eyes, even if I haven't noticed them since. My dad—or me—turning into a white woman ranks high on my list of fears right now, but it isn't something I can share.

Florence rubs the cross at her neck and says, "God, it'd be great if we could call a regular exterminator to release Marion to hell."

I laugh, relieved to have one person who is still on my side, and take out a lighter. Its flame quivers between us. "Ready?"

"Ready."

I flick the fire over one stick of incense, and it leaps to another, burning a bright circle of ash. I light her bundle too before stepping forward, back turned, so I can concentrate. "Cam," I say. It's my plan, but I haven't prepared my plea at all. The dead are easier to talk to when there's no chance that they will respond. Standing in front of the altar is freeing. Standing in the open holding smoke feels damning. "Cam, please, I need help."

Ma qui. In the thousand tabs on hungry ghosts across Vietnamese tradition and others, drawings depicted creatures with swollen throats, small mouths, appetites for feces and rot, and other creative ways of eternal suffering. Marion Dumont has an impossibly long neck. I'm asking for a Cam I might not understand.

Sharp smoke drifts from my hands. In dreams, in her

memories, we can understand each other, but this is real life. I need to speak our parents' language. "Cần giúp. Please." Gray ash tops the yellow and red sticks, flaking away until half of what's burnable remains. "Cần giúp."

"Holy *shit*," Florence curses behind me. I turn.

She is here, in the flesh, so much like the first time she visited me. Her presence blocks out all other scents, as if she's slipped a mask over my nostrils. Cam appears so much younger in her plain white áo dài, a girl's school uniform. She steps closer, blades of grass churning against her silk trousers. Her face is captivated by our bundles of smoke, the mouth opening, nostrils flaring, as she sucks in the floating incense. She inhales it like a cigarette, like food. The neck beneath her collar grows a half inch, and instinct pulls me back. "Did Marion follow you?" I ask.

Her eyes are trained on me while she drifts closer, taking the smoke in hungrily.

Florence, whose face I desperately wish I could read right now, translates as she holds her incense far from her body. "Bà Marion có đi theo Cam không?"

Cam tilts her head and looks so real that I remind myself she has the same core essence as Marion—spirit, ghost, someone who can't let go. "Không bao giờ ra khỏi nhà."

"She never leaves the house," Florence explains, sounding relieved. Marion Dumont is still bound by her agoraphobia, thank god.

I shift on my feet, wishing I could speak privately to Cam. Although I should be used to another person or Google being an intermediary, needing one always makes me feel like an outsider to my own culture. Especially now, when I need to acknowledge the intrusive thought that has rooted inside my brain: *Do we deserve this?* Parasites are everywhere, but it was my ancestors who prepared food for the Dumonts. Maybe Marion's vendetta is personal. With a slow breath, I ask, "Did my family poison her somehow?"

In those false worlds with Cam there were no boundaries, so it's an agonizing wait as Florence translates.

"No," Cam says in English. Relief floods me, then shame that I'd even considered it. She repeats *no* intently.

As if sensing my despair, Florence draws closer to me. Her hand rests on my shoulder, waiting for me to go on. I nod. "Marion muốn gì?" *Want* has always been an easy word for me to remember, and I use it here. If it's not vengeance, then maybe there's something else I can do for her so we can sleep in peace this last week. Only then would it be fine for me to leave Ba here.

Her calmness melts away. Again, Cam inhales the smoke, the first time she appears more ghost than person. Red seeps through her gray-pink lips, sinister rather than beautiful. I prefer her in my sleep. Perhaps my ghost isn't telling me what Marion wants because the possibilities are too vast to guess: she's buried in pine and wishes for France, she wants to see her children again, she hasn't accepted her death.

There's always a cost in speaking with the dead. Incense, an offering of food, burning joss money and paper houses.

"Show me everything," I say to the girl who thinks we are alike.

"Show me *you*." Untangling from Florence, I step forward and hold the incense right over my beating heart. "Giúp em không?"

Mouth red, eyes hungry, Cam nods and reaches for me. When her sharp nail touches my temple, I faint.

———

It is spring, and Đà Lạt is in full bloom.

A girl's hands are in the air, slender and gripping a hat that she uses to chase a golden butterfly. I am suspended, a bodiless specter pulled toward a younger Cam's smile. Her heart-shaped face tips down toward a boy running around her knees as she ushers the butterfly close. Her clothes are worn and old, short enough that her ankles show.

Their laughter is an echo on this bright, pollen-filled day from the past.

A white man watches her from the dirt-stamped street. His eyes are the lightest green, a grasshopper's molted skin.

The scene scatters like seeds, and she is in an áo dài of the finest silk. Her dark hair is swept behind a gold-threaded bridal crown.

Nhà Hoa is younger here too. The brick and wood are less yellow. The mansard roof remains tidy. The hydrangeas though are already tall and stiff. While petals scatter in the wind, a sulky Marion stands at the window beside Roger Dumont.

The other man hoists his bride in his arms and into the house, which opens with the help of his brother's brown men. There's no celebration for this bedding. No trays of fruits and jewelry and roasted pork to honor a family's union, only the inevitable drawn closer.

None of this is what I want to see, I want to say to Cam, but she isn't here with me. Past Cam, yes, disappearing into the house's dark.

⁓

It's years later, and Marion is finally dead. The house has emptied of her husband and children. A bowl of oranges beside the Dumonts' old bed has begun to mold with white and green fuzz. Cam rests against the headboard and picks the top rotting fruit, peeling its skin quarter by quarter. She jams the slices into her maw, juice sliming her chin.

Enthralled by this transformation, I watch as her husband carries a tray of food in. He knocks the orange from her hand. "You need to eat something else," he says, the sounds not matching up to his mouth.

"Pierre, I want to see my family," says Cam. Her cheeks are hollow and dark, similar to Marion's during her sickness. Honey-sweet buzzing radiates from the walls. Her head twitches toward it, distracted.

He squeezes her hand. "They don't want to see you. I've tried my best." His tone is tired, ambivalent. He's said this many times. Sullen, Cam watches the wall. The rotting orange stops midroll, wrapped in dust, and he grimaces. "Maybe we should rehire help," her husband offers. "This house is too much for you alone."

Cam pulls her hand away, banging into the teacup at her bedside. "That's exactly what she wants," she says with a rasp. "More and more people to impress and torture. It doesn't matter

203

what I eat. It's all the same!" Cam bursts to her knees and hurls the tray away, screaming as the buzzing reaches a crescendo. I jump too within this memory. I've never seen her so bitter or angry. "Get out! I hate you!" She lobs another rotting orange at the husband she never wanted. "I hate you! You brought me here!"

Hopelessly, I'm discarded in another memory. In this house of dreams, white sheets overlay every piece of furniture. Only the ghosts remain exposed. While Cam looks outside through the window, the red-haired ghost frets restlessly in the foyer.

The whole house seems to shudder. Marion draws close to the walls with a rare, imploring look stitched to her face. "She's weak," Marion whispers. I move closer to observe the tremble in her voice. "She could've stopped on her own, but she wanted, don't you see?" Though we're barely a foot apart, this remnant of the past cannot sense me at all.

Like before, the walls buzz. Back and forth, house and host speak until eventually Marion wails, "It's not my fault she died!" She jabs an accusatory finger at her sister-in-law, but Cam never responds to this charade.

Outside, seasons pass in the palest shades. All the while, Marion never stops her torment, *You can't get anything right, can you?*

My name is called. Someone cradles my face. A curtain of dark hair caresses my cheeks as I blink. "Jade," Florence breathes, shoulders relaxing, and I glimpse blue sky and the jagged line of pine needles. She smells real: citrus conditioner, touched with gasoline.

Cursing, she rises to stomp the incense that fell from our grip.

"Where's . . ." My voice drifts, my feet returned to earth.

"She got all close to you, then 'poof'!" Florence snaps. "You scared the actual piss out of me, falling over and not responding."

I didn't even know Cam could share memories when I am awake. I check my temples. There's no blood. "I'm okay," I say. "She showed me some memories of when she married into that family and when everyone alive left that house empty. They can't ever stay long in person."

Scowling, Florence digs her boot into more crushed incense. "She tell you that?"

"She told me a while ago." I shrug, though my mind's never been clearer. It's been hard to hear in these memories of hers, but the signs are all there. I just have to follow. Marion or the house needed Cam, but the Lady of Many Tongues couldn't resist tormenting her. The iron balcony at Nhà Hoa is still bent crudely toward the ground, marked by Cam's unjust death.

"Did Cam tell you to stay?" Florence cuts into my thoughts as she leads me back to the house. "Isn't it easier for you to go, then convince your sister and dad after?"

My family is too close to fracturing completely. Their finding out Ba left because I couldn't keep it together would sever any chance of forgiveness. "I have to try. I'm not giving up," I say. Cam will give me the answers that I need. Everything is less obscured now. The threads are waiting to be pulled together. I'm not helpless. "I can fix this, Flo." Her shortened name is sweet and easy after everything we've seen together.

She sighs. "This is a lot. Not you. Everything else." She gets on her motorbike, obviously not joining me inside. "I mean, uh, ghosts *and* aliens are real. I need to think about it."

We stand in each other's orbit, skin scented with smoke now that Cam is gone.

"Thank you for coming with me," I say, and because she's real and she's worried about me, I lean in and kiss her on her forehead.

Florence's fingers graze mine. "I'll see you later, okay?"

22

AS MY DREAMS RETURN, so does the paralysis. After almost three weeks of waking up bodiless, I should be used to it. The panic lulls after my fingers crack, each piece regaining feeling, as if I'd been disassembled during the night and put back together. I expect Marion to appear, slinking from behind the bedroom door, and every second that she does not worries me that she is elsewhere, haunting my family. I never want to sleep, but I have to. It's the only way Cam can show me the past so I can figure out how to beat Marion in her own game.

In the last visit, Cam led me through wild gardens screaming with marigolds not yet paved for Đà Lạt's growth. She shared confused memories of her time in the house, when Marion had first begun to lurk around corners. *The food tasted fine*, Cam told me after, in that limbo space I've started to consider as ours.

And now I'm awake, in the real world that only I can investigate, where sound is both raw and unfiltered. There's a cost to exploring a ghost's vivid memories though. My body begs for rest. My mind is dull and fatigued. As I go downstairs to play Ba's dutiful daughter, I see that the house has remained complicit in good behavior. Nothing new has broken. It gives us no reason to want to leave.

Outside, the reno workers blast music so loud that the windows tremble. They've been working around the clock, almost as hard as me. Hearing familiar songs—even when the Viet lyrics are beyond me—is a balm to my anxiety. I am here, and I can be useful. There are dried and packaged starches to prepare for Lily while I eat whatever meal Ba makes. I'm disgusted with how I'm craving those crispy egg rolls stuffed with jícama, wood ear mushrooms, and ground pork from last night, when anything can be in it.

Within the sitting room, our photographs have been returned to their places on the mantel. The hydrangeas are wicked, spilling to either side of their pots. The overstuffed chairs are landmarks in this lush parlor, and feet dangle from the fireplace. The air is thick with a love song as I shuffle toward the kitchen, ready to boil more bland noodles. Yet something is wrong. I face the room again.

Feet dangle from inside the fireplace.

Is this real?

Have I lost it?

Vigilance every waking moment carries a high toll.

Inside the fireplace are two pale legs. A deceptively cheery ankle bracelet shines on the left.

Screaming, I throw myself in, my forearms around her calves, pulling, yanking. The little hairs on her legs scratch me in return. *When did you start shaving your legs*, I will ask once she's out, and *are you already dead?* Please don't be dead.

The body in my embrace screams too.

"Lily," I say, urgent, once she's freed.

She doesn't see me, even though we're in this messed-up reality together. Her eyes are narrowed on the feather-thin bones in her hands. Ivy has wrapped into a broken bird-shaped thing, vines reaching flowering through the eye sockets. I grind my teeth harder.

"I heard . . ." She trails off, slowly blinking at me. Her long hair is twisted around her neck. "I heard some thumping, then chirping. I wanted to check." Dropping the find, she rubs her hands furiously on soot-covered pajamas. Black smudges across her cheeks to the tips of her ears. Brown eyes behind a wet sheen. Someone ready to cry.

"Let's get cleaned up," I say, gently taking her by the shoulders. She hunches forward, folding herself smaller, and follows me upstairs. That dead thing doesn't move after us. In the bathroom, I help dab soot from the back of her arms and other places she misses. This house has never bothered anyone but me. "Did you see anything else?" I ask when her breaths come naturally. *How did I miss this?*

Her attention snaps violently to me. "I don't believe in ghosts."

"That's not what I'm asking."

"I'm not helping you leave early," Lily continues, unburdening herself of this peace. "I'm not using Ba for money." She throws a damp towel at me before hurrying back to her bedroom. She's never been good in a confrontation. Where my sister lets off steam in controlled bouts, I have always been fond of a direct, explosive attack.

I stop her seconds before the door can slam. Wood stings my palm, but I shrug off her wince. "Don't take anything Dad gives you," I remind her. "Just the dried food. I bought enough for the week." Her expression twists in irritation, and she answers by shutting the door in my face.

The impact reverberates throughout the house. My eyes flick toward the ceiling, then the hallway closet. My sign, it's here. Cam, or something else, is responding. Ever since our arrival, the thumping has demanded to be heard. I should've investigated sooner, when I was less afraid. Beyond the small door with many locks, the stairway to the attic squeezes me from both sides. I press on. As my feet touch the attic floor, sound erupts again.

THUMP. THUMP. THUMP.

The house's spine quivers. It echoes in my body. In less than a week, Ba has covered the insulation with new drywall, smoothing the room into a gray landscape. Marion's writing desk is open, dust stirred from its surface. Nowhere are the baby rats I found last time. Ba has been busy.

I stand by the chimney, palms over rough brick, and feel the tremble of an angry fist. I lay my cheek against this house, the same way Marion did in the past. The urge to speak is overwhelming. "What are you trying to say?" I whisper, touching its well-laid mortar lines.

An imperfection snags my eye: a single brick jutting from the rest. I dig fingers into the loose brick, pulling, pulling, and pulling until my nails start to lift. Fresh pain sears my hands, but I hold my breath and pry the brick apart. The flashlight from my phone illuminates enough to see paper pinned on the opposite wall. In a move that both Halle and Florence would say is extraordinarily unwise, I shove my arm inside the dark hole, fitting almost to the bicep. The air is impossibly hot inside the chimney, though no fire's been lit.

The paper is too high from this angle. I need to make the gaping space bigger. I have to get whatever's inside that wants to be found. A hammer from Ba's lonely toolbox is perfect for that. Its weight is much less than a shovel, after all. I swing it easily against adjacent bricks, scattering concrete crumbs over the dusty floor. Destroying something tangible is therapeutic. Knowing it'll piss Ba off makes it even more therapeutic.

With a section of brick chipped off, I reach in again on the tips of my toes. I'm half expecting a vicious bite, another lost bird's feathers, or the clenching of possessive vines, but the sepia-toned paper dislodges easily. Whereas Marion's collection had been full of parties, nature, and family portraits, this stash of photographs is smaller and carefully curated. Soldiers stare stoically at the camera, proud, outside an unknown village. Locals work a rubber plantation, unaware someone has immortalized their backs. In another picture, dead faces rest on a tree stump.

Eyes closed. Bodies elsewhere.

These are not photographs you hang up.

The Dumont brothers and their fellow officers have a hunter's stance with their bloody bounty. History would love to say these executed prisoners were bandits. I would say, perhaps, that they were home when the strangers arrived.

"Did you all die here?" I ask out loud, when really the question I mean is, *Have I buried you well enough?* And even then, the rotted skulls we hid might not be theirs. No easy answer arrives. My fist tightens around the photographs. Then I realize these might be the only ones their descendants would ever see, and quickly unfold them. All collateral damage, like my great-grandmother in the curtains during another family's portrait.

The hammer drops with a clang from my grip. Alma mentioned before that Marion's husband kept order in Tonkin, which means his actions were under the banner of duty. A small, pained laugh crackles from my lungs. If those earlier photographs were worthy subjects of an academic paper, then these belong to a museum. So many would hang them in exhibitions detailing the history on how colonialism ruined lives, without ever naming those lives.

My great-grandmother, too young and full of wide-eyed wonder to understand the dangers in her life. My grandmother, chasing American soldiers for candy while napalm dropped in a neighboring province. Ba, on a packed boat but alone at sea.

The holes in Mom's family history, despite a half dozen siblings to construct stories from. And Cam, whose loved ones stopped seeing her over a marriage that saved them.

I've been going about it wrong; I don't need to know what Marion wants. Racists don't need reasons to be racist. She lived to be seen. There are so many others waiting to be heard, overlooked and forgotten and written in the margins. My family won't be free if I play by the rules set by others, allowing the pattern to repeat—relentless and hungry.

It was never only Cam and Marion in this house built to outlast flesh.

"You have been here this entire time," I say to the walls, spinning slowly at the attic's center. That's why Cam said *them*. "You've been listening." Cam had been too afraid to engage with the supernatural when she was alive, but a house has no loyalty.

We all learn what we need to survive.

We shape the environment, and it also shapes us. The Lady of Many Tongues has been Nhà Hoa's longest tenant, yes, but others have walked through here and left splinters of their soul—or *vibes*, as Florence once theorized right out of her ass. I laugh, this time joyful. The splinters led me here, much like the red leaves of that hydrangea bush. Stories have been written into its very bones, even if all this house wants is to never be alone again. Marion is selfish and arrogant. She doesn't notice these details, and maybe Nhà Hoa doesn't either. I can be different. There are things this house has yet to learn about me.

And because I am still breathing, I decide which beast to preserve behind museum glass or press between pages of a book that might not be read again. I am alive, and willing, and so this house needs me more than it needs its dead madame. I press my body close to Nhà Hoa's so that it can hear my heartbeat. Then, I whisper: "I will be your host."

larynx

SHE WHISPERS IN THE corners. She's a child of this house, and she says such nice things.

"You're beautiful and others should see you."

"I'm writing a story that everyone will read."

"Was the photo like a thorn in your side?"

"I'll always listen. You can tell me."

This house has always wanted a child.

"I do have hands, see! I can bring you anything you ask for."

They're so resilient in affection, and they always bounce back after a slap.

23

BURN THEM. TURN THE photographs into ash, as if they never existed. Pretend I didn't see. That's how I'll protect my family. Myself. I'm starting to know the kind of person I am.

Leaning forward against Florence on the motorbike takes my mind off the weight in my bag.

She lives on a noisy street in Đà Lạt proper with matchbox houses behind solid gates. We pass a house decked out in red for a wedding, where they've set off illegal firecrackers that bubble upward on crowded strings. I hold on to Florence tighter, as the smell takes me back to the temples during Tết in Philly. Me and Lily watching as close as we can get, Bren in Ba's arms, and Mom right beside him. Their faces lit up. I haven't trusted a smile since.

"You guys have lion statues," I say, deadpan, when our

helmets are off. Twin lions with grinning faces guard the front doors of the house.

Florence's hair falls in a messy swoop down her back, smile misaligned in mischief. "Keep my puss—"

"See, she's back!" a man calls out, emerging from the house in quick steps down. He's in his thirties and well dressed in a pinstripe vest. He points at Florence. "Your fries are burning. You leave oven on."

"Burning as in right now?" Florence groans, pushing me inside with a backward glance. "This is Jade, and that's Tuấn."

"We babysit your fries," he says, exasperated, though his eyes are warm. "We don't let them die." He smiles at me. "Have fun, you two."

"*You two*," Florence says, "don't drink too much." Their talk flows naturally, as if they've done this a thousand times.

Her uncle is more reserved as he passes by us, putting on a gray suit jacket. "Đi bộ qua đó. Đừng lo." His regard is wary, but I don't shrink away from his protective stance. On the road, the couple veers toward the wedding party we saw earlier.

Florence stops waving when a caustic smoke assaults our nostrils. "The fries!" She runs down the hallway, abandoning me in the place she shares with her uncle and Tuấn. It is open under recessed lights, accented in silver, tastefully plucked from a magazine spread. Pictures decorate the entryway in. The few of young Florence confirm that she had a bowl cut as a kid. In more recent ones, she is squeezed between them. There isn't a single frame that seems to be taken with her parents.

My hand searches for a pulse in the wall. Tame homeliness presses back, plain and forgettable. It doesn't talk as Nhà Hoa does.

The fries have been saved by the time I wander into their kitchen. The baking sheet boasts several scorched marks and half-blackened fries, soon swiped onto an oval plate. Florence rests comically large oven mitts on her hips, nose wrinkling. "Not dead, but this is still a punishment."

Leaning on the kitchen island, I pinch a single fry off the plate and drop it half in my mouth. "Hot, bitter, and greasy," I say, looking up at her. "Exactly how I like it."

She laughs, fumbling with a frying pan and some premade patties next. "There'll be a lot of that. I didn't do much cooking in school, and Tuấn's really good at making things homey around here but he's not a cook either."

"I've been eating kimchi ramen nonstop for four days," I say. "I'll only complain if you break out anything instant." My appetite fluctuates too often to care, but it's sweet she remembers my confession for McDonald's at the night market. I would've been happy with her company alone. "I'll help."

We work in comfortable silence while the pan sizzles between us. She gives me space to breathe, and I take that freedom in, letting her house keep us safe. She's my friend and she isn't running, despite all the craziness. We cook the burgers overdone, so there's no pink in the middle where a parasite might lurk. It's then that she asks, "So, what's up with you?"

The word slips out easily. "Nothing." There's a traitorous

squeeze within my chest. When had I become someone who likes to be asked about?

Florence mimics a computer's error noises. "Sounds like bullshit." On the last syllable, she slaps me lightly with the spatula. It leaves a greasy square over my left boob. She cackles.

Her laugh ripples in my chest, as I confiscate the spatula. It's good to be normal again. "You owe me a new shirt," I say.

"Sorry, I don't carry kid sizes," she teases with another glance at the ruined crop top.

"You think about what I wear a lot?" I ask, the same question she asked me when we stood in that small closet together, breaths tight after finding the first set of photographs. She'd come for me then too. She's good at being a friend.

"Maybe," Florence says. "About what's lacking." She means the cut of my shirt, the style of my jeans, but I can't help the heat rushing to my face.

"It's a good distraction," I say. It's easy to hide the fact that your clothes are old when boys' eyes simply slide over them. Better to be a stereotype no one can read, I thought, but lately it seems all I've done is hurt myself. I'm so straight, for instance, that I kissed Halle's longtime crush because I wanted people to *know* I was, so no one would notice I was looking where I shouldn't.

That's a truth I didn't expect to bubble to the surface.

Florence's phone rings, shocking us both. Sheepish, she lifts her cat-eared cell to answer, "What, Gem?" A red-haired girl appears on the screen. In the first half second, they share looks that only best friends understand, something I used to have with Halle.

That hollow space where she used to be grows bigger as I watch them catch up in rapid-fire mode. As I excavate the house's secrets, it does the same to me. I feel exposed and foolish. I slide burgers onto our plates. Bits of conversation stick: catching up for a trip, buying tickets. Is Florence leaving soon?

Then, knowing I'm there, Gemma says loudly: "You're way too nice to people. Don't get involved with that girl."

Although I don't support violence against inanimate objects, I'm seriously considering punching the phone in the face.

"She doesn't have enough abs or boobs and you deserv—"

"Okay 'bye," Florence says quickly, and hangs up. "Uhh, sorry. She's like that."

"It's fine," I say, willing myself to not overthink. I allow the weight of my bag to ground me again. "I want to burn the pictures from the attic." Surprise crosses her face. "My sister has the one with my bà cố already, so the others can all burn. Enough racists are remembered. We don't need to add more to people's collections." War memorabilia, historical exhibits, textbooks, personal family albums, placards, and one-line captions to sum up decades. "Nhà Hoa won't be the next hot tourist destination."

Nodding, Florence sets us up around the firepit on the deck. The flames begin low, then soar with a cleansing brightness that warms my eyelids. I throw the first one into the pit. The paper curls in dark splotches.

"Be still, you racist spirits," says Florence when she tosses a handful from the stack. We watch them turn to ash. I swallow down smoke and still find no relief. We're on the second stack now. That they exist at all is a reminder of how deeply those occupants believed in themselves.

I remember exactly where I placed those heads, so when Florence moves to turn the next photograph over, my hand closes over hers. "That one was hidden in the chimney. You don't want to see it."

We stay there for a long minute, her studying me. "I've protected myself a long time too," she says. "I can handle whatever it is." I ache from the softness in her words. *It's ours*, she seems to say.

I let her and the photograph go.

She holds it up to the night sky. "You burned their faces."

Holes are left where the officers' heads should be, but the people who are dead remain. Separated from their bodies, they've suffered too much already. "I did." With lit incense, I blotted the faces of their killers and all who settled here. I didn't make digital files of any photograph until they lacked all identifying features. "To erase them," I say, "since they're so proud of what they've done." It changes nothing in the past, but this is in my power now.

Brows drawn together, Florence burns it in the highest flame. "That fucking house, man."

"Those fucking people," I correct, because the house led me to the chimney. It knows things, and it will tell me if I'm nice. Cam was always too afraid to listen, but she only had herself to worry for. For my family, I'm capable of doing more. This house wants to be known, so let it. What is a ghost without a house to haunt? I will be Nhà Hoa's confidante and vessel, writing the most beautiful stories for the opening party. I am providing what it needs, so we can't ever be disposed of.

As it has learned, my family are the ones who've loved it most.

Night stretches languid around me and Florence. Close, intimate, and almost normal. We watch the pit until the end, when we're sure nothing has escaped. I hadn't trusted Marion to let me do it back at the house, but here, I am free. I am in control. We shovel ash, scattering it to the wind. "I release you, racists!" I yell, and Florence joins in, our voices drowned out by the wedding's blaring music. I can't tell whether I want to laugh or cry, so we eat instead. The burgers are as greasy as promised, a little taste of McDonald's extravagance. The fries fill my mouth with an acrid taste that I confuse for cold ash. I'll tell Florence my plans tomorrow, I decide. My phone screen flashes with Lily's begrudging reply: *I'm fine.* We'll be okay for this one night. The house knows I'm its friend now.

Later, Florence and I stand in a hallway, me in a pair of her plaid pajamas since I'd forgotten to pack literally anything else. "So. You can probably sleep in Tuấn's room. He usually sleeps in, y'know." Florence doesn't look embarrassed or flustered. She's considering safety. The room next to the master is plainly decorated with a perfectly made bed.

"I'd rather sleep with you," I say. Her mouth perks up. "Platonically. Snoozing, I mean." By then, she's laughing. "I'm so tired right now."

Her bedroom isn't as lived-in as I expect. She nudges aside two open suitcases. Lilac curtains, sheets, pillows, and even walls make their presence known by ruining my eyeballs. "Sorry, uh. When I moved in with Uncle, he had this room designed for me, which, I'm forced to tell you, was *not* by Tuấn. Anyway I was little, then boarding school, so we never updated the bed." I stare at the twin-sized bed. "I like sleeping on the left if that's cool."

It's practice for college, I tell myself, even if I'm not going this year. It's the last thing on my mind. Awkwardly, we climb into bed, blanket pulled taut from one edge to the other.

"It's kind of cold," she says.

"Okay if we get closer?" I ask. Makes sense, definitely not an excuse, since there is an arctic cavern of space between us— farther than when we stood on the deck screaming at the world.

"Yeah." Our spines line up together, our feet almost tangled. I hope I remembered to lotion them after showering, the lone semi-intelligent thought I possess currently. "So," I say as her digital clock blinks lime green. "Your friend Gemma doesn't like me." Great, happy topic to balance out the night we've had. Smooth.

"She's always like that. She's irritated I won't backpack with her this year," Florence explains.

It is the sort of thing I'd never do, but it's easy to imagine Florence traveling and keeping an outdated blog with terrible selfies. "Do you want to?" When the bed shifts under her weight, I turn too until we are on our backs, an inch apart.

"Not that simple," she tells me, when I can see her doing it all. False stars twinkle more green than gold above us. "My uncle wants me to get a business degree from Temple, then come back and help run the real estate stuff. My parents too." Florence pretends to pinch one of the stars between her fingers. "They've always wanted a lot I couldn't give. My parents, I mean. I was always different. Not *I'm different from other girls* different—the *I'm not what my parents expected* kind. They wanted a quiet baby; I was loud. They wanted a fast learner; it took me forever to read. At least now I can sit sort of still through classes." She laughs, but it's not warm. Her hand lowers back down.

"I had the same sticky stars in our old house," I say quietly, and point to the ceiling. "One time, I pulled them off to give to my then BFF, and my dad slapped me—it was fine, I'm fine—because I accidentally ripped off some plaster." I shake my head, sinking deeper into the pillow. "Don't know why I'm telling you this, except to say adults guess what's best for their kids, and sometimes they're wrong. Maybe even a lot of the time." I pause, gathering the last of my thoughts. "You should do what feels right to you. Not what they're demanding from you."

She's too quiet. I must've said something wrong or overstepped, but then she taps my hand, the lightness back in her tone. "And you, going to UPenn really worth all the sneaking-around-your-mom stuff?"

"I've already made my choice," I say. I'll defer a year to make up the money. The school's well known, so I can get a good job after graduation, pay off whatever loans, and Mom won't have to work so much. It's close to home, but not too close, so I can live as I want. Still, in a month, both of us could be living in the same city, without much scrutiny. For once, I want my life to be a little complicated by someone good, and Florence is that and more. "If you do end up at Temple, I can show you around."

Even though we aren't looking at each other, I feel her gaze all over me. It's the closest we've come to talking about time together beyond Đà Lạt. I hold my breath. "You are so stubborn," she says. She's definitely wearing a grin, to my detriment. "Of course. I bet you hold major grudges."

"I do have a list of petty grievances I'm taking to my grave, so I can say *I told you so* in the afterlife."

"Knock. On. Wood." Florence taps her knuckles on the wall above our heads. As if sensing my skepticism, she scolds me, "Ghosts are real, so bad luck's gotta be real." After a second, she asks, "What are you planning to do about Marion? Since you aren't leaving yet."

Exhaustion sinks in, dragging my eyelids down. I'd listened to the house almost all night, collecting stories about how it came to be, but sharing with Florence can wait. The website will still be there tomorrow. "I'm praying for success in chilling out her spirit," I say lightly, rolling on my side to face her. She does the same, palm underneath her cheek. "You're my delinquent accomplice and all—great job so far, by the way—but it's not all we have to talk about. We can scheme later."

"Oh shit," she says. "You want to *conversate* me?" She fans herself dramatically.

Florence has a mole near her right eye that I never noticed before. Tonight, I'm seeing everything new and different. Here,

I don't hear trees at all. Only the wedding's raucous music and karaoke calls into the dark.

"It's a start," I say, voice low. The faintest of blushes spreads over her face. She recovers immediately by launching into the merits of waffles as a dinner item, and we laugh, talking about absolutely nothing and everything like favorite colors and allergy season. We talk so much my mouth dries, and being tired becomes invigoration instead hours later, as if we'd sneaked out of our houses for teenage debauchery.

At the start of another distant slow song, Florence asks, "You ever been in love?"

"What's with the serious question?" I ask. Unbidden, the sharp memory of my diary and all the names written within appear. I almost black out. It was always like-like, or lust, or proof. In my entire life, I've never gotten close enough to love someone else.

"Well, have you? Enough to keep you haunting a place."

A scowl lodges between my brows. "No." My forearm's under my ear, though I never sleep on my side. Mom said people who chết oan sometimes remain as hungry ghosts, and various folklore and legends attach lingering emotions to lingering spirits, but the prospect of staying around for *more* foolishness seems exhausting. "You?"

"Never," she confesses. "But it's bananas that people fall so stupidly in love, you know? What's it like to be so silly and happy? I sort of want to know."

"You're bananas enough already," I say. Even within families, love is an impossible thing to pin down. How can strangers?

"Sometimes, the things we want to hear, it's better that we don't ask for them. It's more meaningful that way."

With a thoughtful hum, Florence pulls the blanket close to her chin. "Well, you're gonna be disappointed, but . . ." Her fingers are delicate as she brings the covers close to my chin as well. "It's time to sleep." She laughs and feigns sleep, at first. My skin is hot where she touched, but it's the parts of me that she hasn't that burns most.

Only Florence can flay me with just one look. Make me peel open with a touch that haunts me long after she closes her eyes.

24

I SLEPT A DREAMLESS night that, by morning, brought me even closer to Florence. Her long hair overlaid mine, a natural deep black over my dyed brown. A gradient of color between us. There's no added weight in my limbs, only a bone-deep easiness that proves this is my first restful night in Vietnam.

We laugh about morning breath and shove at each other, rolling on the plushy rug in her room. We brush our teeth in twin mirrors, the walls behind soft blue rather than Nhà Hoa's watchful birds.

She says something about getting breakfast started, that I should look in her closet for something to wear.

Plaid shirts, bad tees, and torn jeans make up the entirety of Florence's walk-in closet. I pull on the least offensive plaid shirt, worn fabric smoothing over my cheekbones. This cozy routine can continue in Philly, if we want. It's that easy to hope when you aren't surrounded by a house with needs that come first.

Hunger claws at my gut, but a flash catches my attention. Scattered under a pile of clothes is paper, crinkled and familiar. A pervasive, ugly doubt commands my brain. I throw aside the fishnet stockings I've imagined handling in other ways. The handwriting hooks into me. There are unending numbers and drawn lines, immediately recognizable because I've walked them day and night for four weeks. *My house.*

"Jade?" Florence calls from somewhere distant.

Grabbing another notebook, I turn over pages now marked with sticky notes that say everything from *check contract* to *wtf.* The notebooks are his, but the colorful writing is not. I take in a long breath. Why does she have them? Other than that first day and when we hang out, Florence doesn't come over. When did she take them?

Her bare toes appear at the edge of my vision. "Jade." My name's never been so soft, and yet I am a fuse on fire.

"What is this?" I ask. I get up from kneeling, so from her height she's forced to stare up at me. She'll never see me beneath her, breaking apart and confused again. "Is this why you always insist on hanging at the house?" It was never for research. I can't think of why—only that she came into Nhà Hoa for a reason, and it wasn't always for me. Sickness brews hot and shameful. "Do you like him or something?"

Her reaction is immediate. "No! Ew. Listen." She reaches for the notebooks, but I withdraw until hangers jab into my back.

She bites on her upper lip before speaking. "Your dad cheated my uncle out of money. I wanted proof." She points to the short stack in my hands. "He let me in the house once for a tour before you came and never left me unsupervised. You didn't watch me so closely." Florence tries a sad smile that only makes me mad. "I found the notebooks one afternoon. There are numbers written down, and repairs, he never told my uncle about. That house never would've passed inspections without a bribe."

Florence had stolen these things. Snatched them from his room whenever I wasn't looking, took it from the chaos of things he replaced us with. "You never thought to tell me?" I say, gripping them harder. *We could've helped each other*, I think. *It all could've ended differently*, I think. "Does Ông Sáu know?"

She sucks in a long breath. "No." She worries her bottom lip. "Not yet. It's already so close to the opening party. What's done is done, and you—"

"A ghost is my only friend here," I say with an incredulous laugh.

"Do you actually believe that?" Florence asks. "She can be the mastermind behind the haunting, for all that you know." No, just the food, always the rotting food—to warn us, to prevent us from swallowing worms and wings and microscopic terrors. Cam chết oán in this house. She died an unjust death because of Marion, and now she can't even escape her murderer. She wouldn't hurt me.

I look directly into Florence's eyes. "Don't distract from the real question, which is"—I pause, savoring that last little space between us—"how can I trust you?"

There's no immediate answer as I storm into the bedroom and gather my belongings.

Florence charges after me, not backing down from the fight. It must be a trait she got from boarding school. "He's insane, and if you can read even the tiniest bit of Vietnamese, you'd get it," she says. "You'd see for yourself the shit he's writing in these books! He's bad, more than you realize. Between your dad and my uncle, I'll choose my uncle every single time."

My heart clenches at the words spilled in perfect vehemence. I should know better: my family language, the written form, the truth. Why don't I speak Vietnamese well? Why can't I read it? I should've tried harder. Florence learned English, so why couldn't I with my mother tongue? I don't belong here. I'm a wolf in sheep's clothing, as the cliché goes, or maybe I'm an actual banana—yellow on the outside but white on the inside, as people have helpfully told me. Who am I but someone others define?

It's easier to be a stereotype. It hurts when you are yourself. I know very well how bad things are.

"I liked you," I say, chancing one last look at Florence. Her mouth is slight, open, and empty. Her hair flutters at the ends, as if caught midmotion. "I really liked you." What use is it to tell her now? "A real friend would've told me." My glance sharpens to a glare. "Don't bother with the site anymore. I'll do it myself."

Outside, day wakes. Cars beep, unlocked, and it all continues. No one's being ripped apart but me. I walk, and I don't know where I'm going. My phone is at 3 percent. I call Dad.

He finds me thirty minutes later hanging by a tiny shop with one of the few orders I know by heart in Vietnamese—cà phê sữa đá. It's too sweet on my gums as I get in the truck. The gradient of coffee and condensed milk slicks my bloodless hands cold. I think *fuck it* and don't wear my seat belt.

We drive, Đà Lạt spread around us. I want to drain that beautiful sky through a fat straw. It almost makes me cry, but I breathe in and count, slumped in the seat.

"Did you and Florence fight?" Ba asks as we tunnel through the trees closer to the house, swatches of shadow and light on the curving road. I almost laugh. Every awful thing happens in a fucking closet.

"Yes. Good. Great," I say pointlessly. "How's your zombie eye?"

His answer is dispassionate. "Fine." Since there's nothing better to do, I try to see if he's lying. In the short second our twin eyes meet, they are plain whites, not dressed by worms. Maybe he isn't being controlled right now. Silence would still be the preferable bonding experience, but he speaks again. "Look, if you like her . . ."

"I don't."

"Jade, I know," says Ba. "I shouldn't have read your diary all that time ago." That confession throws me back.

I clench my jaw. This summer isn't one for self-discovery or exploration. College, even a year late, will be my new life. Beyond all of this, I get to live in a dorm with other people. Meet new people. Meet people like me. Friends who I'll learn to never let go of. This is as close of an apology as I'll ever get from Ba. Vietnamese parents do not apologize to their children, no matter the circumstances.

"I shouldn't have said those things to you," Ba says, fingers tightening on the steering wheel. "You can tell your mom you're gay. She'll understand."

"I know, but this isn't about that," I say, maybe lying, maybe not. There's no measure of a word for someone like me, and I have to get it right on my first try. Mom can know, and she'll probably love me, but I need space to get it right. My eyes are hot.

If this is his manipulation, then I've fallen half for it. I unzip my bag and pull out the notebooks, scattering sticky notes over our feet. It's easier than telling him I don't belong here, that sometimes I don't feel like I belong to myself. "Florence had your stuff. She said you used a bribe to get the house by inspections."

No denial comes. Just a simple, "Did she tell her uncle?"

"Not yet," I say.

"He's stopping by tomorrow, to look over everything before the party on Sunday," Ba says. "I'll deal with it then."

A chill inches along my neck.

"And remember this, you can't ask your mom to come here, okay?" he continues, jaw tight as though keeping himself from twitching. His gaze flicks over to me, as dread pools in my stomach. I'd almost forgotten that Marion could be in there. "She would never leave. I wouldn't let her. She shouldn't see the house, got it?"

The truck pulls onto the driveway. His fingers tap on the steering wheel, covertly pointed at Nhà Hoa. The house waits, newly clean and summer bright. "Satisfy it and you and your sister go free."

"And you?" I ask, sickness surging in my throat, the question begging to be asked. *What will happen to you?*

"I'm not leaving," Ba says as he puts the truck in park, those motions slow and controlled again. The concerned creases have faded from his face. He holds my shoulder with one hand and the notebooks in another. "This is our family home now."

Ours, as if it can be that simple.

She comes that night. Cam visits me in my sleep. Standing in the woods' dappled sunlight, I say, "Florence lied to me." In this space between dream and memory, my mouth speaks perfect Vietnamese. It hurts me raw, even here, to know the difference between hope and reality.

Cam nods and offers a pale hand.

When I take it, she pulls my body into an embrace. The scent of days-old bouquet chokes me, slow and steady. "It's nice to have a friend," Cam says into my hair. "So you're never alone." I will stay here, where someone understands without explanation. I cling to her harder as she whispers, "Let me show you what's important. She did it wrong with me."

Touching my temple, she takes me—completely—into her world. It goes like this:

This house groans a wet, sloppy cough through broken windows, front doors still swinging. Teenagers run fast to their bikes outside, clever enough to not turn around. They've gotten away, to her chagrin.

Marion circles empty liquor bottles, irate, colored barely

more than air. "You are useless," she says to a stony Cam. Anguish coats her tongue. The Vietnamese bride doesn't answer. She simply moves until she's beyond the doors too, where Marion doesn't follow—*can't* follow. Marion howls, "You can't leave us to die!"

Here floors and banisters exist unpolished; walls unwashed; and all unloved equally. Only the hydrangeas grow, ruined and ethereal, more muscle than root. Light hits the liquor bottle in a high beam that sears my eyes.

A boy kisses me in this dream—no, it isn't all dream but actual memory, mine. Jade's. I remember these hands, strong and sure, and how I thought: *so this is want.* Our graduation caps slid off our heads, almost the only thing we were wearing, and I was meant to say something. My brain short-circuited, because this is me: always more than what my mom expects.

"*Spoil me,*" I said against his lips. "*Open me up.*" Show me how fragile a girl body is. Show me how to make my best friend cry, because she loves you, and I do not, but you want me and sometimes that's just good enough. Somewhere, I'm certain, Cam watches past-me whisper a shameful thing, "*Come closer, Marcus.*"

The pine trees are flashes of solemn white around us. Her skirts swish in the dark air behind her, a whisper of gray. Thick clouds shield a bright moon.

My legs don't burn, despite how much I run. Not like the days of running in the gymnasium, hopping over obstacles and stray feet. No mark had set us off. We simply were always running. Our feet are muddled in the underbrush.

"Camilla!"

Her husband is a shadow of the wood. Cam trips on her skirts, crying out in pain, but she raises herself again, looking back fearfully.

She runs, distressed and bleeding, but Pierre overtakes her with his long legs. He picks her up around the middle, and an animal scream bursts from her throat.

Her mouth takes the shape of French words, but I hear the words I can understand. "She's eating me from the inside! Let me go, Pierre. Please. Please let me go."

He doesn't answer his bride, even as she beats her small fists against his chest.

<hr />

Blink yourself awake. The ceiling hasn't fallen, but its weight lies on your skin. You're certain you still have limbs, but you can't move them. It's an out-of-body experience that's in your body: perfectly contained.

It's morning where you are and night where your best friend is. Where she *was*, because she's not your best friend anymore. You trashed that one, didn't you? You wish you could tell her. She's the gentlest person you know. You wonder if she still is after what you did.

You try to move, but you can't. Your temple's wet with a

tear that conned its way out. You don't feel, but you're certainly crying.

At your bedside is your new friend. Beautiful, cold Cam with her neck in an áo dài collar. The hand touches your forehead. "Shh. Sắp xong rồi."

Almost done, Jade, you are almost done.

25

PALE SUNLIGHT SCATTERS BETWEEN the blinds' slats, striping a section of wall. The pine trees rustle in a dying wind, the last sign of the night's storm. It's past noon now, and I've only just woken up. The dreams and memories from Cam's visit linger in my mind, the contents out of reach. Unlike previous times, I can't really remember them at all. A night wasted, then. Sighing, I check my phone—no new messages from Florence. Maybe this is how the word *crush* was invented: hope blossoming wild under the constant threat of being caved in.

When my feet smack on cold hardwood, the feeling that this will be a bad day gets worse. The skin around my toes crackles, leading to an itch that extends to my ankles. Dark dandruff—mud—flakes from my feet. The blanket bunches under my rough grasp, thrown aside. An array of leaves and grass litter the foot of the bed, nestling a silver brush. Its curving design smiles devilishly at me. I flip it over, revealing spry white hair curled into its teeth.

The antique brush that was this house's, then Lily's, then Thomas's, then Alma's. What is it doing here?

No no no no no.

Blood pounding. House closing in. My feet on the hallway, letting the floorboards creak again. Fingers fumbling golden knobs. Cold splashes over dirtied skin, and the water muddles. Soap lathers between my toes and over the grit on my calves.

When was I outside? No no no.

I slept, I was sleeping, I rested all night. I bury my face in wet hands. Never have I been so awake in my life. I must have forgotten to shower yesterday. I must have, even though my hair smells the same as it always does, a freshly smashed coconut. Stress makes you forget. The site, Ba, Lily, Flo—all of it and more, even though I'm leaving. *We're* leaving soon.

Maybe remorse struck and Thomas brought the brush back, placing it daintily on my bed as Sir Meow-a-Lot would a bloodied mouse. Thomas wants to be liked so badly, and I'd rather be watched than to not know what my body has done.

I clean up and get dressed for the day, declining when Mom's call pops up. Only three days left until the party and my birthday. I can make it until then. Nhà Hoa quiets as I move through it, each motion a secret between us.

Yet I feel as if I'm being mocked. I'm walking toward something inevitable. I pass through the bone-white sitting room and into the kitchen, where steam spools from hot congee. Each bowl is a house of its own with a chimney made of fried bread dough. Lily pokes at the creamy rice soup, glancing up. At least she listened, though it'd be simpler if she learns to say no to Ba. I don't feel like eating, but she's not going to leave uneaten rice. Ba scared us too many times with the maggot-per-wasted-grain story when we were little.

"You're up late," Ba says as he cleaves into a boiled duck. He splits the neck into thick sections. I tip Lily's bowl into my mouth, unflinching. It scalds me all the way down. Without the juicy duck breast splayed in gingered fish sauce, it tastes sad, which is the least of my worries where Ba's cooking is concerned. He detaches the head. "Alma and Thomas got into an accident."

My grip loosens on the half-finished bowl. Each time he brings down the cleaver, he leaves a mark in the handsome bamboo board. I let the remaining soup sludge into the garbage disposal. If there's a hell, I'll be responsible for this waste. "How?" I ask.

"They're fine." Lily twirls the store-bought dough before chewing a bite. "I mean, sort of. Ông Sáu told us when he stopped by earlier." I barely hear her over the blood rushing in my ears. I'd thought the empty bowl beside hers was Ba's, but it must've been his. Is this how Ba's dealing with Florence's uncle? How did I sleep through someone else walking through this house?

"They were coming home late from the market. Alma says they weren't drinking, but . . ." Ba sets a plate with the butchered duck on the table. Its yellow skin glistens with fat, pooling grease on the dish. "They drove off the road to avoid hitting someone."

"And did they?" My question is too calm, too off the point. I should've asked if they're okay.

"She's hurt, and Thomas is still knocked out at the hospital, so ai biết." Whether he's upset due to the potential loss of revenue, or truly hurt by this, there's no telling. Ba's expression doesn't change. "She's not thinking right. She's confused."

It makes sense that they were drunk. Mom's siblings broke the no-drinking-and-driving thing a lot in Saigon, no matter how much of a fuss Mom put up. And Alma and Thomas love to party; during that dinner with us, they spent nearly twenty minutes showing off pictures and videos from their stay in Thailand.

This house's heat is too much with the stove on. "I'm going for a walk," I say. Lily tears open a lychee jelly cup, no longer paying attention, but Ba watches me leave.

Outside, the ground squishes beneath borrowed boots, since his were closest to the door. No one really walks these roads, but I keep close to the trees as much as possible—just in case. Misty rain drifts from the overhead branches. Counting distracts me until number fifteen. Why do I feel sick, when I don't like Alma or Thomas? I don't want them to get hurt, but we hardly tolerate one another. Nothing is owed on either side now, with the brush returned and photographs gone.

At the bend right before their vacation house, the scene of the accident becomes clear. Traffic cones have been left behind, bowled over by people going on with their lives. Metal and glass are glittering gems scattered everywhere, so I take precaution stepping on an undisturbed path. But close to the pavement, the dirt isn't smooth. Among the wreckage is the indent of feet in mud. Not the tread marks of first responders or hitchhikers. These footprints lead back into the woods.

My foot settles beside the print, but this is Ba's shoe, at least a size too big. I ignore the instinct to go home. As methodical as a lacrosse player lacing up her cleats before a game, I undo my boot and slip it off. My sock is new, since Mom bought a giant pack of them at Walmart before we left for Vietnam, and the heel and toes are striped purple. My sock is about the same size as the footprint, so it must mean that my foot is also about the same size as the footprint.

A strangled cry escapes from my mouth. I didn't mean to do that—or this. I imagine it perfectly: a girl crosses a winding road in the middle of the night. Headlights so bright it hurts her retinas. An engine rumbling. She doesn't move, and when they finally notice her, she's suspended and outlined in white, every confusing color that sends their car into the pines.

Is it my imagination or memory? Was I in my body or out? Am I really here? I worry my hands together. I'm walking in a snow globe full of torn rubber tires and car remains, the apocalypse of a dream I didn't realize I had. I made Alma and Thomas crash last night. No one brought that damn brush to me. I broke into their house for it. Someone could've died because of me. Someone can still die because of me.

I wasn't here, really. Or maybe I was: all the color swirls in my mind, flashes of things that happened to Cam and things that happened to me. Does Ba remember what he does? I had thought us safe in the woods, somewhere far from the house, where Marion Dumont doesn't wander, but maybe not all of her needs to leave Nhà Hoa. Whatever of hers that's in my gut is enough.

Telling someone would be the smart thing to do, but it's easier to be an urban legend. People believe urban legends. Ghost wanders road and causes a car crash. It's always the girl who's trouble in stories.

My other boot lands over the print and erases it from the path. I run the boot over and over until the dirt is smooth and without a telling mark.

———

I take my time walking home, testing myself. Will I disappear in sunlight or shrivel like a salted slug? I don't know what parts are still me and what parts have been replaced. Desperately, I want to crawl back into bed and wall myself in with pillows. There's a price in being awake and vigilant.

Hydrangeas have climbed to the roof, slipping leaves and vine and white petal over clay tiles, adding shadow to Nhà Hoa until its shape is unrecognizable across the green lawn. I'm coming through the back garden when Ba's agitated voice emerges from the cacophony of yawning trees.

"Đã mua vé rồi," says Ba. On the patio, he runs a hand through his thin hair. "Okay. Fine then, 'bye." He raises his phone as if to throw it, but his hand is pale with restraint. He turns to me, suddenly. "They aren't coming."

"Who?" I ask. Maybe the party has been canceled.

But his pain seems more acute—a live wire wrecking his control. "My brothers and sisters," he says. His eyes simmer a dark and dangerous thing, more potent than a parasite. I've seen it once before, when he left for his mother's funeral in Vietnam. While I said the Pledge of Allegiance in a classroom in Philadelphia, he buried her after a nineteen-hour flight alone. There hadn't been enough money for all of us to travel. "None of them. I bought them tickets, but they changed their minds." He laughs bitterly. "Days before the opening."

More of him surfaces: tight lines around his mouth as words spill out. "They think I'm spoiled because I lived in the US." His head shakes. "I didn't ask to go." I've only heard the story a few times: The boat leaving Vietnam was overbooked, but the police were close. Not enough room for all of them. Bà Nội plopped him—the youngest and smallest—inside a tiny square of space with her brother and helped push the boat onto water. "I remember our roots here. Why can't they see that?" This isn't Marion or the house. This is a lonely boy all grown up and still desperate to be accepted home.

Yesterday he held my shoulder, and I have the fierce urge to do the same for him now, to reach out and touch his shirtsleeve and press my thumb into his skin in a way that says *I love you*. "You don't need them," I say, but it sounds wrong and unconvincing. "You have us here." Not for long, not forever, but it has to mean something, for once, that I want him to stay.

I move toward the spot where our hands have been preserved in concrete. This house, this land, has at least this mark of ours.

When I kneel down to trace our initials, I see tiny black ants drowning in the rainwater collected in our prints. We're quiet long enough that they die.

"You don't need to worry," Ba says eventually, removing a dropper from his pocket and squeezing tears into his eyes. It's funny timing, except for the part where it's entirely fucked up instead. "I removed the cameras."

The congee congeals into a cold, sloppy mess in my stomach. I'd forgotten about the cameras he installed to catch me and Florence fake haunting this place.

"I already erased the video," Ba continues. Relief floods over me, then guilt because for one morbid second, I wished I could've watched myself leave Nhà Hoa.

"Did Ông Sáu say anything else?" I ask since Florence would've had every opportunity to share about the journals. We have the journals again, but a clever person, especially a savvy tech nerd, would've taken photographs.

Ba shakes his head no. A sharp and wild hope thrashes in my chest. Between my dad and her uncle, she'll always choose her uncle, but maybe there's a chance for me. I'd never thought, after all, that Ba would be on my side, protecting us in the same way he wants me to protect Mom.

"Thank you," I say quietly, awkwardly, before rising on my feet. I look into eyes that mirror mine. *Đôi mắt bồ câu.* Big as a dove's. Three days until the party. We have to make it three days, until we all get what we want. I will be the perfect host until then.

26

BA, LILY, AND I are laughing, the sound so full it bounces throughout the attic. We each have a corner of a fitted sheet, utterly bamboozled over which side is which as we pivot around the four-poster bed set at the room's center. "These things should come with directions!" Lily shouts when we get it wrong again. We're probably faking it now, holding on to the luxurious cotton as a lifeline to one another.

Ba said sorry, didn't he? And Ba wants to protect Mom, and us, and make us proud, and a home in all of this. Repeating this makes it easier to be here. Beneath anger and resentment, there's so much love. *Love makes all things easy*, as one of Mom's inspirational decals would say.

Something's simmering on the stove downstairs. Savory heat snakes through the narrow door and swaddles us. Finally, we tuck the fitted sheet on the bed. My sister's happy that we're in this together, that we're making our handprints encased in cement hold meaning. Lily fusses over blankets and throw pillows while Ba and I work on the walls. I'd fixed the rectangular exit holes on the chimney earlier—sloppily, but enough to pass Ba's eye. The thumping sounds no longer taunt us either, gone since I pried those brutal photographs free.

The walls have been sanded smooth and primed for paper. Caustic fumes from acrylic primer mix into the smell of a delicious meal. We run light yellow wallpaper from one edge, and I stop here and there to listen, ear flat until pincers pinch underneath. This sixth room is largest by far. The house was right: guests will love this room.

When we lean back to admire our handiwork, the paper's pattern becomes clear. It's not white damask as I thought, but curly diamonds centering Nhà Hoa's face over and over again. A hundred Nhà Hoas peer from the wall, and the promise of many more remains rolled up on the floor, ready to be laid out. "I had the wallpaper made special," says our dad. "This is a house the Nguyens made beautiful."

"We have to give the room a Vietnamese name," I say, because it is ours, no matter which ghost claims it.

Ba rubs his chin. "Ngọc bích loa kèn," he suggests. We stare, very blankly, at the oily primer smeared on his face. "I'm pretty sure it means 'jade lily.'"

That he is not sure himself is what makes the name perfect. I smile. "That is terrible."

"It's the best, you mean," Lily interjects, beaming, then faltering as she remembers she should be mad at me. She stands close to Marion's writing desk, now polished and restained cherry, and avoids looking my way. Cream hydrangeas brush the sill over it. "What about Brendan?"

"Your brother's not here, is he," Ba says, because a bone for a good act explains it all. His eyes slide over to me. "Remember to update the website."

Right, the website, which I'll make perfect. Two days until its debut at the party, and now the sixth room has our names. Florence's old name too, since we share the translation, but I'm not supposed to be thinking about her.

"Let's go eat." Ba leads us down the narrow staircase where my vision goes unsteady. My breath hitches in a panic until the world rights itself again. I stayed up all night listening to this house, on guard so my body couldn't be taken. I'm not giving up yet. The hours blend together so much that I realize we'd skipped lunch entirely.

At the foot of the stairs, Lily stops me, all the warmth gone from her voice again. "Mom sent us something. Last week." She goes into her room, and since she can make a home of any place, she's moved her bed away from the chandelier and piled her favorite books and knits in the spot where glass once exploded. She returns with a box, duct tape hanging in tatters. There's a lot we haven't talked about since our fight. If I'd answered any of Mom's attempts to contact me, I would've known she sent a gift. Lily shoves it in my arms. "You're hurting her feelings, so please call her back."

My sister means to leave me behind, but it's my turn to stop her. "I have something for you too." And though I shouldn't, I grab the silver brush from my desk.

Her eyes widen on the antique. "How did you get that back?" she asks. I've removed Alma's tangled white hair and run the brush under hot water as the house's birds watched. I wonder if Lily would believe that a ghost possessed me, that I am truly sorry anyone—including Alma and Thomas—got hurt. I hardly believe it myself.

"Don't take anything from Dad," I say instead. Not a spoonful of honey, not a garnish of mint. Her lips thin out, displeased with my nonanswer, as she puts the brush back on the vanity. For the briefest moment, I wish she'd ask again. She vanishes downstairs.

I hide my disappointment in my room. Sea-foam green fabric pools inside the box. When I take it out, the áo dài cascades delicately over my arm. Branches extend upward from the tunic's edge, sprouting delicate cream flowers. It's gorgeous, nicer than all the ones we tried on earlier this summer. The silk trousers are a bright white. By look alone I know they'll fit my wide hips fine, even perfectly. I hook the hanger over the window.

Insects overflow from the sill. I'd stopped cleaning when the jar was stolen, and time has robbed the remaining exoskeletons of their shine. How lucky is it though for them to die together, fuzzy and warm in a well-made bed.

I can't think about sleeping. I can't think about eating either.

All at once, the swell of aromatics from the kitchen is too

much. I force myself out the front door, shouting back at the house, "I'll be right back. Gonna call Mom real quick."

I'm too tired for this, but Lily's right, of course. She remembers birthdays, holidays, and Bren's recitals at school. She writes letters by hand rather than by email and closes envelopes with stickers. Mom is important, and I have to talk to her. Surrounded by things secretly buried, I know she's my last tether to normal.

The pines run cool this late in the day. By the time I reach the ant colony, it feels as though I've emerged from the deep end of a pool.

"Hi, Mom," I say as soon as she picks up. "I got the áo dài." She turns off the TV in the background, and guilt gnaws on the emptiness in my stomach. Compared to early summer, her smile is less easy.

"Có vừa không? I had to guess your measurements," she says. "Your aunt was wrong about who can wear áo dài. It's very pretty."

I smile. In some roundabout way, she's telling me *I'm* pretty. "I'm going to wear it at the house opening. Where's Bren?"

Mom waves at him off-camera. "Come. Bren. Bren!" She frowns as she refocuses on the phone. "He doesn't want to talk right now." Great, he's mad at me too. Against all reason, Ba is the only person I'm getting along with right now. "Does Lily like her hair clips?"

"She loves them," I say. "You talk to her recently, yeah?"

"Lily would say she likes anything I give to her," Mom says as I toe the edge of the ant colony. "I was thinking . . . ," Mom continues. The ants have deserted the fallen tree trunk for the trees above where they're frozen, mandibles tight on stems. Stalks spike the air, and a thin webbing holds them together in death. "We come to Nhà Hoa. It's your birthday."

"No," I snap. "No way." The warning in the truck was clear. Ba would never let her leave.

Her voice dips. "Why?"

"Because . . . " This is haunted, I'm haunted, Dad's fucked, we have parasite problems, it's not safe for you because I love you. *I love you.* My jaw aches as I work words from my mouth. "I don't want you to. I'm seeing you next week anyway. It's a waste of money."

"That's not a big deal. Money is just money," says Mom. A mattress squeaks from her end as she straightens up with rare embarrassment. "And actually, I'm already in a hotel in Đà Lạt." I'm not an optimist, because shit like this happens. Hope dooms you into making dumb decisions, such as ignoring your romantically challenged but well-meaning daughter's advice to avoid your almost ex-husband who is decidedly still a mess but in a different and probably supernatural way.

"Are you here to see me or Dad?" I ask. They haven't seen each other in person since that one weekend visit, when Ba sucked away all the joy and color from Bren's birthday balloons. Despite all that and our sparse calls, she wants to see him. The longer it takes me to shut it down, the easier I imagine Marion slipping into my place with a soft yes, *yes,* come here. A hungry ghost always needs more, and this house has learned what it shouldn't have. And me, I'm another excuse for her to see him. "It's a birthday. Who even cares? You should have asked me first."

She sighs. "Okay."

"I'm serious," I say, jaw cracking. "I'm not your excuse to see him." I let Mom witness the tiny part of me that resents her too. "This is *our* time with Ba." She recoils from words I've never spoken aloud. I'm sick of holding it together when everyone's intent on reconciliation with someone who abandoned us.

Mom sighs before putting on a dim smile. "Take pictures for me, okay?"

Over ten stressful minutes, I make her promise not to tell Lily or Ba that she's here. That instead of coming to the opening party, she and Bren will harvest coffee beans, white-water raft, or whatever it is we tourists do. Afterward, we'll meet up at the airport and fly to Saigon together. The sun has sunk close to the horizon by the time we hang up, phone burning in my pocket.

When I reach Nhà Hoa's porch, the first thing I smell is the salty sea. Crushed crabs, shrimp paste, and fried shallots. The house is dark inside, except for the dining room. Ba and Lily wait for me at the table. It's six o'clock and everything's been set. Lace linen covers the sturdy oak.

"It's your favorite," Ba says from the head of the table. The insulation's yellow fuzz dusts his brows.

"I don't want to eat," I say, yet am beckoned forward. Lily, with her long hair swept over a shoulder, sits on the opposite side. She looks past me.

I sit. The chopsticks are in my hands. There're floating tomatoes, squishy and juicy, and a broth that's all red flame in a porcelain bowl. White noodles as pulpy as worms on wet pavement. Pressure-cooked pigs' feet, the hairs plucked.

"I'm not hungry." But I eat. The taste melts over my tongue and fills me. When my hands stop, Lily slurps her steaming soup down. Ba watches us before skewering a meatball made from pounded crabs and pork flesh. My sister whimpers into her bowl. I'm so tired I can't fight it. Secrets do not keep a girl fed, and this nourishes me. It reminds me of home, Saturday nights in a warm kitchen.

I eat, and I eat, and I eat.

The house watches from the wallpaper, buzzing, growing loud, overtaking conversation. It's always so pushy. I gnash tendons between my teeth. I don't want to. I'm so hungry. It feels good to not be in control. I tear skin and muscle. The white linen is splattered with the mushy insides of an overcooked tomato. I suck on each knuckle and dislodge it from the whole.

Bones pile at the table's center, the remains of our ongoing feast.

marrow

THEY'RE EATING THIS HOUSE! *They're eating this house.* They're eating this house. They're eating this house! They're eating this house! They're eating this house! They're eating this house! They're eating this house. They're eating this house. They're eating this house! They're eating this house.

How delicious.

27

TO SPEAK OF IT is to invite judgment. To speak of it is to give her power.

So we don't. Not for a while and a night. Lily slept in my room, stomach aching from the animals she ate. She fell asleep holding my hand tight, close to the bed.

In the morning, regret lines our mouths, but the trash is bagged and taken out, evidence left to rot.

We decide to do our hair. Mine, to be exact, since the roots have grown out an inch. It feels safer to be locked in that tiny bathroom, even though it's not. Cabinets close in squeals of laughter, doors crack their hinges in preparation of a day's work, and curtains dance without a single breeze, and underneath it all is its real love language: scuttling legs and grating feelers as enthusiastic as a baby's babble.

"Mom actually had good taste about this one," Lily says as she examines my áo dài hanging on the door. Apart, I sidle close to the wallpaper that deteriorates in artistic patches. It's charming, so it's tolerated to a point. Silverfish find their way into the glue, no matter how Ba seals the cracks. A mildewy odor emanates from the wallpaper's wide pores.

"Are you even listening?" Lily asks.

I wasn't, but: "Yes." I turn my head, jaw aching, and sit on the chair we dragged in. Lily's waist and hips are swamped in my áo dài, but the length is close to perfect. Her eyes squint in suspicion. "I don't think they sell many áo dài with *girl power* spelled out in sequins on it," I say, and after a moment, she relaxes. It's normal to be out of sync and awkward when you and your sister have been fighting for a week.

"If anyone can get it done, it's Mom," Lily replies, lips quirked. We're not used to this, fighting and being without our mom. Is this house an echo chamber for Lily too? A cacophony of voice and chirps sharing opinions that become fact. Nails dig into thigh. I must not ask her. *I can't ask her.* The house is always listening, just as I am always listening now. I have to stay the creature that has scared her most in this house. When my thoughts slip too much, it always grounds me to think of Mom and the ridiculous cursive or all-caps decals. In a way, it's my true north. There's a home away from Đà Lạt.

We snap a poorly lit photo of Lily's fancy pose for Mom, sending it with at least fifty fire emojis. Exiting our chat, I scroll past my message to Florence again.

SATURDAY 2:33 a.m.

Me: I know you didn't tell. Thanks.

I don't quite remember sending it but having seen it, of course I sent it. I miss her and the silly comments in our code. She didn't turn Ba's bribes to her uncle, though I doubt more every day that a bribe was ever needed. This house is perfect, superior to the abandoned villa Florence and I visited, and better than the flimsy, boring houses newly dotting Đà Lạt.

"We're gonna do one section at a time," Lily says once she's changed out of the dress. I set the phone to one side. "I watched many YouTube videos on this." Since I'm the one who touches up Mom's roots every few weeks and she isn't allowed to color her hair yet, her eagerness to play with hair dye borders on diabolical. I swat her gold-plated hair clips away, but Lily waves the butterflies around my crown like I'm a flower to be pollinated. "I don't care if they get dirty. They're mine, I decide what to do with them," she scolds. I relent.

We sit in the bathroom as we did that day she got her first period, only she's painting my hair cold. "I talked to Mom yesterday," I say, keeping my tone casual, as though I hadn't insisted that she not come to my birthday. I'd wounded her feelings on purpose, counting on her sincere shame. Chemicals sting my scalp.

"Good," she says. "And Dad?" On instinct, I grind my teeth together. Responsibility has always fallen on me for his behavior. In the mirror, her side profile is unreadable. "He tries harder with you than anyone else."

It's a statement, not a question. The utter wrongness of her words sinks in, churning stomach acid. I carry his burden, and so it's fair that he should have some of mine as well. A camera is nothing compared to a skull. I inhale sharply. "He does not."

The brush jabs hard behind my ear. "He totally does. He made a deal with you."

"It was his idea," I say, explaining how our parents' separation sans divorce had screwed up financial aid and how when I called, my visit was what he asked for. Of course, I'd interpreted the invitation in the simplest terms: a half-assed attempt to bond.

Lily sighs. "And you couldn't tell me."

Grimly, I turn to her. "Mom would put off seeing her family another decade so we could eat *and* be educated. What other choice was there? She deserves to start living her life again." Not in sacrifice for us, and definitely not for me.

"But then you started pranking the house," Lily says, "to leave sooner."

"Because of the real haunting," I say, though she's partially right. I had wanted both of us to leave sooner and with the money, if at all manageable. "Some of those things, yeah, were me and Florence, but there's more that's not." I listen for the house's protest, but it's silent except for our breathing. It's already everything I've told her before.

She hesitates, probably considering ripping hair from my scalp. "Obviously before last night"—her lip trembles—"I was avoiding Ba's cooking, because it's weird that he wanted to go all Chef Dad on us, and you said not to eat. But now I don't even know, Jade. Yesterday was weird. I needed to opposite-vomit? Cramming all of that . . ." She trails off, mimicking shoving invisible food into her mouth with a nervous laugh. "This place is creepy."

"It's a place with a story," I say carefully. My immediate reaction to my sister believing me should be relief, but all I sense is dread unspooling under the birds' glossy eyes and the silverfish's clicking maw. The stories must wait. They will grace the world on opening night, as intended, for the widest audience. "I never do things without a reason."

Lily snorts. "I know you have reasons. They're just not all good ones."

I raise my brow. "I'm sorry that I scared you the other times, but I needed to convince Dad. Didn't do any good. He's made up his mind."

Lily pins me with a skeptical look. "You are exactly like him, Jade."

"What the shit does that mean?"

"You settle on an idea and don't let go," Lily says, unclipping another section of hair. "Like, that time you decided you don't like Oreos but ended up eating half a package by yourself."

"I was stressed out studying and needed a sugar rush."

"How you keep insisting Sir Meow-a-Lot isn't your cat."

"He isn't."

"He is, you big softie. *You* found him and brought him home."

For fuck's sake, you do one nice thing and people remember. "I didn't plan on keeping him," I say. Luckily my phone lights up, an excuse to tap out from this character assassination.

SATURDAY 11:35 a.m.

Florence Ngo: I was never going to

There're so many things to say that a keyboard can't capture. Under my breastbone, something is loose and wild. I can't leave without seeing her. Quickly, before I change my mind, I ask if she wants to get ready together tomorrow.

When I shut my phone and look up, Lily's smiling at me. "And her," she says with finality. "You were so determined to hate her."

"I was not," I argue, unsure whether to be angry or amused.

"You know," Lily says, brushing the dark roots of my hair, her voice a whisper. "I love you, no matter what." Her volume picks back up and happily. "All my friends are queer."

This is the moment, isn't it? My sister outgrowing me and finding the words I've always fussed over. Who cares if they're in English or Vietnamese, when I can say them out loud? "Love you too," I mumble. Maybe this is why our parents never tell us anymore; it's too much like saying mud is dirty or the sky is blue.

"And I love Dad too," Lily says, unabashed. "I'm not going to leave him alone here. He belongs back home with us. Let Ông Sáu play caretaker, or Alma when she's better."

"I know." I'm trying. I want to. I had glimpsed him in the truck, that sliver of care still inside and that desperate need to belong. I want to belong somewhere too. I always have.

Lily places the brush and hair dye down. "Okay. I got everything."

My head burns with dye, but I smile. "Want highlights?" I ask, and she brightens. Mom made me wait until I was sixteen. Switching places, I unknot the silk headband from her hair.

Lily jerks away. "Ow, sorry. My head's been a little sensitive."

I frown. "I barely even touched you." That same earthy smell wafts from the walls and mixes with the chemical scent. "Is that why you've been wearing your hair down?"

"Yeah," she says. "I think it's a pimple from leftover hormones or something."

I set the folded fabric on the sink's rim. "Let me see."

"Really, it's no big deal," Lily backtracks, but as gently as I can, I finger through her hair. Each pained noise she makes brings me closer to it, the thing that's making my heart beat harder. In this house, nothing is coincidence. The thumping stopped once I found what was hidden in the chimney. My sister, sleepwalking again, marked her height against Marion's children. The food rots, no matter the refrigerator's age, and now these walls release their animal scent. I part along the flat seam where the headband was, and Lily hisses.

The welt's as ripe as a seeded grape. Its center is white, bulbous, as if pulled fresh from vine. It oozes clear liquid as something shifts inside.

"Don't move," I say, but to whom? It or my sister? Faced with whatever I couldn't protect Lily from, I want to scream. The sound threatens to rip me apart, but I have to get myself together. We are so close to the end, and Ba cannot be trusted to pick up the pieces if I disappear completely into this house's halls. Lily deserves more than this.

Alarm rises in my little sister's voice. "What is it?"

"It's not a pimple," I answer matter-of-factly, reaching for my

261

toiletry bag on the shelf. Lily tries to stand, but I hold her in place where I can see it stewing. Seething for being found early.

How do I know that it's not yet ready in the warm cocoon of my sister's head?

Who told me that?

Her gaze drifts upward in the mirror. "What are you doing?"

"Don't look," I tell her before squeezing a glob of hand sanitizer onto tweezers. The cloyingly sweet gel coats the metal. I don't know what I'm doing, only that I can't leave it where it doesn't belong. I'd been focused on our food, but there are other ways an unwanted entity can slip inside. I should've known after all my research how easily one can be colonized: infections begin as innocently as licking your fingers clean of salt.

This house has Marion's cruelty. It toys with me. *Ce sont tous des parasites.*

Anything can happen to the people I care about, if I don't willingly open myself up for dissection. "I'm sorry," I say. In the mirror, my reflection is holding Lily in a headlock. She cries out when I touch too close to the welt's red rim, struggling against my grip. I'm holding my sister in a headlock. "You have to stay still." Even though she's scared, I squeeze into the wound and use the tweezers to pinch one white end. I tug, unleashing a spot of blood that makes me want to hurl. I hold my breath.

The larva expands its rounded body, too young to squirm in these metal pincers. I can't split it open. I don't want to know what happens when something's half-dead in you, so I keep at it gently, soothingly, until this impossibly bloated body emerges from the hole in my sister's head. "Don't look," I say again as my hand shakes with terrified adrenaline.

Lily can't contain her high panic. Once I let her go, she springs forward to try to catch me—to see what's been eating inside her skin.

But I'm faster. Flipping open the toilet seat, I throw the larva in. Its bulky form splashes as I flush it away, other hand shoving my sister back.

"What was that?" Lily asks, shoulders pulled to her ears as she hugs herself.

I clench the tweezers harder. "Are there more?"

"More what?"

"Spots that hurt or itch," I say calmly, though I run my tongue over my gums and teeth, searching for any stray legs. The shower curtain shifts, though nothing's touched it. This house can't be left in boredom. It gets too many ideas.

She shakes her head. The tweezers roll from my fingers and ping against tile. I pull her into my arms. Tears wet my shirt. "Was it lice, Jade?" Lily asks, sniffling. She knows it isn't, but she's learned from me too when a lie serves us and when it keeps us going. "You can't tell anyone I have lice."

"I won't," I say into her hair, staring defiantly at the birds. She's embarrassed, of course, but no one can blame themselves for where a mother decides to lay her eggs.

28

LATE THAT NIGHT, I whisper to the floorboards. *You're special and people will know it.* Ba finished the sixth bedroom an hour ago. By moonlight, he'd packed away all the tools in the truck because this house is perfect. Soon it'll be my turn to unveil the final touches—carefully curated photography, lovingly massaged descriptions. When Nhà Hoa's maw opens for the tourist season, the insects will have their fill of someone else.

Lily will be safe; Ba, soon after.

A hand takes mine. Its presence is a shock of green-veined white, and yet the bones and grip are as familiar as my sister's—because of course, I had fooled myself into thinking it was Lily holding my hand to sleep, needing me when she was scared. Each finger has slipped between mine before. My eyes follow the stretch of its attached skin to the body underneath my bed.

She is dressed in blush, fallen like a petal on the rug. The blunt bangs part under gravity. Cam wears a scar on her forehead and a small smile on blood-red lips. She's been hiding underneath my bed, always close to me. The hand squeezes mine, and her other cups an ear to the ground. I'm listening too.

Something chews. Something gnaws.

Cam says the words in Vietnamese as the floor sighs against my ear.

"Mine."

She held me to sleep, I think, because we're dreaming of a hillside where she picks wildflowers. Her áo dài sways in the wind, beautiful, and I wonder if I'll be the same in mine.

Then, she shows me dreamscapes of where I've never been in Đà Lạt, that in real life have been lost to construction. Somewhere, in my world, are her relatives, the children of her siblings, but they'll have all forgotten her name, in the same way that I do not know my mother's mother's mother's name. There's no place to find them anymore.

There are orchards that we walk, her always a step ahead and smiling and so real that my heart aches knowing where her life ended. She never mentions Lily or the egg in her head, whether she suffered the same.

She doesn't show the bent balcony to me again, even when we slip—briefly—into a memory of her playing hide-and-seek with the Dumont kids. They were sweet, mostly, and dumb: they had an obvious fear of checking under their beds.

She's sorry she never spent much time with my family, and so like last time, they are fog-white specters haunting the kitchen. The Lady of Many Tongues dances about the sitting room, commanding past Cam to wind up the old record player again and again.

Darkly, Cam shares with me the rubber plantations her parents toiled in. Such great Michelin tires made under starved Vietnamese hands. We walk through cathedrals where she was told she must lay her sins, but it's me who hears them, me whom she trusts with a whisper that starts with *who I could have been*. To be married, she converted in more ways than one.

From one blink to the next, we dream back into my room. The night-light's plugged in, and I see clearly how the flowery robe hangs from her shoulders, its silk edge over the hard lines of her collarbones. Her hair is mesmerizing and almost blue.

"Come here," Cam says, mouth soft.

There is something animal in the way I want her—chest as fragile as an overfull teacup. I still don't know her well, but like a dream, she's every girl I ever wanted and was afraid of. They teach us boys want and girls are the ones who are wanted, but what about people like me? Quietly burning in want and to be wanted.

Bright with moonlight, she gestures for me. Even the hydrangeas outside reach in for her, searching for any tiny crack in the windows' glass. "Bring me your heart," she says.

Marcus had touched me like he was sure, and I want to return that favor for someone else, and why can't it be her? She's a ghost, and this is a world of no consequences.

I can pretend we have choices.

The daze overwhelms me as I step forward, so close to that absence of smell. She takes my outstretched hand and places it on her chest. Ice-cold panic rips from my fingertips and straight to my gut.

She doesn't let go. Cam smiles.

The grip never relents, only grows stronger, more forceful. Skin splits under my hand as golden-brown eyes darken into winter's undergrowth, a rotting green.

Her forehead lengthens, and her hair bleeds, framing a different face, Marion's face. Crueler than her portrait, the real thing. It is her I am touching, her chest I'm caving in.

My jaw locks tight over the scream clawing up my throat.

"Donne-moi ton cœur," Marion simpers, then laughs, sending an echo through the house. Silverfish burst from her punctured chest. Their long-lashed legs sweep my skin. They're eating me. I'm sure they're eating me. "Behave, little rat," says Marion. Gray tombstones line her gums. "Flatter it all you wish, but this is still my house."

She lets me go, and I scramble back into bed. She melts into nothingness. The insects fall, blue and silver flashes like snow drifting under night. She has slipped into my dreams, or maybe this is me awake.

Marion has worn Cam's face, and I no longer know who is real and who is not.

29

THE EARTH SWALLOWS RAIN and leaves the surface clean, where Ba and his workers lay flat stones around the house. We must keep the partygoers' shoes impeccable so when they depart, it's only Nhà Hoa's beauty that they remember. Not the soil it rests on or the earthworms struggling through it. That way, these will be grounds they want to walk again.

My hands cannot touch anything soft.

Marion's spongy flesh haunts each fingertip; my knuckles know the wet weightlessness of pudding. *Always the drama queen*, the house had gossiped about its first tenant. She wants nothing more than to be the grand host, so of course I must be kept in line.

Florence arrives in the afternoon—and I'd forgotten that she would—smiling as she raises a plastic bag full of junk food and rapidly melting ice cream. I don't want to be alone, and yet

I don't want to be with her. Whatever's left inside this house can't be counted on to tether me: the still-fraying relationship between me and Ba, the healing between me and Lily. And Cam, missing. Cam, not answering the incense I burned outside my window. I let ashes eat the petals below, even though it makes the house angry.

"You moved the furniture around," the real girl says. Florence plops down on the neatly made bed, which has been moved to the wall opposite to its original spot. The dresser has been reoriented as well, and the mirror polished to a gleam. The desk has been dragged from the window. I guess I did move stuff. She throws me an ice pop and grins. "Happy birthday!"

I'd forgotten that too, with all the fussing over Nhà Hoa's debut tonight. "Thanks," I reply before forcing myself to recall one of Mom's inspirational stickers. *MINDSET IS EVERYTHING.*

"Hey," she says, head tilted to catch my eye, a tinge of embarrassment on her cheeks. "I'm not gonna go anywhere you can't see me."

The journals. I'm sure Ba's learned his lesson too. There wouldn't be anything for Florence to find, but I appreciate the sincerity. "Why didn't you tell your uncle everything?" I ask, that last bit of curiosity burning in my mind.

"What's done is done," Florence answers, unwrapping a deep purple ice pop. "And you deserve better than to be dragged down with him." In her tone, *him* is grotesque. She's being unfair. Ba's doing his best with the losses he inherited. "It doesn't help anyone anymore. Besides, all our hard work on the website would be for nothing and it's amazing—or it better still be, after whatever you've done unsupervised the past few days. My uncle's driving me bonkers right now, anyway."

Undone, I laugh. It'll be okay; Florence thinks I'm someone worth sparing. Every moment of work put into this house has paid off, and now the website will have its audience. Sitting close, we spend the next hour finalizing the website, based on her uncle's last notes. We test the reservation system with fake punny names, utterly enthused by each other's cleverness. I have saved my descriptions for later. She doesn't know what tonight really means to this house. I stay in this moment, where our lips are wet with sweets and laughter. We don't speak of what will happen when summer's over or how I'd offered to show her around Philadelphia. Mom's text wishing me a *happy birthday* is left on Read.

With a few hours left, we start getting ready. I flick a lighter on, letting my eyeliner soften in the flame.

"There is such a thing as liquid eyeliner," Florence says, skeptical over the fire hazard.

I drag the eyeliner along my lash line. I've always loved the soft heat. I leave the corner tipped upward. When I'm done, Florence is still watching me in the mirror. I raise my brow at her. "Doesn't it look good though?"

Anger isn't enough to dull the way she peeled me open that night at her house. She'd only brushed my chin, for fuck's sake, but I'm pushing her to look at me again, and closely.

Today, she forgoes her bomber jacket, which is a beloved gift from Gemma apparently, and pulls on a knotted T-shirt and a long leopard-print skirt. The slit on the side runs up her thigh. She's settled on the bed, maroon-socked feet wiggling, as I change into the áo dài.

"Need help?" she offers, quiet, as if something were listening and waiting for us to cross the line.

I raise my arm in reply as Florence closes in, fingers deftly fastening the bodice. My arm lowers against her shoulder, resting against the soft wave of dark hair. She patiently buttons me in, and the fabric stretches taut across my chest, somehow containing my rapidly beating heart.

She doesn't pull away when she's done, and neither do I. Her eyes travel down the length of my áo dài, to my feet, and back up again to my smirking mouth.

The stare goes on until there's nothing left for us to do but move. I pull her closer, our noses knocking into each other, and then the tension fades—so many parts of me unwind under her touch and so many others come alive—to the kiss, the single hottest spot in my memory. I wonder if there are others that might burn for us.

We come up for air. A tiny giggle escapes us both.

"You've ruined grapes for me," I say, eying her lips, still stained purple at the center.

"Well, you didn't ruin coffee for me," she replies diplomatically, fixing my collar. "It was already terrible."

"Oh really?" I lean in again. "Can I make it better?"

"You can try harder."

I kiss her more deliberately, desperately, a strange hunger ripping through me. My fingers tangle in her hair. Oh, how I love that—the feel of her hair in my hands, the feel of thin fabric over nothing.

Too much, too little, occasionally volatile, and still she drinks me in. She pushes me against the wall, and I drag her with me.

Her hands are on me too, warm but not soft. I feel her breath hitching under my lips, the shudder of her spine. I feel bones underneath skin, ridged fossil—

I gasp.

"What's wrong?" Florence asks, lids heavy. I wonder if she tastes blood from the way I've wrecked my own mouth in anxiety.

"I don't . . ." The dream crashes hard. My fingers crushing into Cam's—no, Marion's—chest, soft as cheesecake, and searching for something I can no longer name. "Sorry. This isn't." I move away, toward the window where the hydrangeas lie waiting below. They would catch me if I fall. "This isn't me." It's more a question than statement, but she doesn't understand. I can't imagine Florence being afraid of anything, and definitely not of herself.

"What the hell does that mean?" Her voice trembles, close to fury.

I panic. One truth in exchange for me covering it back up. "Aren't we using each other anyway?" I ask. "You said you were bored and needed something to do, but really you wanted to get back at my dad. Excuse me if I decline being the thing to do."

"Don't turn this around on me. It is not about doing or being bored. This is about you, scapegoating how you fucking feel or don't feel," Florence says angrily. "Can you admit your own fault in your decisions? Or is it all some cold-hearted ghost bitch inside you? News flash: Have you considered that it may be just you? And your dad, actually?" She snatches up her jacket and leaves, the door echoing closed behind her.

Once more, I am alone.

tendon

THIS HOUSE HAS GOOD bones.

Soil is vacated for better feed, walls are unburdened with memory, and floorboards abandon their old arches for new footfall. It buzzes in anticipation, gathering itself so tall its nails rise—certain to catch a toe or three.

Please let it be three.

There are lonely years to make up for. Its love is abundant, wrapped in flower and vine so it won't spill in the road from which the guests have begun to arrive.

This house has good bones. *Come, and see.*

30

NHÀ HOA IS BEAUTIFUL. Glowing lights hide the house's blemishes in shadow and accentuate its best—the wild hydrangeas, the creamy yellow walls, its absolute presence. Guests park their vehicles out front and follow a delightful stepping-stone path around the house, where vendors have set up food-and-drink stations. French and Vietnamese cuisine are presented together: macarons next to tiny goblets of chè ba màu; delicate rice paper filled with fresh mints, noodles, and just-cooked shrimp, then their counterpart in puff pastry and cheese; and so much more slivered and arranged for a feast.

Ba's more charming than I've ever known him to be, and our guests devour his company. "You'll have to book a night," he teases whenever someone asks for a tour inside. And they do— they find me in the crowd and insist that I turn our reservation system on.

Soon, I always promise, predictably flanked by my sister declaring loudly that I am the birthday girl.

Their eyes slide over my perfect áo dài, from the small side buttons Florence pinned for me to the tips of my flats poking out from the trousers. *Happy birthday*, they say, then disappear into the real party.

Until the website goes live at nine, it's been impossible to relax. All the coffee in the world couldn't replace the time I've lost dreaming or in limbo. Throughout the evening, I check the site code on my phone again and again to make sure every word is still there.

"Dad's going to love it," Lily says, mistaking my anxiety for genuine effort. Discreetly, I search for the hole in her head, but she's pulled her dark hair back with the butterfly clips. They glimmer under the warm light, a distraction. "The business cards are almost gone, look!" She points to the dwindling stacks on each cocktail table. People eagerly await access to the URL for a chance to win a free one-week stay at yours truly, Nhà Hoa.

The vicious urge to tell her the truth about what's coming rises, then drowns peacefully in my mouth when I glimpse open windows. Even with the throng of new bodies, this house is listening to me.

"Let's go say hi to Ông Sáu," I say as Ba's business partner comes into view. We pass the garden where bushes soar, laden with ripe tomato and cucumber. Green and red chili peppers hang from weedy branches, dragged downward like a girl's earlobe. A half-eaten chili is on the ground, yellow seeds spat out by a boastful guest. Ông Sáu and Tuấn mingle easily between expats and locals but do not look pleased to see me. "Is Florence coming?" I ask at the same time as Lily's cheerful greeting. Her elbow jabs into my ribs.

"Nó bệnh rồi," Tuấn answers. We both know she isn't sick. I haven't given Ông Sáu reason to like me, personally, but Tuấn's iciness stings in particular because he and Florence are close. She must have shared what I said, or maybe he guessed. I'm a quick read, probably, with the threads of my head so loose.

There's a bucket of baguettes, I'm tempted to text Florence, but it would be cheap. Laughable. Any excuse to connect will be transparent after that distressed dismissal. One summer—that's all this is meant to be.

"Alma isn't here either?" Lily asks, craning her neck to look around.

Ông Sáu shakes his head. "She's still at the hospital with Tommy." My insides churn. I can't worry about anything or anyone else outside of this house, but it's been four long days since the accident. Even my optimistic sister frowns.

From the side, Ba approaches in his handsome white-collared shirt and suit trousers. His jacket has been draped over a cold guest's shoulders since the beginning of the night. "Should we get our speeches ready?" he asks after checking the slim black watch on his wrist. It's almost time.

"You or me trước?" Ông Sáu asks as he sets aside his beer.

"You first," Ba replies. "And, Jade, you turn the site on when I signal." When I tell him I'm ready, he beams at me with pride. It's all coming together as planned. While they prepare for the official unveiling, I move through the crowd with Lily taking the lead, as though our ages have been switched. This last half hour unfolds with uncharacteristic clamor. No thumping chimneys or squeaking floors, just real voices submerging Nhà Hoa. Snippets of conversations catch on my eardrum.

—il y a des villas plus jolies—

—Thomas not doing well—

—thức ăn lạ—

—swear those flowers leaped—

It's not my turn to speak yet, so I'm silent as we linger between the dessert table and our biggest offering. A roast pig is splayed as a centerpiece, mouth open as if stuck in a perpetual scream. Its hindquarters are carved indelicately where knives snag on globules of fat. Lily takes over cake distribution, putting others at ease with her charm—however bad her Vietnamese or French. She thinks if this becomes a success, Ba will hire help to leave at this house and come home.

I count the candles on my promised birthday cake, the only way to rein in my thoughts. Glances crawl over my body, at the silk of clothes Mom ordered for me. Clothes made here, worn here, incidentally marking me as a mascot. I won't wear them again.

The live band finishes a rousing song to applause, which heightens when Ba and Ông Sáu step onto the patio with their fresh drinks and microphones. The crowd shushes one another during Ông Sáu's introduction. He switches between Vietnamese and French often to rippling laughter. No one else notices Ba cracking his jaw from side to side. His grinding bones fade into background noise.

As the house's excitement grows, so does mine.

"Thank you for attending Nhà Hoa's opening," Ba tells the crowd, grinning. "We've spent the past year renovating this extraordinary house and are thrilled to receive our first guests in October." The fairy lights brighten across the lawn, basking our guests in a stark glow. "It has a long history here in Đà Lạt. The first proprietor of this house planted the very hydrangeas you see today," he continues, gesturing toward the climbing blooms. "Many of you probably passed this house before and have seen how they've endured. My mother's family—the Bùi—worked in this house when it was first built. I'm proud to have restored this house with its original furniture and appropriate modern luxuries, and we welcome you to stay with us in the future. Now, my daughter—"

A giddy smile coaxes my lips into submission. This is my cue to make the site live. Nodding obediently, I change the settings. *My turn.*

He smiles too, because this is the moment that Nhà Hoa is officially open. So many chins and cheekbones are lit blue with electronic screens as people visit the website. Ba raises his drink as he says, "Enter the lottery by midnight and you can win a free vacation here at Nhà Hoa." I begin to move around the crowd, and Lily follows slowly as she clicks to the website. "But don't wait too long or we'll be booked up."

A third of the group chuckle, but the rest are unaware of all sound. The whispering begins during this awkward lull, gaining steam as Ba's face shifts in confusion.

"Putain!"

"What were they thinking?"

"This is not funny."

"Có thật không?"

My smile widens. Lily grabs my arm, trembling, with a browser open for me to see. The familiar page refreshes with perfectly timed hover animation:

They say all old houses have death in them, but what of houses that begin in death?

On the page where our esteemed guests are meant to enter the lottery, I have instead detailed the house's history. All of it— what I knew and what I gleaned from Cam's memories and this house's buzzing.

It's rumored that during Nhà Hoa's initial construction, a worker fell from the roof and broke his skull. The first hydrangeas grew from blood-fed seeds. The house has had its taste, and in those early years it dabbled as serial killers do: birds, cats, squirrels, dogs. This house knows what is a believable accident. It's clever, it's manipulative, and it had a teacher to observe in Marion and Roger Dumont.

As restlessness roils through our guests, Lily keeps scrolling and asking, "What is this? Jade, did Florence put this up?" Next to Ba, Ông Sáu's mouth takes the shape of a curse.

The Bùi family served in Nhà Hoa, all squeezing into the one bedroom on the lower floor, and endured harsh treatment from their employers. The matriarch of this family was tasked in housework, cooking, gardening, and even child-raising. Her employers' twins fed from her breasts, leaving nothing for the little ones in her own family . . .

Ba searches for me within the mass that's devouring the house's unseemly life.

How many times does a community have to say he/she/they/it looks so normal before finding the rot? When someone tells you your worth over and over again, you begin to believe it. This house is better than the land it sits on. Better than the houses around it.

The photo gallery is the best touch, since blacking out the Dumonts' and officers' faces makes it all the more ominous, in case dead peasants aren't enough. My great-grandmother's portrait in the curtains, however, remains ours alone, tucked away in Lily's bedroom among her favorite things. After weeks of failing to convince Ba and Lily, I revel in the guests' disgusted gasps.

Marion had the arrogance of someone given power. No one could disabuse her of the notion that some things shouldn't be eaten raw. Ill and agoraphobic, the madame of the house's paranoia and cruelty became a hotbed for abuse. Her sister-in-law Lê Thanh Cam, local and then semifluent in French, cared for the Lady of Many Tongues until her passing.

Haunted. Ma quỉ. Hungry ghost.

By then, maybe she and the house weren't so different in nature. One death wasn't enough to sate their appetite. The buzzing began soon after, a sound made only for the young Vietnamese bride. As the food rotted away, so did she. Trapped without family, or love, Cam died the most unjust death: pushed from the balcony. The original ironwork still bears that mark, ready to be tested again. Nhà Hoa does not want to be alone. It does not want to be forgotten and irrelevant, like its madame.

The swarm's cross talk intensifies. Ba's face has reverted to stiff cardboard and creased eyes. "Jade," he calls after me, but I don't stop. Their horror allows me to stand tall in the house's shadow, strengthened that I've done right. No one will stay here. Surely no one will dare.

What's buried under Nhà Hoa now that this house cannot stay quiet?

As people play the audio clip at the end, my shaky voice spills from their devices to narrate the end of the web page. The list reads like movie credits of the lives lived or lost here:

Construction worker
Unidentified individual #1
Unidentified individual #2
Unidentified individual #3
Lê Thanh Cam
Bùi Minh Sang
Đào Anh Loan
Bùi Thiên Long
Bùi Phi Nga
Bùi Thanh Trúc

From a dozen phones, my voice stumbles over the Vietnamese, but she's trying. She did her best to respect their names. Slowly, the off-sync audio files end and the party steeps in silence. While some have left, the rest watch Ba moving angrily through the packed bodies.

Why is no one running?

Why isn't Florence's uncle demanding his money back?

Why—

"My daughter," Ba laughs sharply when he reaches me, "loves a good prank. It's her birthday today. Maybe that got to her head." He laughs again, causing those standing closest to join in.

I pull away from the hand resting on my shoulder. "I hate pranks," I yell when I mean to be calm. I can see scrutiny replacing the terror from moments ago.

"She's been up to it all summer," Ba says, spinning a charming story. "You know, putting in smart bulbs, writing ominous messages, scaring the absolute shit out of me. *Ooooh*." His exaggerated ghostly call inspires more relieved laughter.

No no no no.

I hold my phone up with the enlarged website. "It's true," I say. "All of it's true. Everything I wrote about actually happened." My tone slips in its urgency. "Ghosts are real. *Ma are real*. I found those pictures in the attic." Lily sticks to my side, but she trembles under our dad's gaze.

"You can make up anything on the internet," Ba says cheerfully. "Stock photos, AI faces, Photoshop." His hand waves dismissively. "She didn't want to share the party, and I should've listened." My head shakes vigorously. "I'm so sorry for my daughter's interruption. We'll have the proper website up at a later date."

In that moment of suspended belief, during which everything shifts, Ông Sáu and Tuấn soothe the situation over by offering a real party in the city, drinks on them. The crowd finally moves, but it's not what I wanted.

I try harder. I tell them more. I plead. So many sentences start with *I* and end in no one who believes me. To make it worse, I begin to cry.

Under their snarling judgment, I am the girl who cried wolf, the liar, the American. All me ruining the fun.

Noise clutters my head—guests leaving, windows snapping shut, and my inner voice repeating *believe in yourself* like a malfunctioning greeting card. Inside, the house's ceilings and roof threaten to snap my neck in shame. I promised to be its host—better, calmer, and more competent than Marion. It promised me a place to always return to. Believing in my skill, it told me stories to spread its fame, and I betrayed it.

I wipe my wet face in a towel. The black-and-white-attired staff have abandoned their stations, leaving trays of food unserved. Salty nem line up as a pink crosswalk, the embedded slices of garlic in the shape of moth wings. Doughy bánh bao lie in concentric circles on a platter. Sunset orange flesh embellishes cream cheese heaped on peppery crackers. But it's cheap grape and coffee that haunt my tongue, desperate to be scraped clean on an oyster shell.

The door slams shut as Ba and Lily enter. "Mày không nên làm vậy," he says in quiet rage, the pretense gone.

It's Lily who I speak to first. "I couldn't tell you because *the house is always listening.*" She stares at me: a hysterical stranger. The Vietnamese gums in my mouth as I regard Ba. "My dad should've taught me better." I say the words like I am big, like turning eighteen has made me an adult. "This house isn't good for you, or us. No one should stay here anymore."

"This house is *perfect*," Ba says louder, undoing the top two buttons on his shirt as sweat collects on his brow. "And it's ours. I *told* you."

"Come with us," Lily finally says, drawing herself between us, a picture of reluctant bravery. She doesn't want to be blamed for what I chose to do. "Let the other people figure it out."

"You think that's for you to decide?" My sister jumps under Ba's harsh tone, shoulders rising in the way they used to when our parents fought on the rare occasion that Mom had had enough of him. But no, he focuses on me only, red veining his eyes. "All the money is in this house. You understand? We needed to be booked one hundred percent and more to make it back."

Outside, cars and motorbikes start without a care as my stomach twists. It's empty, the last thing I ate already melted and gone. All the money he got building houses for other families, spent on a place that can never be owned. College, and Mom, will never see those payments again. My future, the one I planned for, gone, but that's not what hurts. I had given that dream up already.

Ba had never planned for a resolution. He's manipulated me from the start, never caring for how this will end.

"Why did you ask me to come here, then?" My rage is silent, akin to grief, a body in anticipation of loss. "I knew I shouldn't believe you about the money, but you had no plan at all, did you, to make it right with us?" In the deepest parts of my heart, I had hoped for more days like the one at the lake, when we shared and talked and remembered.

He snaps, "I'm doing this for all of us."

"For yourself," I say, swallowing down tears. "For *your* family." The one he is always chasing, the one that can't be bothered to board a plane and see what their little brother has accomplished. While I unearth his heart, it's also shedding light on mine. "They're not *my* family." Aunts and uncles and cousins I wouldn't recognize on the street. "They don't even like you."

His palm connects with my cheek. I'm disappointed when my skin doesn't fall apart to reveal someone else who's better equipped for this.

"Stop it!" Lily shoves herself between us. "We care about you, Dad, and this place is creepy. It makes us—it did things to us, didn't it, like right now?" She still wants to mend this. She wants our dad back.

But this is the final purge, and I'm thankful when Ba speaks, because I can't break it to her. "I left you, Mom, and Brendan because of Jade." Ba doesn't hesitate when he deals this blow either. "Your sister told me to leave. That she couldn't deal with me anymore, after your grandma died, when I needed someone to tell me to stay."

At the wrong time, I laugh. "Con là con của ba." *I am your child.* "I was thirteen." I don't look at Lily. I can't look at Lily, or I will say nothing else. "I wasn't old enough to get what you were really asking. You packed your own bags."

"You aren't denying it?" Lily asks, whatever else she wants to say fading.

"He asked me if he should." My voice rings inside my skull. "He wanted to go."

What did I expect to happen, again? Contrary to my very nature, I had not thought at all. Simply acted, and cowardly: letting Ba tear out pieces of a different diary, crumpled and uncared for.

Lily hiccups, head tilted to her chest so I can't see the way I've damaged us. "You should have told me."

We're all haunted by the things we should have done. For example: I should be saying sorry. I should be begging for forgiveness. I should ask if I can hug her, if she'll ever call me chị for the first time and again. She runs away from me, out of the house.

"Now I fix your mess," Ba says. The door shuts again, and I am the only living person in Nhà Hoa. Without my family, I throw myself into sound: a motor starting, the refrigerator's hum, my breathing. The past returns to consume me.

Once, Ba put a pair of shiny shoes on my feet and told me they were magic. That they made me special and unafraid. Even then it wasn't his first lie.

To this day, I can't look at glitter and not find myself flung back thirteen years, standing in the school hallway while a white girl sneers, *They're just from Walmart.*

That time, I made myself believe in magic, in riches, in bravery bestowed.

This time, it was Ba. I'd ignored all the signs. I'd asked no smart questions. I'm getting what I deserve, because I believed in my father. I loved him enough to hope that he loved me too.

tongue

IMAGINE A DEVOURING IN reverse. From the bowels they surge, feet undigested and through starlit entrails. Their laughter is new and quick while limbs are marinated drunk. So close to this mouth, and yet it stays empty, salivating.

It's not fair. Bad, *bad* girl. It's not fair to be left hungry and second choice with a foul memory. This house trusted a petty thing, a form so beneath it, and yet she must be reminded. She must fix what is wrong.

This is your home, the windows choose to rattle. *Look at me.*

31

HOW MUCH CAN A heart endure twice?

It's a storm that begins within: whipping my lungs with everything that matters and all things that don't, the impact as heavy as hundred-year-old trees. Mouthfuls of shame, anger, and love, resentment, all of it pooling at the corner of my lips. Spit threads to the floor, connecting me to the house.

My palms push into eye sockets, trying to close it all up, but I see a bruising blackness. It stinks of bleach. A refrigerator door left open, maggots on a beautiful girl's chest. Too much, not enough; I'm always one or the other. Now, Lily's done with me too.

Cries echo back at me—some mine, some not. This place still wants me.

I run. Through the house and its doors, over the ridges of tires digging in mud, and over pine needles. Into the woods where we buried the skulls. A father-daughter bonding activity short of murder. I smell bleach. I see his hands cleaning without gloves and how they must hurt. I need to get away. I need to be alone. I need to sleep.

I am the only one he has ever hit. He is the only one who truly knows me. I carry the burden of being the first child, and it sinks me into the soil. Unwashed linen, comforting and earthy, as close to home as I'll get. I squeeze my eyes shut until I'm dreaming.

Mom washes my feet as masked women grind shellac nails to dusty beds. I remember this. She dips her hands in green scrub, then dresses my legs in the texture of sand, working calluses to their fresh baby skin.

I was born not talking, so I don't now either.

She's laughing and telling other strangers, "My daughter got into UPenn!" Her eyes are kind and demand more from me. "That's an easy commute."

The massage chair slams its fist into my spine, then liver. There must be blood involved.

I'm leaving, fake me says. *I never know how to be myself around you.*

In this dream, Florence kisses me first.

In another, she kisses me again.

And I say sorry. Halle pauses our show and takes my hand, the dust from our Cheeto-ridden fingers shedding. "I know you didn't mean it."

It's that hour when I can't tell if it's sunrise or sunset: the horizon is steeped rooibos in a blue mug, clouded with sugar. Lily's favorite, and she isn't here. It's just Ba and me and open water, my boots—the right size—heaving through. It isn't Vietnam at all but some shitty human-made lake back in Philadelphia.

It doesn't matter, in the end.

"You remember how to knot the line?" Ba asks.

"Loop it like a shoelace," I answer, and I do. My fingers move fast, even though it's been years, and throw it into the lake.

My fish line is suspended, then yanked, almost tearing away. Ba laughs, "Bring it in!"

As he taught me, I hold the rod in a perfect right angle and wait until the fish slows down. The key is to be patient and tire it out. I reel and wait. Repeat. His large brown hands wrap mine, and I am his child again, in the safety of his arms.

"Dad," I say. "I love you."

Bubbles break the lake surface, drowning me out, and I think: catfish, and we'll braise it with fish sauce and chili peppers; snakehead, and we'll split its scales and salt it under the sun; trout, and we'll stew it fermented and topped with headless prawns.

The body moves closer, a sliver of dark brown and warm ivory. Water parts, spilling within itself, and I see so clearly.

It's Jade. It's me with the đôi mắt bồ câu, clothes cutting red marks into her skin. The me with the hook in her mouth gasps.

———

Suddenly, I am in her place, emerging through cold wet. Arms pull mine up. Ba has gone. Lily's not here. I am alone with a dead Vietnamese bride. Crown lit in a brilliant khăn đóng, she's wearing her matrimony best.

Red is for celebration and good luck, so Cam must be my charm.

"Where have you been?" I ask, arms wrapped around myself. "Are you real?" Even here in this limbo world, I remember whose rib cage I broke. Don't bite the hand that feeds you, but what if the ghost you trust turns into the one you don't?

Hurt flashes across her face. "I've always been real." The cadence doesn't match the movement of her lips, and I accept this for normal. I have nothing else to lose.

"You could've done more," I say, the pain of never being believed dull. "Haunt everyone else the same."

A little more of her neck slips from the collar when she shakes her head. "Your heart is most like mine."

It doesn't exist, I want to say, but lies are as exhausting as truth. I push back, "You could've told me straight up what would happen, at the start of all this." Our eyes connect, and a

292

question burns through me. "Can she only control one of us at a time? Well, at least." Me and Lil, taking turns to slurp soup, is an image I'll never forget.

"They are always listening," says my bride. Marion and this house, chicken and egg, no one knows which rotted first. "You shouldn't have written everything down that way. You've made them angry."

Always with Cam, it's *should not, could not, do not.*

"I did what the house wanted." I made a promise I actually kept: to make it known. Giddy with joy, Nhà Hoa couldn't predict how I would tell the story. "It's beautiful. It's legendary. No one will forget it." The guests read those names and saw that real people—servants and workers and unknown faces and Lê Cam—suffered in this house. For a short time, someone besides me had believed. Cared.

She walks into the water. "My mom told me once that marriage is like wearing clothes," says Cam. She rarely shared about her life before Nhà Hoa, so I wait, the fog so thick that I step closer to keep her within eyesight. "But family is a part of you. They are your arms and legs.

"I saved my family by wearing clothes, but they lived without me. You see the lie?" Cam asks. The gold lines of her áo dài no longer glitter under a false sun. Bitterness laces her tone and the angle of her body, ready to fight. "You can survive without an arm or a leg, your ear, nose. You can survive losing a lot of blood."

Sick gathers in my chest. "Say what you mean, Cam."

She casts a sidelong glance over me, her lips redder than

293

cherries and fresh-bloomed poppies. "Family isn't always necessary. It can be you, or them. One day you'll have to choose.
Don't choose like me," she says, not hesitating anymore. "Đừng
quay lại." She's as beautiful as the day she was married, and
equally as sad. "If you go back, I can't promise that you'll be able
to leave."

I'm wrecked by real cold soaking my clothes. Half-conscious,
my head aches bad. Pine needles rake long lines down my cheeks
as I turn, vomiting undigested food and too much coffee. The
woods outside Nhà Hoa remain quiet. My mind races with
dream and memory, settling on Cam's warning.

She told me to not turn back, to treat family as disposable
body parts, but where can I go, if not with them?

Fog diffuses moonlight, coloring everything gray, as I sit
up. Touched, my phone screen flashes on with Halle's and my
face. I've been asleep nearly three hours. No calls from Ba or
Lily, both probably still out undoing my trouble. Lily's disappointed face has been burned inside my eye. It's worse than
when I held her in the bathroom. At least now she *knows* why I
had to pinch a living thing from her head.

I always have a reason, but she might not listen, and why, *why*
am I the one who always has to explain? It should be their turn
to deal with it. I force my sleeping legs to move and grasp at a
nearby tree trunk.

Cam said she chose wrong. She stayed with the officer and
his brutal family to save her own from a harder life, but she also

craved home. Sometimes, she went looking for it. Asking for it in a tortuous limbo. She split herself in two parts: wife, then daughter.

That's where Cam and I differ. When I make a decision, I go all in.

Fake haunting. Playing games. The website. In an orderly fashion, I did my best to ruin this house without damage.

I take another shaky step. All those faces that judged me tonight, they are next. Ba isn't giving this place up. I imagine them staying in the Lovers at War master bedroom, pissing in front of glossy-eyed birds, and bringing the unexpected back to their own country, burrowed in their stomach lining or soft brainy bits. Sickened and called back to the place that started it all.

Ba and Lily will stay forever as hosts and servants.

This is a house the Nguyens made beautiful. It's our legacy, the mark we'll leave in Vietnam. It's how we know we belong, but I'm done begging for validation. Ba and Lily forget that Bà Cố didn't die here. The girl hiding in the curtains grew up to have Bà Nội, who had Ba, then Ba and Mom had us. We've survived without this house.

All my life, labels have been armor to deny others the truest parts of myself. I can play unhinged, hysterical teenage girl. What I won't do is let a house dictate our lives, so even if they despise me for it, *I am all in*. There's no guessing which parts of me Nhà Hoa has changed, but I still have choices.

stomach

TWO YELLOW EYES ROLL forward, and its windows shudder. That noise, that engine, this house knows what it is. A dinner bell. Yes, it's time again.

Hydrangeas swallow the motorbike whole. *Crunch*. Softer now! *crunch, crunch*. She doesn't turn around. The fear ripening at her back is too bountiful.

"Jade?" Her voice is so delicious, native born and foreign trained.

"Over here," this house says in its daughter's creak, deep in the belly.

She steps inside.

32

I DON'T HAVE SHOES on. The soil lets me know quick, with thorny branches and stinky moss. I walk fast anyway, uncaring for what bites my feet. Between unanswered calls to Ba and Lily, I've put together a list. There is one bullet point under *Solutions* so far: burn it. Cursing, I try Lily's number again. The little sleep I got outside the house replenished my brain cells, but every thought still leads to fire.

Short of renting a bulldozer, this is the most unrecoverable, cleansing way. As more calls go unanswered, my panic rises. Yet an unexplained tug draws me forward so firmly that I trip over tree roots and mounds of dirt.

The closer I am, the stronger it is.

To find their way to one another, ants leave a pheromone trail. Lost ants, ants with bad inner compasses, and those ants that went out hungry, follow this scent. Nhà Hoa is signaling me, I think, in a similar way. Neither Cam nor Marion have a scent when they appear in person, but I am alive. Perhaps in running away, I'd shed some of myself and now it's leading me home.

Home.

What a wonderful word that means I don't have to be alone anymore.

In the mist, the exterior lights shine as bright orbs. At the edge of the woods, I stop. Tiny napkins scurry across the ground, blown from the abandoned party. The house has darkened, stretching unfathomable shadows. Underneath must be walls, but this is a monstrously gorgeous version of itself. In a matter of hours, the climbing hydrangeas have overrun its face, petals a vibrant white.

The house has noticed me, of course. Nhà Hoa's growing coat of vine and leaves shivers in a way I understand. *They're waiting for you*, it promises, and I move forward for an embrace. No heat comes from Ba's truck when I pass. They really are home, and that's the most important thing right now: to be reunited, all of us, as a family.

I lean into the plush greenery along one section of wall. The house's whisper is lower here, but the vines tighten instinctively. Flowers caress my cheek, and I hear: *stay.* Their sugary scent fills my nostrils. "I will," I reply, because I've always needed sweet to balance me out. My hands curl into the foliage, where a dozen ladybugs crawl over my skin.

You'll never have to lie again, the mesmerizing black dots spell.

In this world, everyone is mad at me. Everyone has too many questions, and I don't always know the answer, or the truth. The only escape is inside this house, because it knows me and doesn't judge. It can make us forget the things that have hurt us. "I'll take care of you," I whisper, hugging the hydrangeas harder. "I'm sorry."

If flowers could bleed, red would soak my áo dài's sea-foam green for how tightly I hold them. Against the curling leaves the silk is a bright contrast Mom won't get to see, because I've never given her the chance to forgive me. To know me. To decide if she still loves me. "Mom," I croak out loud, my head pounding and eyes too dry and raw. She isn't here because I told her to stay away, because it isn't—

Leave them behind, the house demands against the shell of my ear.

Cam said something similar, but that's why I am here. To be with Ba and Lily again, my arm, my leg. In a household split as ours, everyone chooses a side, but I don't want to anymore.

"Mom. Bren." I say their names as fervently as a chant. I've been ridiculous, forgetting that there are people waiting and a home plastered with ridiculous inspirational quotes elsewhere.

This house tells me it is perfect, that I am too. *You will never have to hide here.*

That is a lie. Cam has always had to hide who she is to survive. Our deepest secrets give it power and leverage.

"Halle." I hold on to their names, desperate, as I back away. Iridescent beetles drop as I smack my impossibly heavy ears. As if drawn by a magnet, the leaves continue to reach for me, limited only by their vines. Inside, potted hydrangeas smash their heads in watercolor blushes against the windowpanes. Ba and Lily are still in there. What promises did this house make to them? I tear myself back, blocking out the house's call with my voice. "Mom." I fumble with my phone again, past the note that says to burn the house, and dial from my favorites.

It's past midnight now, but she'll be awake, reading her books on the e-reader we saved up for her last Christmas. My jaw tenses, twitching with anticipation, when it connects.

"Đừng nói," I say. Don't talk. Please don't talk first or I'll lose my nerve. I press the phone to my ear, close enough to hear air-conditioning and Bren's soft snores in the background. I used Vietnamese, so she knows I'm serious. The house gnaws at me, replacing my instinct to run away with the desire to walk right into it. But I can't leave my family and Halle behind to live some fucked-up version of a perfect life with Lily and Ba. "I've been lying to you."

The inspirational decal from our bathroom comes to mind: *Be Brave. Be Bold. Be BeYOUtiful.*

In a way, being me is what got me into this mess. "There's no scholarship to cover everything at UPenn. Ba's supposed to give me money for staying here with him, at least the first year." I talk rapidly to her silence. "I didn't want to make you worry or take out loans. You've given me enough with what you have. You've sacrificed enough."

Will she scold me in Vietnamese or English?

I weigh the words in my mouth, pretending they're heavy enough to send me down a roller coaster. Each time I had thought of coming out, I'd imagined Halle with me. No-nonsense, sweet Halle, who knows the names of every boy and girl I ever wanted. Except for the one, now, and the other already dead. "Halle's not my friend anymore because I did something awful with someone she's crushed on for forever. Not even because I liked him, but because he liked me, and . . ."

It doesn't take even a second for an answer. "I'm your mom, I know." Her voice is gentle, but I need to say it. Being sure and clear and honest is my way of fighting through this. The fewer secrets I share with this house alone, the less it has to manipulate me with.

"I wanted to distract myself from who I want to be with. One day," I say, probably not making any sense. My sweaty palms meet silky fabric, drying on the áo dài. "I like a girl."

An intake of breath: mine or hers?

I can't bury myself for her, or anyone, or a house anymore. I deliver the finishing blow. "I told Dad to leave. He asked me the day before he left us, if something isn't happy, is it okay if it goes? Yes. I said yes, because I was tired of picking up his beer cans and him ignoring all of us. And that's where your fish went too. Right into the Delaware River." I wonder what hurts more: that I did this to her and hid it, or that Ba asked me to. "I don't want to be stuck between you two anymore."

"We can . . ." My mom starts to speak, then stops.

I feel as if I've thrown up stones, each containing a morsel of me or memory I've tucked away. I have picked the worst time to have feelings. I laugh and say, "But I need your help. I'm in so much trouble, Mom. This house is haunted. Something's wrong with Dad, and Lily—" I break for a moment, biting my lip until it bleeds, looking everywhere but Nhà Hoa. Power tools, paint, and fuel litter the back of the truck.

I don't smoke. I don't drink, really. I'm only a girl who's had a lifetime of bad thoughts. Enough practice, like studying for a test. A lighter should be easy. A lighter *is* easy. I burned those photographs from before. This will just be a bigger flame.

"I need you to call the police, anyone who can help," I say, the plan coming together in relieved anger. "Because I'm going to get them out of there. I'm going to burn this house down." The gas carton's contents slosh around when I pick it up. "'Bye." I end the connection before she can be angry with me, tell me I'm absurd or straight, or convince me not to hurt Ba's house.

After twisting the cap off, I throw arcs of fuel on the front steps. My phone vibrates, but I ignore it. "Dad! Lily!" I shout. "Come out, if you can hear me." I toss one empty bottle aside, yelling for them again as the drenched steps shine. I can't take being so close, so vulnerable to the house without drowning out the whispers more.

How can I expose this house and still keep myself safe? *Hypocrite, bad daughter, slut*—"Halle," I say when her voice mail greets me. It's noon back in Philly; she'll check this message right after.

"This is Halle Jones. I can't come to the phone right now, so please leave me a message and I'll get back to you." At the very end is a snort of laughter—mine—before it cuts off, because we'd recorded proper voice mail greetings together one afternoon, in case college admissions called.

"Halle," I say again, shocked to still hear past-us. It helps me keep emptying whatever bottles I find over the porch. "I'm sorry. You don't accept that." I simply want her to know the truth. "I shouldn't have kissed him back. I fucked up. Bad. I haven't liked him since, like, elementary school. He was just there that night. It's BS, because it was graduation, and I still wanted everyone to see me as not . . . different. There's nothing wrong with being different. I was always scared of my mom knowing, you know, in the same way your mom scares you. What's worse than your mom being disappointed? She never really paid attention to how good I was doing, as I was doing it, but I knew if I messed up, that would be that, but—no, just. This is coming out wrong. Halle, I want to say I'm sorry. I know you didn't shut me out because of Marcus alone. I'm sorry I threw it in your face, like you were blowing it up. I put being scared over being your best friend." There's a loud clunk from the garden from someone moving fast—*Lily, Ba*. They must have heard me. I squeeze my eyes shut. "I'm okay—okay, Halle? Thank you. Let's end with that."

Our breaking apart is less a wound and more growing pains. Halle has other destinations while I find mine. It is done, which is enough, and I feel drunk from telling the truth, that unbridled joy surging through me. They're close now, I hear them, and with them beside me, I will set this house alight, and we will leave.

I'm running toward the shuffling feet around the house when a hard, solid plank crashes right into my face, slamming the bridge of my nose. For the first time on this foggy night, I see stars.

33

GRASS, MUD, AND STRAY dandelions kiss along my sides, brushing against a temple that throbs. Nothing comes into focus when I blink. Only a blur of light and sound register, the birds restored to their trees, cawing and hooting into the night as my attacker lets out a heavy breath and spits.

I rub my eyes clear and catch the full brunt of the next whack by accident.

"You're not getting away," they mutter. I know this voice. My tongue toys with the name, unable to enunciate. Multiple points of pain attack my skull, as I'm eaten alive from the inside by forces I still don't understand. My vision recovers poorly under the rapid swelling. Our would-be guest of honor dons torn vine and leaves over plain slacks and a tea-stained blue sweater, filthy with loam from the garden bed. Her white hair is a wild halo as she stares down at me with bloodshot eyes.

"What are you doing?" I ask—dully since it's obvious. She's hurting me, and by the angle of her weapon, she won't stop. Somehow, I'm upright again and shrinking away into the dizzying landscape.

Alma stalks forward in a determined gait, ignoring the question.

The house shows no other sign of life, but the pungent fuel reminds me what must be done. "Where's my dad and Lily? Did Marion put you up to this?"

Screaming, Alma slams the plank my way. Wood splinters into my palms and sinks deep as she shoves harder. My fingers dig into its edge. I stumble as she swings it crosswise. "I came for you. *You* made us crash," she snarls. "You made us crash." Her muttering continues in a wretched sob. "My Tommy."

"I'm sorry," I say, the words automatic as a way to deescalate. While she has me trapped, there's no telling what's happening inside.

Alma's voice shakes, as does the plank separating us. "Sorry doesn't bring him back."

I'm dropped in an ocean of freezing water. He can't be . . . But I saw the aftermath on the road myself. There'd been a lot of metal, glass, and rubber near where my footprints were left in mud.

"You were headed toward us, weren't you?" she says. "Looking for my Tommy." What she accuses me next of, however, snaps me out of shock. "You had your eyes on him, didn't you? I saw how you looked at him."

It's always easier to think a girl has motive than for a man to take responsibility. Disgusted, I say, "Because he's a creep."

"Don't you dare call him names," says Alma. "He's dead." Snot dribbles from her nose to her chin. She must've run through the woods to exact her revenge, not caring who or what she would have to fight to reach me. "He died because of you, walking around at night practically naked." She sputters in thick globs, rambling on and on.

I've officially joined Đà Lạt's urban myths: girl in barely any clothes causes car accident. An emptiness yawns within. Unfulfilled hunger. It's inappropriate to be so hungry or disdainful, when I should be remorseful instead, when I should be talking reason to a woman plagued by grief, but I have already established that I am bad at this. "It was Marion Dumont," I say. "Not me."

"Don't be stupid," she sneers, throwing all her weight into ramming me against the house. The impact sings over my body, and the hydrangeas try to soothe me once more. "I already saw your deranged little website. I don't believe you."

It's almost a relief to hear those four words. Ba had reprimanded me at the party, but the expressions on our guests' faces were colder. It wasn't only my unapologetic writing that disgusted them; it was also the tears I cried. With renewed strength, I yank the board from her grasp. When she stumbles close, I smack her hard twice before running from the hydrangeas that had begun to curl around my calf.

"Do you know how expensive it is to renovate a 1920s home

that was left in disrepair?" Alma asks, staggering as she follows me out from the house's shadow. Her murky eyes glance toward the gasoline-soaked steps. "Thomas and I put everything into this house. You're not going to ruin that too."

It clicks in my mind what she wants to do now that he's gone. "You can't sell this place," I say as I back against the truck. Even if it were purchased by someone else, that doesn't change the fact that my family toiled here. "It's ours." To live, to work, to burn. We decide for once who remains.

"*I* funded it," says Alma. "*I* know more about the history here than anyone. Absolutely insensible land laws, considering how our capital funds this whole country . . ." Her muttering fades as she sees the truck cargo. Grinning with pure delight, she picks up an item from Ba's things. A power tool comes alive. The silver drill bit whirrs, as sharp as a dentist's tool. The drill strikes the plank, a viper in her hands. I may be young, but she is taller and quite fit, probably from all the skiing, golfing, tennis, and hiking they did in retirement.

I trip when she scrambles closer, the thin wood between us cracking slowly as she aims for my cheek. With a groan, I force the plank to my left and roll under the truck. She shoves the drill after me. "You're a nasty, rebellious teen getting back at your father," she says as her bobble head bounces with each wild swing. "So spare me your lies."

The drill bit punctures fabric. My dress collar tightens against my throat. I scream, army-crawling forward. The back panel rips in a perfect vertical line. "Dead people walking. Ghosts. Ridiculous!" Alma keeps shouting in her rage, swiping hard with the power drill. It bites into metal, adding the smell of something oily. Black fumes. Gasoline. All the precursor to a burn.

Liquid snakes into my clothes and muddies the ground into a sloppy mess. A headache threatens to split my skull in neat halves as I gag, escaping to the other side. She catches up seconds later. Glancing from house to my dripping form, she smiles and throws the power tool aside. "That's the one good idea you've had," she says, bleeding nose turned high. Her tone is saccharine sweet. "Be a dear and burn away from the house."

"Fuck you," I say, lunging for her, as she draws the lighter out. I might not outrun her, with all the blood rushed to my head, with the whispers still trying to sneak inside, but I can fight. My fist connects with her face. Bones to break, elastic skin to pierce into—I don't hate hurting someone in a way that's not lying, not when anger blooms in my chest over the way my home's been claimed.

Alma wants this house so badly, and yet it chose my family to lay its eggs in. What makes us vulnerable? Are we weak? No, that's not it. Why any Vietnamese, really, other than that we have always been conveniently here living and working while others profit.

I was born far away, across an ocean, in the same country that raised Alma. It's sickening how others might think we're the same when my family tree started here.

The house is silent as it watches us fumble for the lighter. I can't believe a thumb war is what's keeping me from blazing up.

The worst thing has already happened to me, and this is

simply shit stuck on my foot. As I am finding out, fighting the elderly is an untapped skill of mine. I propel us close to the slick porch. "No!" she yells, wrestling the lighter and tossing it angrily from me. I reach behind me, fingers scrambling across the porch edge until I find a piece of metal.

"*You* didn't build anything," I say. Ba's wind chimes are heavy in my hands, ironically still dismantled from that day I caused Alma and Thomas's accident. The metal rings upon impact, and I kick her legs out. Grabbing her by the sweater, I shove her into the steps. The force reverberates up my wrist. I have her by the scruff of the neck, easily avoiding her nails that search for leverage. I smash her head through the spindles. A hairline fracture starts in the aged wood. Groans bubble from her mouth, but she's still reaching for me with gnarled hands. Her head's rammed again into the spindles, until she stops moving.

My chest plummets up and down with heavy rasps, as if there are invisible hands trying to resuscitate me. Here's a cause for celebration: Alma stuck between broken balusters, blood shining under fairy lights. The arms do not move, limp as a doll's against its torso.

No one watches from the darkened windows.

The house, Marion—neither helped me do this, and I smile.

34

I'M A VICTORIAN DAMSEL. I'm a ballet dancer. I'm a suburban teenager. I'm every person who survives: clutching a weapon and the last of their mind. I'm also every person who doesn't survive: nonvirgin and named yellow, unrepentant fighter against the elderly and dead colonizers. There will never be statues or universities in my honor here.

One hand grips a crowbar, and the other clasps a two-gallon gasoline can taken from the truck. I've ripped the largest splinters from my palms, but the tiny ones that require tweezers stay, digging deeper. I stare at the house with its windows dark. My áo dài catches on a breeze, dirtied but as gorgeous as any gown. Dirt clumps my hair into thick bands. My eye has swollen up, obscuring a quarter of my vision.

The balcony's French doors snap open, swinging as warning and invitation. "You're so dramatic," I say aloud. Ghosts don't spare anyone on drama, I've realized, or maybe it's Nhà Hoa still fired up from the party. It's part of the spectacle.

At the front steps, I lean down to inspect Alma's body. Overgrown leaves shift by her beaten face. Alive.

Fuel slicks the porch and shines in untended pools. Not wasting any more time, I unplug the can to pour within. Before I finish, I have to make sure Ba and Lily aren't trapped by the house. The door is ajar, snagged on the abundance of climbing hydrangeas that have claimed outside. I crouch low to avoid their touch. After getting jumped by Alma, it's better to be safe.

This house encases me whole, hotter and more humid than hours before. Every single thing unlit. Every noise quieted, as though the rats have had their fill. The light switches are dead. I'm already sweating by the time I shut and lock the door, in case Alma gets up.

When I turn around, green eyes find me again. Marion Dumont stares from her portrait. No one answers my call, so I have to go in deeper. An old house like this settles over time, and it might have taken Ba and Lily into its crevices. My heart is exhilarated with excuses to talk to my sister. Dear Lily, have you seen the rats? Doing quite well, are they not? Destroying everything? Have we considered that this place should not be saved?

The welcome mat caresses my feet, which rub in until freed of the biggest clumps of dirt and grass. I set the gas can down and run a hand on the wall beneath the staircase, feeling for every dent that proves it is not perfect. "Where are they?" I ask, and nothing answers. I bring the crowbar back and smash against the panel. I peel it back, opening this house up for its sullen insides, its dark secrets. Wood plummets to the floor.

This house never would've passed inspection, Florence had said, and it is true.

Ants overcrowd the walls, staked through their heads by the fungus that controls them. Most have perished, releasing spores to poison the whole colony, but others crawl through tunnels leading far into Nhà Hoa. Ba had passed on houses in the US for less.

Then, I overturn the gasoline, dragging a slimy trail through the sitting room. I check the fireplace for my sister's feet. I drown the potted hydrangeas. I blink, and blink, waiting for my family to appear in the dark—or her, Lady of Many Tongues. I've seen half-wrecked buildings, scorched and wet after a firemen's visit; I don't want that. I need more fuel.

I toss the rattling can. Ba says a grease fire can't be put out by water, so maybe that's true. The kitchen will have oil. I have to make this place combust any way I can now that it knows I'm no friend. The leftover trays from the party have been flung off the counters. Something has stepped on them, turning appetizers to viscous waste.

No time to wonder who or what.

I kneel by the cabinets to grab all the oil. Ba has provided a variety—olive, vegetable, ghee, sesame, and even avocado. I throw the first glass dispenser. It breaks in one great gush. When I double-check for more, I find a jar. My jar, the one that's been missing from my room. It was full of dead insects the last time I saw it; it's empty now.

Theorizing about parasite-infested food can be an academic activity; witnessing the proof that Ba—whether under the house's or Marion's influence—supplemented our meals with bugs is nothing short of a nightmare scenario.

With stomach acid eating at my throat, I check my mouth for splinters and sprouts. My skin tastes like American fast-food grease. My finger comes out clean, except for the blood running from a bit lip. I rise, arms full of my chosen weapon. A creak from the back room puts me on high alert. "Dad?" Again, no answer.

Movement rumbles the ceiling, so I empty bottle after bottle up the curving stairs. My silk trousers are soaked from the bottom up, moisturizing my dry heels. The walls beg me to listen again, but my head swims in fuel and oil. Ba and Lily have to be upstairs. My family will be upstairs, and before I burn this place down, I need them.

Leaves rustling, hair being brushed, tiny legs scuttling. This house is alive.

"You've returned," Marion says in French-accented English. In this hallway of closed doors, she stands outside the only open room, the master. Through the balcony, Đà Lạt's cool night finds its way inside: pine and hydrangea, wet earth, smoked pork, and again, gasoline. Her dress is a velvety smudge.

"Lily!" I call out again. "Dad!" As my voice echoes back, Marion holds me still and awake. She demonstrates her control over me by plucking each taut muscle until the bottles and crowbar clang on the banister.

"You've made a grand mess," says Marion as her neck

stretches. "Fooled this house all you wanted, but now we both know you, useless rat."

I look everywhere for a sign that they escaped, straining to gloss over her abandoned torso. Perhaps it's better that there's no indication they've returned at all. If I am by myself here, Marion can compel me alone. "Cam," I try instead, closing my eyes. "Cam. Help me." She's warned me before. She's given me clues where she could. She's shown up for me, and I need—

"What hasn't she told you?" the Frenchwoman simpers. Her absence of smell dulls each accelerant on my body as a bony cheek slides over mine. Against my ear, she whispers, "It was never only me."

This memory is different from previous excursions. The world materializes in slow blinks: floors first with oak boards steadily shaped; sheer curtains wrinkled by rough hands; severe masts arched from bed to ceiling; and porous walls brimmed with whispers. Then, at the master's center and backlit by sunrise, a young woman straddles her husband.

From a corner, Marion grins, and I know suddenly that this is a ghost's memory.

Cam's expression is blank. The glint in her eyes is borrowed, shining from the blade she sneaks from the pillow beside them. Her husband is too enthralled by the flowery robe hanging from her emaciated shoulders to notice. She stabs down and spills blood. She stabs and his big hands try to find her throat, but it's too late.

His sloppy gurgle joins the walls' low murmur as I begin to shake. In all her memories and our dreams, she's never shown me the precursor to her death, the way she first murdered her husband.

Marion's voice is soft and encouraging as she coaxes her sister-in-law to rise. *Come on, Camilla.* In a daze, Cam slips from the canopy bed and pulls the sash from her waist. *Come, dear,* Marion says from the balcony. I shut my eyes before I can see her neck break.

When I finally look again, Cam heaves upward from the bent iron, one arm clamoring over the other to take turns lifting her long neck. The robe's sash stays tight on the railing where her body hangs. All the while, Marion laughs and laughs, unaware that she's made a terrible mistake.

This house will be alone for a hundred years. Neither will be happy.

And Cam, she is a hungry ghost, and not even my incense can fill her.

I'm standing in the kitchen. The lights have come back on, and in front of me is Ba with a searing gaze. While I lived Marion's memory, she must've moved me. She helped me find my family. "I got it fresh," he says, palm slapping the thigh-sized red meat laid out on a large cutting board. Its bamboo is ready for another knife mark. Fat marbling streaks through the meat, as white as airplane exhaust.

I giggle. In this house of dreams, I can have everything I want. Its buzzing tells me so.

He sets out another cutting board for me, and I take up a knife.

Lily enters from the back, dazed, while Cam walks behind her. Supervising. Those golden-brown eyes—so awake—rest on me, explaining, pleading, full of shame. It was her all those times. The brush, me walking on the road, a hand in mine to sleep, it was all her. Marion told no lies there.

Married at seventeen, dead at twenty: there's a nursery rhyme somewhere, a warning for girls who follow.

From her protective hands, my sister drops dead grasshoppers under my knife. *Look at me.* For a moment, awareness flickers between us. "Don't listen," I murmur to her, but she leaves for the dining room, set to task. Cam lingers closer to me, dousing the grasshoppers' earthiness with nothing, blotting the meat's blood soak with nothing, pervading all other scent with the staleness of a plastic bag.

"What else did you do?" I ask. I don't blame her for her husband's murder, not after his crimes and Marion's urging, but Cam actively concealed it from me. She worked with the house to hide it from me.

"Chị bảo vệ em," she says.

An incredulous chuckle fights its way out. "You didn't protect me." I strain to yell, but the shame has lodged inside me. The party bombed. Lily is not okay. Ba is witnessing the failures of my lust. "Tại sao?"

317

She is quiet at first, so much that I expect her to fade away, but then she answers in halting Vietnamese and English. This house isn't the only one learning from its tenants. Cam has been listening to me and Lily and Ba, absorbing our tongue in bits and pieces. "I not want hurt family, nhất là em." Her diction is slow and clear. "More time we đi chơi, less I feel lẻ loi. Less lonely. We the same." I shake my head, though I know intimately how much less lonely it's been to live a dream or in limbo to escape real problems. "But they not. Marion take. Người Mỹ take. I take back."

A shiver runs down my neck. Cam reclaimed that brush by puppeteering me to Thomas and Alma's villa. This plea, however brave in this mishmash of languages, isn't an apology. Ba carves the thigh, pointedly not staring at us. "That why you told me not to come back? I'm a đồ chơi to you," I say, fed up with being someone's plaything.

Her áo dài is a gash at the periphery, ripping closer until her dead hand rests on mine. "No," she whispers, words in a perfect rush of excuses. She warned me earlier she couldn't promise I could leave if I came back, so why did I return; she knew she couldn't stand to be stuck here with only Marion, so please understand. Fingers squeeze into my palm as she says, "I not let her hurt you anymore. Ở lại with me. I want you, Jade." Those four words tug deep, especially my name in her mouth—that barely there *d*. I don't respond. If I stab her with the knife, she won't even bleed. No escape. No future if I stay.

When I keep silent, she adds, "Last food, okay?" My world begins to get hazy and simple as she leaves me behind.

"I suspected," Ba says, somehow the most clearheaded among us. "But didn't know. She stays away from me usually." He didn't care, as long as he got what he wanted.

Dazed, I cut the grasshoppers' heads off—since no one likes being looked at when eating, really—and slide them from the cutting board in one swoop. They bounce around the sink. In even pieces, I split legs and arms. Their paper-clip thighs get an olive oil massage. It's important to let these tough things rest, but they'll be tender enough.

Oh. *Oh.* I've done this before. While Ba's been feeding me, I've been feeding Lily. My pride in being able to provide a comfort crashes into numbing realization.

There are so many ways to make a meal not vegan.

The afternoon after we went fishing—our last *real* happy day—wasn't at all what it seemed. Brined in soy sauce and fried with tofu, diced grasshoppers don't look very different from lemongrass.

In small ways for a long time, Marion had me in her palm. My sister is another victim of Cam's fucked-up and unclear warnings.

Beside me, Ba's knife work is fast and imprecise, rushed compared to our usual dinners. The clanging is hypnotizing. Sautéed less than a minute, the meat still drips raw in the middle. All as it should be. Each morsel, slick with lime juice and fish sauce, is carefully arranged on a bed of crisp and fragrant herbs. Grasshoppers have been mixed in as perfect garnishes by my hands. Translucent onions ring the platter.

Unable to help myself, my mouth waters. The contents

of my stomach are still in the forest, leaving me empty and starving.

Flatworms. Tapeworms. Parasites the size of loose thread. Deadly little things.

Last food, okay? my bride had said.

"Shit," I curse, and stumble away from the platter. Cam's or Marion's or the house's compulsion weakens, and I immediately run to the other room for Lily. Waves of pain rock my head. Acting in the moment is as draining as doing every calculation, but I didn't come here to die. Soft candles shed light on the grand table, set for a feast. My sister oversees another girl, whose hands have been tied from behind. A rag has been slotted tight across her mouth. Her hair has a cool, unwashed shine. "Flo," I say, shocked by her familiar profile. I didn't notice her on my way in at all.

"Dad needs us here," Lily mutters, blank-eyed, when I gently push her aside to unbind the ropes around Florence's wrists. Words are muffled, urgent, rushing me along.

The rope twists and turns, an indecipherable mess. As calmly as I can, I tell Lily, "Get out and I'll catch up with you. Don't listen if something talks to you."

Confusion slips onto my sister's face, but she repeats, "Dad needs us here."

I take a deep breath. We'll have to do this the complicated way then, me dragging everyone out. Florence's head tilts so I can undo the gag. As soon as she's freed, Florence coughs and spits, "Your bride knocked me out."

"I guessed," I say, wondering whether Cam had done it

before or after warning me to stay away. How long has she been planning this? I pat my pockets down, but the phone's gone, probably lost during the scuffle with Alma.

Florence leans forward, catching my uninjured eye. "I heard what happened at the party, so I looked for you."

You came back? Like that day in the attic, Florence had come to rescue me. No one's saved me before. I want to kiss her again, to wreck that purpling mark on her neck.

"Maybe untie me first?" Florence says next, as though she can read my messy expression under all the bruising and puffed skin.

My strength isn't enough to undo the knots, no matter how I fumble with the ropes. Perhaps her best friend is right about me, after all, for my lack of muscles, for the trouble I am. Florence is in this position because of me.

I look around the room for scissors or a knife, and finding neither, I seize my sister's shoulders and shake her a little. "I'm serious, Lil. You need to go first and call someone for help." Her brows scrunch together as she works through my command, half turned toward the exit while also clutching a tall-backed chair.

It's Ba who responds first, emerging from the kitchen with the platter we prepared together. "We're all needed here, Jade," he says as the porcelain dings against the table, signaling dinner. As if determined to finish his toast, he raises Florence's cat-eared phone and taps the screen on. "We're not done yet."

35

MY DAD THE CHEF, my dad the renovator, my dad the fisherman, my dad, *my dad* is all I can think to counter this nightmare. Even in soft light, his eyes are red, bulging, while his jaw works itself more on his left side, clenching and unclenching. Beer wafts from his body, and for once that is not what I'm afraid of.

"It's seriously over," I say, drawing out each word, fixating on the plate of food. I stand between Ba, and Lily and Florence, unsure if at any moment Lily will stab me in the back. Or maybe I will do the honor under Marion's hand, though the ghosts aren't here in full form yet. They last only so long, like damp incense or an untrimmed wick. "Lily and I are leaving. With Florence. That's it." I force myself to look at his worm-filled eyes. "I'll fix the website. Have your house, Dad, and your guests. Your ghosts. We're done here."

"Ông Sáu thinks this is a bad house now," Ba says as he casually scrolls through the stolen phone. "Where do you think he got that idea?"

"Anyone who can see?" Florence offers.

"Or hear," I add. Until tonight, I hadn't seen the ants within the walls, but all along they have been there, as real as the rodents that gnaw our wires. There has been a feast without my knowing it.

Ba points to Florence. "She was planning against us this whole time, and you let her at every opportunity."

Lily shuffles to join him, but I grasp her sleeve tight, answering, "Planning against *you*. But I published that web page myself. It's only what the house told me, so it's true." All at once, the lights burn too bright and threaten to break into mouthfuls of glass. The buzzing reaches another octave in our ears. The house is angry, so angry, and I have to wonder if it learned that from me over our late-night conversations.

His jaw clenches again as he says, "You focused on all the bad parts, like always."

No, I exposed this house for what it is. Because it had suffered enough of Marion's moods and failings, it needed a chance to be full under a capable host. I was meant to make its glorious stories known, but I listened for the splinters—the details casually thrown aside of those who passed through its walls and did not survive.

Ba does not understand that I am trying to save us.

"Who did you bribe to get this house past inspections?" I ask. "There'd be nothing to plan if you were honest."

"Don't start with me about honesty," Ba says, and I feel the slap on my face again. I'm certain the shape of his palm still mars my cheek, that a fortune teller can read his fate from what's left there.

"So what?" I ask. "Are you going to murder-suicide all of us?"

Florence coughs. "You really shouldn't give him ideas right now."

Lily slips out of my hold, whirling around to yell at me and Florence. "He's not going to hurt us!" Dense heat weighs her hair down, the golden butterfly clips barely moving. She can't see that he already has.

"All houses have a little death in them, given time," Ba says. "There's no need for more, which is why we're going to settle this right now." He places Florence's ridiculous phone on the table.

"I've been having dreams too," I say, another confession leaving my lips freely to bide time. "What has she shown you to convince you that this is what you want?" I move closer. "Because from what I've witnessed, there's nothing romantic about our family living here. They were servants. *She* called *them* parasites. Bà Cố was too young to understand." Her parents protected her is what I like to think. They didn't want to force her to grow up by feeling less important than anyone else. It's the same reason why I've hidden Ba's worst from Lily and Bren, but I'm done with excuses. "She was a horrible person to our family, and now she's playing games with all of us."

Lily sucks in a shaky breath as I stand close to them both, begging to be believed. As I'd learned, Cam withheld the truth from me. Ghosts have their own agenda, and we fall into the roles they can no longer fulfill. "Marion wouldn't know moderation, even if the skill dropped out of her ass. She murdered the last person she sank her teeth into.

"I know you want to belong here, and to feel a part of it," I say. "But there's nothing good here to rewrite or give your life up for. This house only cares about itself. Never wants to be empty. It doesn't matter what name it takes or whose care it's under." The worst thing is being unsure whether Ba's behavior is all due to Marion's influence or his ambition, born out of pain. I can only keep trying. "Please come with us," I whisper.

We breathe in the same abnormally perfumed air, and yet he doesn't cede any emotion to my reasoning. To my pleading. His jaw tenses. "No one is leaving," he says. I swallow down disappointment as his attention shifts toward Florence. "Your uncle won't pull the investment if you say so. If I have you here. So we'll get him on the phone and resolve this. But first, Jade?"

"What?" The word is spat out, but the body has moved without argument. My scratched-up fingers wrap around chopsticks. Cam's heart-shaped face flickers into focus near Ba's, curiosity tilting her brow. Lily pries Florence's mouth open and squeezes as I would a fish hooked to my line. A muted scream comes from her throat as she thrashes as much as she can in her seat, eyes wide at the raw slab of beef hanging from my chopsticks.

Like that day we ate and ate, I am simply moving: following commands from my body. Like mouths that do not match the language they speak, my body does things I do not understand.

Beef drips on Florence's cheek. A single beady eye stares down from the grasshopper head stuck on it. I'd missed one. Of course I did.

That's when something chimes, as sharp and sweet as a golden temple bell. My breath stalls as a round piece of metal smashes into Ba's head. He groans, and then there's the chime again ringing throughout the room. Cam is gone. The floors creak, and a shadow makes itself known.

"Mom?" Releasing Florence, Lily runs and throws her arms around the woman standing over Ba.

Weeks have passed since I've seen her in person, but it's absolutely her. No apparition can divine the accuracy of the tie-dye pajamas that she obviously rolled out of her hotel room in or the '80s-style windbreaker zipped over them. Lily and I have the exact pair. Of both. Shock blossoms over Mom's face as she stares from the pan in her grip to Ba knocked out on the floor. "Oh my god. Is he drunk?" she asks.

I drop the chopsticks. "Where are the cops?"

Mom arches a sculpted brow at me. "You told me you were going to burn a house down. I'm not calling the police on my daughter"—and this next part, she says loudly—"who is my daughter, no matter what."

I am equal parts tormented and euphoric. The former for coming out in a haunted house and the latter for my mom accepting me. Still, seeing Mom is a shot of adrenaline that rushes blood into my ears, blocking out restless whispers. But the bounds of my joy soon bump against the walls of this house, because I remember exactly what Ba told me before.

If she came, he would never let her leave.

"Why are you here?" I ask, unable to stop my voice from trembling. I failed in making her angry enough to stay away.

Mom, with Lil clutched on one side, drops the pan and hurries over. "I already told you," she says. "You're my daughter." Melting into her hug is almost muscle memory, and it takes all my restraint not to cry. I'm always underestimating what she, the bravest person I know, will do.

"Hello," Florence says finally, face red from mishandling. "Maybe we can catch up after?"

"Sorry," I say, jolting to retrieve the knife from the platter. I'm careful to not nick her skin as I cut the ties. Leaning close, I say again, "I'm sorry, really, for everything."

"He's not drunk," I hear Lily defend. "He only had a few beers at the party."

My hands slide over Florence's freed ones, briefly, in an embrace that's more. Everything I want to say. As there's no time, I choose the most pressing priority. "I still really like you a lot." The words I wanted to say as soon as I knew she'd come for me. "But we also need to get the hell out of here."

She steadies herself on the chair. "I know. Next time I'll text when I hear about you screwing up my website." She smiles, and I have to stop myself from leaning in.

"Bren's back at the hotel. What's going on here?" Mom asks again, clearly not understanding the bucket of shit we're in. "The white lady on the stoop did *not* look okay." Or maybe she does then, but she loves us enough to not ask questions before smacking our dad down.

At the threshold between kitchen and dining area, Ba groans.

As one mass, we bolt for the front door. I stop, however, in an uninvited shadow. Marion descends the staircase in a mourning dress, pale eyes sharpening on our unfolding escape. She bares her gray teeth in fury. I break away from the others, yelling, "Go, go, go!" My feet slide over slippery floors as I make for her painting. I seize it from the wall. Ba chases after Mom, Lily, and Florence, disappearing beyond the overgrown hydrangeas.

"Come here, you colonizing bitch," I shout. I don't know if she can leave this house—I can't trust anything Cam has told me—so it's better that I don't let her try. She drifts down the steps, head snaking ahead to see the portrait clutched in my hands. She looks upon herself. "This isn't your house." I'm an afterthought, and that is her mistake. "We're not your servants." I smile and then add the most ironic line of all: "Go back to your own country."

I punch through her portrait, which, honestly, fucking hurts in the most satisfying way.

Marion lunges for me. The golden frame hits the floor, skidding over oil and gasoline. Her neck curves around the staircase, letting her head corner me first. It sneers at me, cruel and foul, until the rest of her lumbers close and her hands—her real hands—slam me into the wall I excavated.

The ants that are still alive crawl over my skin, heftier in number than the silverfish from our last encounter. Their tiny legs march on my frozen body as the ghost threatens my chest cavity. "Mon cœur est ici," she utters with her dark tongue. *My heart is here.* Pain flutters over me, swift as light, like the sun through tree branches while Ba carries me on his back at the park. *Here*, where I can witness age leather his face, where Mom can smile without guilt, where briefly we are all together.

"I will never be forgotten, but you will be nothing at all," Marion snarls. She reaches in, driving deeper than a broken underwire bra. My dead face will buy another hundred lonely years as Cam's had. Each year that passes, my death will become more folktale than warning. Someday, more Marions will come upon this house and see again what is there to take.

Another long neck coils around Marion's, the tangle of their flesh terrifying and unnatural, as they wrestle for control. The pressure releases, and wincing at the piercing pain in my chest, I move. I shake ants from my limbs and race for the exit, looking back at a ghost I could've loved. Cam, who tried to warn me and then couldn't let me go. They stumble and they fade.

Outside, Đà Lạt embraces me. It licks sweat from my aching body, my throbbing head. Oil trickles from my hair. The house's heat scrapes my back, urging me to return, and I almost do, I almost forget, before I see Mom putting herself between Ba and the others.

"Stay away from us," she shouts at his persistent stride. He's greasy with fuel and limping as if he'd fallen.

We're out, my mind repeats. *We're all out of this house.* I run down the steps and approach from the side, hands raised in peace. "We can all get in the car and work it out later," I say. Ba's pace slows for a moment while Mom's protective stance relaxes. "I don't think it's as strong out here."

Bewildered, Mom squints at how Ba and I stand, angled as though the house is a participant in our conversation. "Who are you talking about?"

Ba considers me with that unreadable look. "We're all here now," I say gently. "Together." I nod my head, gesturing toward the road. "We'll go pick up Bren and leave this all behind. We're family. Please." His eyes are soft again, I can admit that much. He's exhausted too, underneath.

"No one is leaving," another voice growls. I'd forgotten all about her. I catch a full view of Alma, our personal Marion. Wood runs jagged along her ruptured cheeks, and she bleeds freely into the little scarf tied neatly on her neck. Her hand shakes on the rescued lighter. "Found you." She laughs a deep barking sound.

In the next breath, she tosses the flame my way. My drenched áo dài is easy kindling. I hear my mother mourning me before I am even gone. I can't believe the last thing I'll see is Nhà Hoa looming behind a woman I don't even like.

A dark smudge passes me, covering me. Ba takes the brunt of a tiny fire that becomes so much more. It eats through cotton and starched trousers. A strangled cry bites into night, and I wish it was a dream. Screaming, Lily and Mom rush and tackle Alma. Lily's golden butterflies glitter in this light. Someone holds me from the side, but all I can see is fire. Orange, and red, the smallest parts blue. A marble of color: a gift.

Slowly, Ba turns around. The fire rises, but he doesn't make a sound. Why is Đà Lạt not raining? Why does it not pour, as Ba says it does in July? Does the sky not know we are hurting? How can it not hear the tenor of my scream? His eyes are surprised because maybe even he doesn't believe what he's done. Yet they are still soft, writhing in some other pain, and it's the same as the day at the pier. He spreads his arms.

Ba is a burning house, the doors open to me. "Come with me, Jade."

My dad leaving, my dad asking for me, my dad reaching for me. That was always the dream, wasn't it? To be wanted and taken along. I'd always wanted a second chance to not let him down when he needed me, but *this* isn't what I imagined.

Cam appears beside him, her neck returned to the collar, unapologetic in the way she invites me. "Come, Jade." I barely see her at all next to the blaze that is my dad.

"Ba thương con," he says, and my heart swells until it breaks and bleeds around my still-warm organs. In this house of dreams, I can have anything I want. His protection and care, a girl to love, a mark on Vietnam. So many things whispered at the altar to burn into ash.

"Ba," I say out loud as the tears come, unwanted. Salt stings parts of me already broken. "I can't, no. I won't go with you." The words choke me. This choice to live without him, because he never should have asked me. He never should have regretted saving me. "Ba." I call him again. My father burns on the front lawn of the house where our ancestors served, every part of him crackling disappointment. He drops his still-smoking wallet aside. He walks up the steps to Nhà Hoa, flames spreading from his feet to the banister and to the door covered in white hydrangeas, where Marion Dumont shouts at him to get out.

Florence hugs me close, the grease of her hair rubbed against my cheek, and I grasp her back, desperate for any tether to what's real. She holds me tight. She doesn't let me go. Mom does the same with my sweet, sobbing sister.

Ba looks at me one last time, then closes the door.

———

Human flesh burns the same way as any other meat, but a burning house screams in a thousand languages. Within wood, steam eats its fill and grows until it bursts in kernels of sound. It thunders on: *pop, pop, pop, pop*, until it breaks, slanting under its own greedy heat. Floorboards pucker, nails ripped and left behind. Metal remains upright but sizzles when the first pipes break, *clunk* as clumsy feet might. The gutters flare up like a strep-red throat that our bare hands dare not clean.

The flowers burn worse: heads fall to the ground, then light what's under too. Leaves sear thumbprints into concrete, desperate to escape. Others empty their insides against tile in green streaks. Vines wither, letting the last of their carbon go in soft breaths, as ragged as someone pulled from life support. The house cannot stop roots from digging in—a patchwork of smoldering veins that encase it whole.

I imagine the little Nhà Hoas in the attic wailing, paper curled as if on a scissor-sharp edge. It would rot from yellow to deepest black. We should have torn out the insulation. We should have done many things differently. Walls are toasted clean to the tippy top, a triangle of fire that ruptures its glass eyes. Even brick cracks, one by one, like fractured bone. Of course, everything inside it dies: the rats, the ants, the silverfish.

Ba.

Their screams clog my ears, but the loudest is mine.

I never stop to breathe, even once.

36

SEPTEMBER, AND THE MORNING sky is apricot pink and orange, a blur of fuzzed skin. The bus station in Đà Lạt is bustling with tourists and locals buying last-minute souvenirs and water bottles for their descent into the jungles of Vietnam.

Our taxi lingers in a place not meant for staying. I squeeze Lily's clammy hand, then tell Bren and Mom I'll take a minute. They watch me from the window. They always watch me these days.

Florence waits for me outside a double-decker bus, holding a large soda with two fat straws. A redhead stands next to her, the proportions of her neck normal, in black sunglasses. She sticks her tongue out at me before climbing inside the bus. Florence shakes her head. "Yo."

"Yo," I copy unconvincingly.

We smile, our shoes connected at the toes, our hands cold alone. I've held hers twice since the house's opening and closing, with our knees touching and hair smelling of smoke. At the hospital, they pumped me and Lily full of antiparasitic drugs and antibiotics. Our bodies recover, but nothing is the same.

Some days, I taste my tears and I want more. To know it's real, no matter what the doctors say, requires a level of anxiety I'm capable of, but repeating it over and over again can't be good for me. We'll need therapy. Mom cries when she thinks no one can hear her in the bathroom, and Bren doesn't understand. Lily goes from loving me to hating me to loving me, as sisters do. I keep Ba's wallet on my body, always, to feel its weight. Bà Nội's photo stays folded inside the front pocket, and I've added another: in it, Florence is sticking her tongue out in the V of her fingers. Blue-and-green plaid covers the curves of her shoulders. A filter enlarged her dark eyes anime-style. It's the tamest one I have of her.

Florence and I went back once together, even though Mom didn't want me to—because that place is bad, and because Lily would want to come and never leave. An unfortunate accident is the official determination after Alma lawyered up and a bribe likely changed hands. But we'll always have the truth.

I went back, riding in the passenger seat of the car Florence borrowed from her uncle who, unsurprisingly, loathes me. Without explanation, I left incense to burn by the side of the road. At that distance, I saw the edge of blackened remains and the pines' dappled brightness; enough. I left other food too: an aloe drink, a sponge cake, and bánh mì. They're not his favorites since I never got to ask what his favorites were.

And me and Florence, what's more to say? All stories end.

"Go on, convince me to come with you," Florence says, leaning into me. She's not going to university, after all, and neither am I. We straight-up missed student orientation (and me, a lot of tuition bills), in addition to not really wanting to. *A gap year*, she wrote in a text. *To see what else there is.*

"All right," I say, my eyes on hers. "I love you."

She flinches.

I laugh. "I thought so." The things given because we asked aren't the same, much like a father asking for his daughter to stay for the final time. "How about this, then?" My lips find hers, and they are gentle—we've learned to be gentle. I know honesty now.

When we pull apart, Florence grins. "Geez, your lip balm blows."

"It's coffee flavored," I say with a smile. "Maybe you'll change your mind when you grow up a little."

"Maybe," she says, walking backward, cheeks flushed. "See ya then."

"Take care, Florence." I don't say 'bye. I don't know how. Neither English nor Vietnamese can name the way I feel—the sentiment deep in my chest. It aches, but it's sweet, like swallowing a sugary candy. Like something that might keep me full.

One day.

heart

THIS HOUSE IS RUINOUS ash, spread thin on soil.

The walls, split fruit and crumbling as age-old mulch, stand only in memory. She walks these lines, seen from the road as a trick of light.

Unnamed, cinder blows and the buds of something beautiful take root.

There will always be another.

ACKNOWLEDGMENTS

Before a story becomes a physical book, it is touched by many people through various drafts. Even more people have enriched my life, giving me the tiniest wonders to make a story emotionally true. I am lucky to have them.

My literary agent, Katelyn Detweiler, is an absolute gem—thank you for championing my work and celebrating even the smallest milestones with me. My editor, Mary Kate Castellani, sharpened this book around its edges, making it better and better in each round. Kei Nakatsuka asked a question that led me to rewrite one of my favorite chapters to become even MORE favorite ("marrow"). Thank you both for understanding the story I wanted to tell.

I couldn't ask for a better team than my incredible publicists Faye Bi and Nicole Banholzer, marketing geniuses Erica Barmash and Lily Yengle, and school and library marketing fearless leaders Beth Eller and Kathleen Morandini. Others at Blooms-bury took special care of this book, too: Donna Mark, John Candell, Phoebe Dyer, Alona Fryman, Erica Chan, Oona Pat-rick, Laura Phillips, and Nicholas Church. My UK team knocked it out of the park with introducing me to international readers and creating the cover of my dreams. Hannah Sandford, Stephanie Amster, Laura Bird, Mattea Barnes, Thy Bui, and Elena Masci—thank you all.

Booksellers were among the very first to welcome and support me. Alyssa Raymond, Bridey Morris, Carrie Deming, and Rayna Nielsen—your kind words carried me as *She Is a Haunting* found its earliest readers. Endless gratitude to Children's Institute, Southern Indie Booksellers Alliance, California Independent Booksellers Alliance, Pacific Northwest Booksellers Association, New England Independent Booksellers Association, Mountains and Plains Independent Booksellers Association, and Midwest Independent Booksellers Association for inviting me to your shows. It's an honor to meet people so passionate about stories.

My first reader and accountability partner, Lindsay Fischer, saw the absolute worst draft and yet said she could see it as a finished book. Thank you for not immediately unfriending me. My earliest cheerleaders—Alyson Kissner, Kate Dias, and Sarah Mye—are the most generous friends who put up with a whole lot of whining.

I must shout out my writing group, Writers' Block, and espe-cially Sandeep Brar and Melissa Pinhal, for maintaining a space that is fun, safe, and inspiring. Can't wait for our next writing retreat!

My next writing community emerged from Author Mentor Match. I owe so much to my mentor Alex Brown, without whom Jade's ba would've built fifty porches and nothing else. Get her book *Damned If You Do*! Wen-yi Lee, I would haunt any house with you. Hands down, best DM I got on Twitter. A huge thank-you to my workshop buddies at Rainbow Weekend and Tin House, especially instructor Mark Oshiro, for precise critiques and support when I was most unsure.

To my partner, Daniel, the first person who told me to chase my dreams, I love you. You always give me time and space to do what I need to. You are my home.

Almost everything good in me is something I learned from my family. Y'all know who you are but I guess it should be in print too: Andy, Nhan, Tri, and my anh hai Xuyen, whom I miss every single day. My mom deserves pages and pages but I'll save that for the greeting cards I put through Google Translate to hear her make fun of me. I love you most.

By the time my bà ngoại passed away in the last days of 2020, she knew I was writing a book but not how much of it related to family. I revised much of *She Is a Haunting* with her and this grief in mind, of everything and everyone I would never know completely. Still, the time with her has been some of the best: playing hide-and-seek in her house, getting (lovingly) yelled at, receiving lipstick-stained kisses on my cheek. I'll always remember you.

And finally, thank you, reader, for spending a few hours getting lost in this story with me.

© Heather Wall

ABOUT THE AUTHOR

TRANG THANH TRAN writes speculative stories with big emotions about food, belonging and the Vietnamese diaspora. They grew up in a big family in Philadelphia, then abandoned degrees in sociology and public health to tell stories in Georgia. When not writing, they can be found over-caffeinating on iced coffee and watching zombie movies. *She Is a Haunting* is their debut novel.

Twitter: @nvtran
Instagram: @nvtran_
www.trangthanhtran.com